The Hour of Witches Book 2

I0778113

WITCH POSSESSED

KRISTA WALSH

RAVEN'S QUILL PRESS

OTTAWA, ON

Copyright © 2025 by KRISTA WALSH.

All rights reserved. No part of this publication may be reproduced, distributed or transmitted in any form or by any means, including photocopying, recording, or other electronic or mechanical methods, without the prior written permission of the publisher, except in the case of brief quotations embodied in critical reviews and certain other noncommercial uses permitted by copyright law. For permission requests, write to the publisher, addressed "Attention: Permissions Coordinator," at the address below.

Raven's Quill Press

www.kristawalshauthor.com

Publisher's Note: This is a work of fiction. Names, characters, places, and incidents are a product of the author's imagination. Locales and public names are sometimes used for atmospheric purposes. Any resemblance to actual people, living or dead, or to businesses, companies, events, institutions, or locales is completely coincidental. No AI was used in the creation of either the content or cover of this book.

Cover Design: Deranged Doctor Design/2024

Editor: ShelfPotential

Witch Possessed / WALSH -- 1st ed.

Paperback ISBN: 978-1-998398-18-8

For everyone who reads Alyssa and thinks
"Yeah, girl, I get it."

Chapter 1
Alyssa

THE MIXING BOWL-SHAPED clock ticked away where it hung to the right of my kitchen counter, the little swinging cupcake keeping beat with each passing second.

I stood in front of the sink, my hands braced on the granite, and stared into the stainless-steel depths of the drain.

Damn, it needed to be cleaned.

The compost bin beside the sink also needed to be emptied, but for the past few weeks, I'd had an aversion to crossing the driveway beside the house to get to the little shed where my downstairs tenant and I kept the recycling and garbage bins. Funny what getting abducted one time could do to the psyche.

The laughter of a studio audience filled the room from the TV behind me, and I couldn't help but feel they were laughing at me instead of at Chandler and Joey's antics.

Which… well, fair.

What else could the universe do except laugh at me as I stood in my kitchen pretending to wait for the kettle to boil so I could make a cup of tea I would forget to drink when I was actually putting off getting ready for work because I was afraid of what my night might bring?

Ha ha, Alyssa Mooney's a coward, ha ha!

I spun in a circle and flipped off the universe for its mockery. How would *it* like it if a place that had been a second home for six years had begun to feel more like a stifling cage than a pub, eh? How would *it* like to have all the routines and predictability of its world turned upside down?

Who was I kidding?

It was the universe.

It would freaking love it because unpredictability was its jam. Fucking up people's lives and leaving burning trails in its wake? Aw yeah, that was a successful Thursday. Bring on the chaos of Friday!

I groaned and buried my head in my hands.

The kettle clicked. I ignored it. Why waste a teabag?

With a final scream of frustration that I hoped didn't disturb Ann or her orange demon cat downstairs, I kicked my way through the laundry on the floor and stomped into my bedroom. It was time to be a grown-up. Get dressed, pull myself together, and go to work.

I was already an hour late. Simon—my best friend and the most amazing business partner and bartender in the entire world—would be at the pub getting ready for the night. Picking up my slack.

Off came my plaid flannel pyjama bottoms and my graphic tee with a turtle witch on it, leaving me standing in my plain purple underwear to peruse my empty closet. I needed to fold laundry.

Hell, I needed to do laundry.

Anxiety and overwhelm were taking over my life.

I grabbed a pair of mostly clean jeans off the floor, then tugged a too-large black Mooney's Pub T-shirt over my head. To avoid looking like a complete slob, I tucked the T-shirt into my waistband. Now I looked like I'd walked out of the 90s, but it was better than telling the whole world I'd had to scrounge the rejects of my wardrobe just to appear decent in public.

In the bathroom, I did my best to avoid looking at my reflection as I pulled my highlighted brown hair into a ponytail and added a dash of mascara to my eyelashes.

Because that would keep people's attention away from the wreck that was the rest of me.

Genius.

As quickly as possible, I turned off the light, grabbed my jacket off the hook by the door, and pulled on my black running shoes—not the trendiest selection, but most comfortable for a nine-hour shift spent entirely on my feet.

Only once I was ready to go did I drop onto the edge of my saggy blue sectional and resume my earlier blank staring into the wall.

Five weeks ago, my life had made sense. It hadn't been exciting or, frankly, all that interesting, but it had been predictable and *mine*. I'd liked it. I wanted it back.

Then Dara Josef-Levesque, a fae duchess, had put a bounty on my head for the murder and magic theft of one of her people—and a regular at my pub—which had put my existence into a jeopardized tailspin. I had no idea why the woman had been so determined to see me dead, even after she'd been presented with evidence of my innocence.

In that particular crime, at least.

I could only be grateful that she'd relented in the end.

Thanks to the efforts of Trace "Not His Real Name" Wyatt, the bounty hunter who had chased me down, thrown me in the trunk of his car, then sacrificed every single one of his values to save my life.

As if it had been nothing for him to do it.

Sure, Alyssa, I'll make deals with demons and relive my worst memories of taking souls into my body to make sure you're still breathing tomorrow morning. Love to help you out, let's grab coffee sometime.

And as if my guilt weren't already strong enough that he'd

done it, he'd hauled his ass into my pub two weeks ago looking like those demons had grabbed him by his ankles and dragged him through every single pothole on Carling Avenue.

But the bastard had disappeared again. No texts. No calls. No sudden appearances outside my place of business. Not even another friendly abduction. Just silence.

Was he dead?

I couldn't help but worry he was dead.

I didn't want him to be dead. Not when I had all these unresolved feelings and thoughts and questions about every-thing that had happened between us.

But if he wasn't, what else could his silence mean?

The first time he'd disappeared—for three weeks after the showdown at The Scorpio Lounge—I'd assumed he'd checked me off as a job complete and moved on with his badass bounty hunter life, driving across the country in his repaired SUV, taking names and bringing in marks.

Then he came into the bar looking like death, saying he'd spent most of those three weeks in bed, and I was relieved he'd finally managed to stumble out to come say hi.

Now he was gone again.

The way he'd looked didn't inspire a lot of confidence that he was belting out some Top 40 hits as he sped along the Trans-Canada Highway.

No, instead my brain had been playing variations of him

curled up on the floor somewhere. Wherever he stayed when he was in town. Was he with his friend Chip? I couldn't see the paranoid hermit computer genius with the horribly on-the-nose nickname bringing Trace bowls of chicken noodle soup and making sure he had enough blankets, but it was better than the idea of Trace being by himself in some lonely hotel. Lying stuck on the floor reaching for a phone that was just out of reach? Screaming in agony as the souls he'd absorbed adjusted to their new prison? Vomiting blood as his body shut down at the invasion of so much extra magic interacting with his teleki-netic power?

I pressed the heels of my palms into my eyes to stop the influx of intrusive thoughts.

Work. That would be a great distraction. Pouring drinks, saying hi to my regulars, finding new and creative ways to kick our live-in sloth demon off his stool at the end of the night. An attempt at normality. Perfect.

It took an effort to convince my legs that my brain knew what it was talking about, but I finally managed to stand up and shuffle my way to the door.

Turn handle. Open door. Walk down the steps. If I had to live the next little while with a read-along instruction manual in my head, so be it. At least I wouldn't starve to death buried under a pile of dirty laundry.

I hauled myself into my electric Nissan and drove the

five minutes to Somerset Street near Elgin. It was a stretch of road lined with pubs, but Mooney's was the only one that catered primarily to the supernatural crowd. Specifically to the public servants from Supernatural, Magical and Occult Affairs Canada—or SMOAC to those in the know—the secret government department that handled any and all matters supernatural across the country. Those guys were my bread and butter, and I looked forward to the banality of hearing the crowd gripe about committee meetings and budget papers.

Most of them would have already come and gone, grabbing a quick pint or a bite to eat before they made their way home— or back to work—the rest looking for a quiet night to drown their brain cells before getting back to keeping the country running tomorrow.

They rarely made messes, weren't assholes to me and my staff, and kept the electric bills paid. Right now, that sort of low-key energy was exactly what I needed. Busy enough for me to keep my thoughts off any imagined unpleasantness but not so stressful that imaginary problems were better than the real ones.

I parked behind the pub and entered through the back door, waving at Simon, who was serving drinks along the short side of the bar, before ducking into the office to hang up my coat and shake the snow from my hair. It was the last week of March, so of course we were having the first of our last winter hurrahs.

Once I'd tied my pouch apron around my waist and filled it with the usual notepad, pen, lip gloss, I left the peace of the office for the steady flow of business in the pub.

Daily Davis, our resident sloth demon, was on his usual stool in the corner, blue cap pulled low over his eyes, pint clasped between his hands, gaze focused on the television. No one reacted to him being there, one person going so far as to bump into him as they passed by on the way to the bathroom. They looked around confused about what they'd hit, and I shook my head. Davis was a pro at going unnoticed. He was a staple in the pub, and I was sure my familiarity with him was the only reason he didn't escape my view anymore. Good thing, too, or chasing him down to pay his tab every week would be that much more of a challenge.

"How's it going tonight?" I asked Simon as I slipped behind the bar.

"Fine," he said shortly. "Where've you been?"

I raised an eyebrow at him, but he didn't look around to catch my curious stare.

I didn't know what to make of it. Simon and I had known each other for six years. He was my best friend, and I'd never seen him like this. His mood swings had been off the charts lately, ranging from enraged to peeved with very little movement in between.

His bad mood had to be the half-succubus's fault. Almost two weeks ago, he'd spent a day with Reverie, and suddenly my Simon was no longer the chaos demon I'd known but someone I barely recognized. I wanted to call him on it. And if he refused to acknowledge it, I wanted to track Reverie down and demand to know what she'd done to him.

It bothered me that he hadn't confided in me, but even I could admit I hadn't been in the right headspace to take on someone else's problems.

Oh goddess, had he tried, and I'd brushed him off?

New guilt piled on top of the existing guilt. I suspected if I stepped to the side, my guilt would retain its Alyssa shape where I'd been.

"I was working through some stuff," I said. "I'm sorry if it was busy."

"It wasn't."

He pulled a few more pints and slid them across the counter to the postgrads sitting at the end of the bar. They raised their glasses in thanks, then turned their backs on us to chat among themselves.

Along with the public servants, we were close enough to the University of Ottawa to bring in the student crowd as well. Bigger pains in the ass and lousier tippers, but the sheer amount of alcohol they consumed kept us in the black in a way the more responsible adults did not.

Them and Davis. When he paid.

I made my rounds through the tables, helped Simon behind the bar, and fell into the rhythm of the evening. I'd been foolish to sit around at home worrying about problems I couldn't solve.

Hell, worrying about problems that might not even be problems.

So what if Trace hadn't checked in? He had no reason to.

As he'd made perfectly clear, I'd been a job.

A job that had shared a wildly intimate moment fueled by some gross demon pheromones in a nasty demon sex club—but a job nonetheless.

He'd finished that job. Presumably been paid for it, though I wondered how much of a recommendation he'd received from Dara considering he'd trapped her behind an invisible wall, stolen her mark—namely, me—and gone out of his way to prevent her from killing me as she'd so clearly wanted to do.

Tearing my thoughts away from that particular path, I returned behind the bar and did a pass on cleaning up.

I'd just finished stacking the clean glasses on the shelf when the pub phone rang. I grabbed the cordless handset—one of the antiquated quirks of the pub I hadn't had the heart to change—and answered, "Mooney's Pub, Alyssa speaking."

"Pip—don't—!" A cry, and then a different voice saying, "Miss Mooney?"

I stood rooted to the floor, my hands going so numb the

phone almost slipped out of my grip. I tightened my hold on it, but the rest of me had yet to catch up. The first voice had belonged to my grandfather. He was the only person who called me Pip. Finally, I found my voice. "Yes?"

"Your Gramps seems to have given away the surprise, but that should speed things along." The voice was distorted, barely understandable. "You have something we want. If we don't get it, your dear old grandpappy will be breathing his last before the end of the night. It's that simple."

My free hand clutched the edge of the counter to hold myself steady, and I shifted to put my back to the room. I should have moved to my office, claimed the privacy, but I knew if I took a single step, I would collapse into a heap.

"What do you want?" I asked through teeth clenched tight so they wouldn't chatter.

"We've heard rumours, you understand. Rumours about a certain amulet?"

I closed my eyes as the room around me swayed. "The amulet broke. It doesn't exist."

It was true. The amulet had been activated when the witch Clyde Corrick had attempted to steal it, and in the process, the fist-sized tourmaline had shattered into a million fragments. The souls, which was what I assumed interested my anonymous caller more than the ugly necklace itself, were currently sitting within Trace Wyatt.

"I don't believe you," the person on the phone said. Because of course they didn't. "You'll bring it to Dundonald Park at two a.m., alone, or the cops will find Gramps' shrivelled corpse among the used needles."

The line went dead.

I hung up the phone, floated mindlessly into the back office, slammed the door shut, and screamed.

Chapter 2
Alyssa

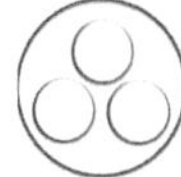

THE DOOR FLEW open as Simon barged into the office. "Are you all right?" He searched the room for any threat before his gaze landed on me.

Were his eyes… glowing? The light in the room certainly made it seem as though there was a red tint to his usual amber irises. Not a little concerning. But not even symptoms of his demonic self waving hello was enough to distract me from the greater panic building in my chest.

"Someone's kidnapped Gramps. They're holding him for ransom." My voice shook, but I managed to get the words out in one monotonous string. "They want the amulet."

He pulled his lips back to bare his teeth, and his bronze chaos magic wisped around his head. "Who are they?"

I made sure my own magic was safely tamped down, not wanting it to brush against his and turn our office desk into a giant octopus or a suffocating marshmallow—with him, one never knew. "I didn't recognize the voice. Couldn't even tell you if it was man, woman, dragon. But they think I have the amulet, Simon. They told me to bring it to them tonight or they're going to kill Gramps."

My lip wobbled, my voice shook, my hands trembled. Dammit. I'd been trying so hard to stay strong. Now I was one vibrating mess as the impossibility of the situation fell on my shoulders. I sank to the floor in a crouch and wrapped my arms around my middle.

"Crying won't change anything," Simon said. "It'll be way more useful to track these fuckers down and tear them apart."

His lack of empathy was a bucket of cold water to the face, and I was no less disturbed by my usually gentle friend advocating for a bloody massacre. Still, he wasn't wrong.

I rose to my feet and cleaned my face with the back of my hand. "I guess I should thank you for pointing that out."

"Where will you start?" he asked, ignoring my hurt feelings and churning panic. I needed to know what was wrong with him, needed my friend if I was going to get through this.

But no, I would have to stand on my own and figure this out for myself. Later, once Gramps was safe, I would push the issue with Simon.

I straightened my shirt, giving myself a moment to collect my thoughts. "Not much I *can* do about it, is there? I don't have the amulet. It was destroyed. I told them that, and they think I'm lying to keep it from them." I propped my hands on my hips and forced myself to meet Simon's eye. "I'll have to meet with them and try to explain in person. With luck, they'll bring Gramps with them and I can rescue him before anyone gets hurt. I'm not without defences of my own."

He crossed his arms and a low growl rumbled in his chest. "You can't go by yourself. If they got the upper hand on Gramps, you'll be dealing with some strong witches. You might be able to take one or two of them alone, but if they come as a coven, you're screwed."

"While I appreciate your faith in me, I don't know what my options are. They told me I have to come alone or he dies. I could call in the rest of the family. We have time. I'm sure Dylan and Brody could try to be stealthy."

I tried to imagine my brothers creeping around and couldn't do it. They were more the barge-in-and-deal-with-the-problem types. My cousins Mallory and Avery might be better options, but Avery would be with the kids and Mal was getting ready for a business trip in Munich. And of course my parents were currently on their way back from an Alaskan cruise and wouldn't be home for another day or so.

"I'll go with you," Simon said, pulling me out of my mental

contact list.

I blinked at him until my thoughts cleared. "You need to stay here and watch the bar."

"Fuck the bar. I'm not about to let you walk into a trap when I can be there to help you."

There was my Simon. A glimmer of him, anyway, if a bit more overprotective than usual. Lacking any of the warmth and cuddliness my old friend usually showed me, but I'd take the rough edges over the prickishness of a moment ago.

I dropped my hands from their peevish stance and rested my fingers on the edge of my desk. "Thank you. Really. But you know how your chaos magic gets when you're around too many witches at once. We'd be just as likely to hurt Gramps as they are."

Simon's chaos demon nature made for a sometimes amusing but always interesting turn of events whenever it came out to play. Especially if there was any other magic in the area. I'd seen people be liquified, watched flying projectiles transform into winged rats, nearly been caught in floorboards-turned-quicksand. The only power his didn't interact badly with was Reverie's, which was the only reason I could see that he enjoyed spending time with her.

That and, you know, the obvious. She was half succubus, after all. I didn't want to pry into the details, but how could that woman not be a bomb in the sack?

Simon grunted his acceptance and leaned his shoulder on the door frame. "What about Jet? Or Madison? I doubt SMOAC would take too kindly to witches trying to get their hands on illegal power."

"Which means they wouldn't look too kindly on me or Gramps laying claim to it either," I pointed out, but I mulled over the idea of calling either of my friends.

Captain Bridget Dawson led one of SMOAC's task forces. Madison Prince was an executive in the minister's office. Both of them would have connections that would no doubt be a great help but were just as likely to turn around and have Gramps arrested for hiding the amulet in the first place.

But if I asked Jet and Madi to keep their help off the books…

"It couldn't hurt to get a consult at the very least." I looked at the clock on the wall. Fifteen minutes had passed since the phone call, which left me more than a few hours to sort my shit out.

Maybe even sneak in a Plan B. Or C.

If I could work my way to Plan L or M, I'd feel a whole lot better.

"Good. They're sitting at the bar," Simon said.

Well, that was convenient.

Simon turned on his heel, and I followed him out of the office, pasting my professional smile back on as I navigated through the crowds and took my place behind the bar.

A few concerned looks came my way from people who'd watched my little freak-out, but other than some encouraging smiles, they left me alone.

For which I was grateful. While I appreciated the crap out of my regulars, most of them weren't my friends. I poured their alcohol; they drank it. Occasionally I met with them in the office to heal minor wounds they didn't want to bother the supernatural clinics with. That was the extent of our relation-ship, and I liked to keep it that way. Made pushing them to pay their tabs at the end of the month much less complicated.

Jet, on the other hand, wasn't nearly as tactful. As soon as she spotted me, she waved me over. There was no drink in front of her, and Madi was tapping her debit card against the cherry-wood bartop, so I guessed they'd just arrived, but somehow— no, not somehow. Of course Madison knew something was wrong. As a powerful empath, she'd probably picked up on my panic from down the street.

"Tell me," Jet said when I reached them. Her shoulder-length brown hair was pulled up in a ponytail, and she wore her usual outfit of black leather jacket over black T-shirt over black jeans. She believed it let her be ready for anything, but I suspected she enjoyed the I-can-kill-you-with-my-pinky-finger vibe she gave off.

I looked around the pub to ensure we had a moment's space,

then dropped my voice. "A witch just called and told me their coven is going to kill my grandfather tonight if I don't hand over a talisman filled with illegal magic that used to be hidden under the safe in my office but is now broken and nonexistent."

There. Had I summarized the shithole well enough?

By the expressions on both Jet's and Madi's faces, I had, though I wasn't sure how they'd react. Accuse me of a crime against the country? Threaten to shut down the pub? Tackle me in a big hug?

If I had to choose, I'd go for the latter, even if it would mean letting someone other than Simon behind the bar.

"Do you know which coven made the call?" Jet asked, going for option four, which was to morph into uber-professional mode.

I shook my head, grabbed a glass, and filled it with her preferred craft beer. "I didn't recognize the voice, but it sounded like it had one of those… voice-changing features to it? Kind of robotic?"

Madison pulled out her cell phone, and her French-manicured nails zipped over the keyboard. Unlike Jet, she was dressed for the office in a crisp cream pantsuit and a lavender-hued blouse that brought out the deep tan notes of her skin and the honey in her hair. "I'll reach out to some people, see if the security office can trace the number."

That all sounded fantastic and more than I'd expected, but

it didn't remove my worry about The Big Problem.

A group came in aiming for the stools next to us, but Simon headed them off and guided them farther down the bar so we weren't overheard.

"You don't think the security officers will wonder why there was an illegal amulet hidden under the pub?" I asked.

Madison answered my question by letting her thumb hover over the send button. She exchanged a look with Jet, and the two women sighed. Madison slipped her phone back into her purse. "I'll admit, it wouldn't go over well."

Jet arched an eyebrow. "Can you tell *us* why you have an amulet like that hidden under the pub?"

"Had," I corrected. "If that helps at all."

"Not really."

After these two had helped me out by costuming me for my visit to the reeking demon sex lair called Club Crescent during my flight from the law and the fae duchess who wanted me dead, of course I'd filled them in on how I'd cleared my name and removed Corrick as a threat to my future... I'd just left out a few details.

Now it turned out I needn't have bothered.

"Right. Well. Okay, it's a long story. Local history long. Building of the Rideau Canal, souls stuffed into an amulet to help smooth out some worker rebellion, power-hungry witch not releasing said souls when he said he would. Welcome family heirloom that got passed down through the generations, advertently or inadvertently helping the Mooney family get what we wanted out of life." As though it was no big deal. "To be fair, Gramps did try to destroy it after he decided not to use it again. Result—the amulet couldn't be destroyed, so he stashed it under the pub where no one would find it."

Madison's eyes widened. "That's how you got the pub so cheap!" The mystery of the pub had nagged her for years.

"It is," I confirmed.

She frowned. "And that's why Clyde Corrick was after you?"

"You guessed it in one. After centuries of keeping its magic to itself, the wards around the amulet weakened and lit up the pub like a beacon." Someone approached the bar to order a drink, and I waited until they left to continue. "Corrick thought that by shouldering me out of the business, he could get his hands on it and, I don't know, take over the world or something. Whatever. He failed, and the amulet was smashed."

I held back the tiny fact that the souls that had been contained in the amulet weren't freed during said smashing but were now whirling around inside Trace Wyatt. The last thing that guy needed was SMOAC knocking down his door— Chip's door? His hotel room? Where he slept in the backseat of his car? Did he even have a place in town or had he left the province?—and asking him not so politely to hand them over.

"So you see? No reason for me to get in trouble. Or Gramps, really. He tried to do the right thing."

"After years of not," Madison pointed out.

"Can we really hold someone's history against them when it's clear they've made an effort to change?" I asked in my most hopeful and optimistic tone.

Madison pressed her lips together and gave me a look that said she wasn't about to answer that question.

"He could have handed it over to SMOAC and let us deal with it," she said. "We have whole units dedicated to dealing with supernatural objects like that."

I pinched the bridge of my nose. "Believe me, by now he knows how badly he messed up. I was nearly killed because of the decisions he made. I think that's punishment enough."

Jet elbowed Madison's arm. "Quit messing with her. You know you're not going to call security on her *grandfather* because of something her ancestor did hundreds of years ago."

Madison watched me until finally she shook her head. "No, I won't. But it doesn't leave us with many options in the way of help. I can go with you to the meet tonight if you want. Stick to the shadows. Do my best to smooth over everyone's emotions and make sure it doesn't come to a fight."

Her empathic powers were truly the stuff of legend.

"Would you?"

Unlike Simon, whose control over his demon power was

spotty at best, Madison had honed her skills into an art. She was so tightly bound that I wasn't sure how far her ability extended.

The woman scared the crap out of me, and I loved her.

I looked at Jet, but she shook her head. "I'd love to join the party, but if I show up unofficially, I can't do anything, and if I show up officially, all the details will need to go into a lengthy and thorough report. Gramps is safer if I stay far away from this."

I got it. I really did. As the captain of the A-team task force, Jet was bound by the rules and regulations that came with the responsibility. She wasn't the type to cross lines if it put any of her team in trouble.

"Give me a call when you're on your way, and I'll meet you en route," Madison said. "Hopefully at least one of them will be willing to listen to reason."

"Thank you, Madi. So much." I chewed on my lip and caught Jet's eye. "I don't suppose you could do something else for me? Something unrelated to this. Maybe not."

"What?"

"Could you look into a woman named Hazel Blackwood? She would have been arrested for magic theft around nine years ago and sent to Moongrave Prison."

After she'd framed Trace for her crimes and sent him on the run from SMOAC and the Alberta Witches' Council for three years. That woman had been his everything at a young and impressionable age, and that betrayal had left him twisted in more ways than I'd been able to untangle. I knew the story as Trace had told it, but I found myself wanting to know more about the woman who'd worked so hard to ruin his life.

"Sure, that's simple enough," Jet said. "I'll get back to you on that."

Madi frowned. "You think they might be connected?"

My shoulders slumped, and I rubbed my brow. "I don't see how they could be if she's still in prison, but I hate coincidences. We're dealing with all kinds of spirit magic right now. I want to know who we might be playing with."

I thought of the voice on the line, and a chill rippled through me. Somehow I didn't think they would listen to anything they didn't want to hear.

But at least now I had backup.

Hang on, Gramps. I'm coming.

Chapter 3
Alyssa

THE REST OF my shift went about as well as expected.

I dropped a bunch of glasses.

I tripped on a customer's foot and spilled beer all over her shirt.

I mixed up orders.

The standard can't-get-my head-in-the-game crap most newbies suffered. Not veteran servers. Except, of course, on a really bad night.

Hello, Bad Night.

Part of my problem was that I kept shooting looks at the clock over the bar. Usually I forgot that clock was there. It was mostly for customers so they knew how long they could stick around before family or overtime called them away.

Tonight, those red LEDs were the albatross around my neck. The numbers changed too slowly and too quickly all at once. I needed to go get Gramps before anything happened to him, but damn, I was not looking forward to meeting with that coven and trying to explain to them—again—that the amulet was gone.

What would I do if Madison's empathic abilities weren't enough to hold them back?

What if she couldn't affect all of them at once? What if, as she held off one witch, another was ready to snap Gramps's neck and leave him in the park like they threatened?

My stomach lurched, and my grip on the pint glass slipped. I caught it before it could fall and smash all over the floor, but not before the beer splashed across my chest.

Great. Now I would show up to this meeting reeking of alcohol on top of everything else. Because that would encourage these witches to believe I was telling the truth. And what would happen if I got pulled over because of panic driving? I was making this so much worse for myself.

I set the glass on the table, ignored the customer calling to me that this wasn't his beer, and rushed into the office to catch my breath before the black spots in my eyes spread across my entire field of view and my anxiety took over. Having my patrons watch me crouch in the middle of the floor and hyperventilate with my hands over my ears was no good for business.

You'll figure this out, Mooney. You've been through worse.

And I had, hadn't I? I'd been framed for murder. Barely a month ago, it had been my life on the line because of this stupid amulet that never should have existed in the first place. Or at least, that should have been destroyed as soon as its original purpose had been completed.

So fuck you, Great-Great-Gramps. Your bad decisions have messed things up for the rest of the family. Hope you're happy.

I tightened my ponytail, scrubbed my hands across my face, and patted down my apron to make sure my pen and pad were still readily available, then I opened the door to return to the bar.

Simon stood in my way.

"Go," he said, and for the first time all night, he sounded like his usual self.

"Excuse me?"

"You're going to go insane if you stay here much longer—and at the rate you're smashing glassware, we'll be serving paper cups for the rest of the night. Besides, by leaving now you'll have a chance to stake out the park before anyone else shows up. I've got things covered here, and I'll close up early. Go."

This was the chaos demon I knew and loved.

I checked my phone on the desk. It was one o'clock in the morning. An hour before the meeting, which would give me lots of time to make it to the park and find a place to lie in wait.

Grab whatever advantage I could find.

"Thank you," I said through the tightness in my throat.

He nodded, and without giving it a thought, I threw my arms around his waist in a tight squeeze. He hugged me back and pressed a kiss into my hair. Then he let me go and gently pushed me back into the office. In another second, he was behind the bar, and I was rummaging through the tiny closet in the corner to grab a clean Mooney's Pub-branded T-shirt. I'd been going through so many of these lately I would have to buy stock in my own product.

Still, it didn't stink of booze, so at least I wouldn't give my presence away from down the block.

I grabbed my coat, slung my purse over my shoulder, and made my way to the back door. Giving Simon a wave, I stepped outside into the frigid late-March morning.

My car was only a few feet away from the door, but I made sure to hit the unlock button and take off at a jog to clear the space between the pub and the driver's side door as quickly as possible. Ever since the attack on Mooney's, I'd been uncomfortable being outside alone in the middle of the night.

No wonder, really. One only needed to be shoved into the trunk of a car once to appreciate how crappy an experience it was. Even so, I berated myself for being a scaredy-cat every time I ran. I was a witch, for the goddess's sake. It didn't matter that I hated causing harm and did my best not to use my magic for anything other than emergencies or helping people—if anyone tried to grab me again, that would fall under the *emergencies* category.

But no matter how often or how sternly I told myself I could handle anything the world threw at me, here I was, rushing to slide my fingers under the door handle, planning to throw myself into the seat and lock the door as soon as it closed.

The second I got the door open, however, a tendril of magic tickled the back of my neck. Not an attack, more like an introduction, a poke in the side from someone letting me know another supernatural was in the parking lot. I closed my eyes to the sensation, sinking into the familiar tingle along my skin. I half turned to look, and sure enough, I spotted the thread of silver power brushing against me.

There was only one person I knew who had that particular shade of magic, and my traitorous heart gave a few extra thumps at the realization that, after so much time, Trace had come out of hiding.

But where?

I searched the shadows for the source of his telekinetic power, but he'd hidden himself well.

From me?

Smart man. Because the longer he played this game, the more my worry for him fell apart and my anger took hold.

All these weeks picturing him holed up somewhere wasting away. All those sleepless nights wondering if he'd ever show up again or if I'd catch the news story about Canada's acclaimed bounty hunter being found dead inside his car.

But what if there was something wrong? Was that why I couldn't see him anywhere? Was he nearby but too weak to step out from wherever he'd tucked himself away?

Again that image came to me of him curled up on the floor of some shabby hideout unable to reach his phone.

Anger and anxiety warred within me, and with cautious steps, I followed the trail of silver magic away from my car towards the pool of darkness near the dumpsters.

Was this stupid of me? Yes, it most certainly was.

For all I knew, the group who was holding Gramps hostage had their own telekinetic witch in their ranks. Or someone who could mask their magic to make it appear however they wanted it to. Or my panic over Gramps's situation had pushed me into hallucinations and there was no magic. I could be about to stumble over a surfeit of terrified skunks, and wouldn't that be the head on the stale beer that was my night?

The sound of boots shuffling on asphalt sounded behind me, gunshot loud on the nearly silent street, and I whirled around to find Trace Wyatt. Standing. On two legs. Breathing.

He stilled at the sight of me, one arm wrapped around his

middle, the other half raised in a loose hello. For a moment, we stared at each other, until he cleared his throat and offered a casual "Hey."

That was when I lost my shit.

Chapter 4
Alyssa

HEY?" I FLUNG a spell at Trace that stirred the air between us and shoved him backwards. "Are you kidding me right now? *Hey* is the best you can do after two weeks of zero communication, when the last time I saw you, you were crawling out of the pub like a wounded dog?"

I shoved him with more magic, and he stumbled, only just catching himself before he could fall on his ass. I wished he had. He would have landed in a melting puddle of mud and slush, which would have left him cold and uncomfortable for hours.

He held up his hands in a show of peace. "I know. I'm sorry."

"Oh, well, all right, then. If you're *sorry.*"

A third shove was apparently all he was willing to tolerate. A wave of silver magic pinned me against the nearest dumpster. So gross.

"Yes." He panted. "I'm sorry."

I worked my purple atmospheric magic beneath his silver net to try to free myself, but in the time it took me to get a hold of my power, Trace closed the distance between us and gripped my shoulders. The contact, the squeeze of his long fingers—so solid, so present, so *real*—made my insides quiver. The scent I'd come to associate with him, a mix of bergamot, musk, and a hint of coffee, made my mouth water. Damn this man.

"I should have called," he continued, "and that makes me the asshole here. I own it."

At the genuine remorse in his tone, my anger washed out of me. Who was I kidding? The heat of it had been fuelled by worry, so it wasn't like I was about to go nuclear on him or anything. The tension in my shoulders eased as they fell away from my earlobes, and I nodded my acceptance.

Though the moment his silver net released me, I gave him a last half-hearted shove. "You *are* an asshole."

That earned me a smile, which I answered with a grudging one of my own. I wished he'd come to me under better circumstances. We'd left so much up in the air the last time he'd come into the pub. We'd toasted to whatever came next, and I had to admit to myself that I'd hoped *next* might include something...

normal. Dinner, maybe. Or at least a cup of tea. The occasional text chat to update each other on what we'd been up to.

I hadn't realized until he'd disappeared how much I enjoyed his presence. Those nineteen hours had been the worst of my life—up until then—but he'd made them bearable. At times, even enjoyable, which was a weird thing to consider.

To have him near me now did uncomfortable things to my chest and other parts of my body, but there was a not small amount of hurt feelings that had woken as well.

"So why the break in radio silence? You need me for something?"

Oops. Was that a little bitter? Because it sounded a little bitter.

"I needed to make sure you were all right." He stuffed his bare hands into the pockets of his heavy black parka. "I've heard… rumours."

I crossed my arms. "Rumours? About a coven of witches who grabbed my grandfather and are holding him ransom for an amulet, the contents of which happen to have taken up residence inside *you*?"

He grimaced and pulled a hand free to rub his stubbled jaw.

Now that my fury had ebbed, I stole a good look at him, and based on first impressions, my worries had been well founded.

He might not be curled up on a floor reaching desperately for his phone, but he didn't appear too far off. The bruises

I'd noticed under his violet eyes two weeks ago had deepened, and his cheeks were gaunt. He'd pulled back his chin-length strawberry-blond hair in his usual style, but the strands hung lank against the nape of his neck. His coat—a new coat? It certainly wasn't the peacoat I'd borrowed and repaired five weeks ago—hung loose on his shoulders, and every movement he made was slow and intentional, as though it pained him to shift his joints.

"It's true, then?" he asked.

I considered lying to him. He looked ready to collapse without me adding the weight of my worries onto his back. But what if the coven believed me about the broken amulet and started poking around into what had happened to the souls it had contained? Trace was already in a dangerous position by holding on to them, and ignorance of this new threat could leave him more vulnerable.

I scuffed my toe in the slush and watched water pool into the empty spaces. "They called me tonight. At the pub. In the middle of my shift. Can you believe the lack of respect for my schedule?"

The sarcasm and forced flippancy prevented my teeth from chattering with returning panic and rage, yet by the expression on Trace's face as he cocked his head, I wasn't doing that good a job of hiding either.

That was a joke. I knew damned well I wasn't hiding

anything. It was a miracle I wasn't a sobbing mess huddled against the trash bins.

"What's their deadline?" Just as he'd been throughout most of my mad dash away from the fae duchess, he was a pillar of steadiness. As though no problem were too great for him to handle.

Then again, this was Trace Wyatt, after all. He'd been a bounty hunter for the better part of a decade, travelling across Canada in pursuit of some of the country's supernatural most wanted, taking down marks and reaping the rewards. I imagined he and Chip faced situations like these all the time without spilling a drop of coffee. Destroying the villains and claiming fair maidens. Collecting favours from coast to coast.

I tried not to think too much about the fair maidens part. Nothing like a slap to the ego to know that you were one among thousands in the eyes of a handsome, confident, roguish man.

How pathetic was I?

"I'm supposed to meet them in an hour to make the exchange." I rubbed my hands over my arms to warm myself up. My anger at Trace had kept my blood rushing, but now that it was gone, I remembered how freaking cold it was out here. "Want to come for the drive? Watch me get my ass kicked?"

The question was out before I could think it through, but as soon as it was, I appreciated how much safer I would feel if he were nearby.

His eyes flashed. "You're going by yourself?"

Despite my recent ego check that I had no reason to think I meant anything to him except as a failed mark, my stomach fluttered at his show of concern.

"No. Madison is supposed to meet me there. Hopefully she'll be able to empathize our way out of this mess. Turn *them* into the sobbing wrecks. Then we can all head across the street to Tim's and grab a doughnut. Good way to start the day, don't you think?"

"I'll drive," he said, and turned to the street where his SUV was no doubt parked.

I started to follow him, but when he wobbled on his feet, I tightened my arms across my chest and stopped short. "I don't think so. Sorry, my friend, but I wouldn't trust you to drive me across the parking lot in your condition. When's the last time you slept?"

He stopped and looked at me over his shoulder. The hunch of his posture deepened, and he passed a hand over his eyes. After a moment, he nodded. "All right, you drive."

Dundonald Park was only a few minutes away, so it might have made more sense to walk, but if I succeeded in getting Gramps, I wasn't sure he'd be able to make it back to the pub without trouble. At least with the car, I could drive us to my place and get him patched up before sending him home to my parents.

Though for the coven's sake, they'd better hope he'd remained unscathed.

I led the way to my Nissan, and Trace climbed into the passenger seat, slumping so low, I was surprised he didn't slide onto the floor.

I shot him a sidelong glance and did my best to sound neutral as I asked, "Are you going to answer my question?"

He kept his gaze on the window. "Which one? I can hear about thirty buzzing through your head right now."

This man knew me too well.

"Let's start with the one I asked out loud. We can work through the others after I finish screaming at you for what I suspect your answer will be."

"I slept tonight, so no screaming required."

"For what? A whole ten minutes?"

"I actually managed fifteen."

"I'm sure that's blown the rest of the week out of the water."

He rubbed his eyes again. "I think on Tuesday I grabbed thirty."

"Someone call Guinness World Records."

He chuckled and burrowed deeper into his coat. I turned up the heat. It felt strange having the tables between us turned. Last time we'd driven together, I'd been the one shivering in the passenger seat, wearing nothing but my jammies and Simon's borrowed sweater. Trace had kindly turned his SUV into a sauna, even when he'd been on his way to drop me off to be killed by Dara. Such a gentleman.

We drove in silence for a while, giving me way too long to mull and muse and gradually spin myself into a maelstrom of emotions. Emotions I might not even have deserved to feel, but dammit, I couldn't not feel them. He'd come to mean too much to me to turn away from him.

"Seriously, Trace, why didn't you call me?" I asked softly, needing to get out at least part of what had given me almost as much insomnia as he was suffering. "Are you at least staying with Chip? Or with someone you trust who can help you if you need it?"

He snorted. "You think Chip would help me? The second he learned I'm carting hundreds of lost souls inside me, he doubled the wards around his house and primed the place to explode if I come within ten metres."

"Jerk." The antisocial bastard had better be glad I didn't believe Trace because I would be on the phone giving him crap so damn fast.

But again, what did I know of their friendship? Sure, they shared dorky nicknames and acted like besties, but maybe they hated each other. Maybe Trace had evidence that Chip secretly loved smiling and their entire relationship was based on blackmail.

I knew so little about Trace. One day together did not solidify confidante status.

Come on, Alyssa, grow up.

I gritted my teeth and glared out the windshield.

Trace shrugged and leaned his head against the head-rest. "I'm not the most stable person to be around right now. Emotionally or magically. I probably shouldn't be in the car with you. But this meeting—these people—"

He interrupted himself with a yawn that made his jaw crack so loudly I flinched.

"And you shouldn't be going through whatever this is," I waved my hand at him in a vague gesture, "by *your*self. How can I help you?"

"Do you know how to get rid of hundreds of lost souls in a way that won't unsettle the balance of the city?"

I swallowed hard. "You can't just... release them into the air?"

"Not unless we want them winding up places they shouldn't be. Taking over bodies that aren't prepared for them, getting absorbed by people wanting to use them for less noble reasons than mine, overpowering transformers and blowing out electricity across the entire city."

"They can do that?"

"I have no idea. Maybe. These spirits are strong. Probably

because they were stuck in an amulet for almost two hundred years. The gem smashed, and it was like a pressure cooker exploded."

"I didn't realize spirits got stronger the longer they stuck around."

Trace shifted in his seat and rolled his neck. "Not all of them. You could walk through an old house and there might be a lingering soul with their feet up on the coffee table in the living room, but they're content to be there, so they give off a comforting vibe. Someone decides to tear down the house, and that same spirit could slip into the contractor's head and force them to drive their car off the side of the road."

I cringed as I remembered a time, not so long ago, when I'd done something similar. Was he referring to that incident or was it simply a poorly chosen example? Was he still upset about the damage I'd done to his car?

Not the point, Mooney.

"So you're saying these spirits are pissed at being crammed in a necklace for two centuries."

"You were in my trunk for thirty minutes. How pissed were you?"

"Pissed enough to blow up a few transformers. Fair point."

I didn't know nearly enough about spirit magic. Mostly because it was illegal, and therefore the knowledge was locked tight somewhere in federally regulated vaults. But I knew some of Trace's history. Yes, Hazel was wasting away in Moongrave and he'd gone on to save the country one bounty at a time, but that didn't mean he'd forgotten the tricks of the trade. No matter how much he might wish he could.

"So how do we get rid of them?" I asked. "My great-great-grandfather promised to free them when he was finished with them. It turned out he was a lying SOB, but was he lying the whole time, or is there a way to do it safely?"

"There is, but it's not as easy as a spell and a tip of the hat. There's a whole ritual to it, with tools and equipment and accessories. You need a focal point, a way to release them directly into the energy of the world. Back into magic itself. I've only performed it once, and I don't feel confident throwing it together by myself. I've been reaching out to people for help, but…"

"Not a lot of people eager to get involved with a famous bounty hunter trying to lure them into admitting they deal in illegal magic?"

"Something like that, yeah." He sounded so tired, and as he slumped into his seat and rested his head on the window, I wished I could offer something more than encouragement. After all, it was my ancestor's fault that Trace was in this situation. The least I could do was try to make things right. Even if my family would be horrified.

My sister would freak out in her usual Drama Queen fashion and dive into a hysterical rant about how simply asking how to release the spirits would bring SMOAC to our door to lock up our whole family. Dad would be curious about the process but uncomfortable about his middle child getting involved, and Mom… Well, Mom would try to heal him in her own way.

Struck by the idea, I reached across the console and rested my hand on Trace's. His skin was warm and clammy, and I wondered if he was running a fever on top of everything else. But there was also a familiar spark that surged between us, a rush at the feel of him, and I applied more pressure, wanting to get closer.

He started at the contact and stared at our touching fingers as I pushed a dose of magic filled with healing intentions into him. A cloud of purple, wispy as cotton candy, rose in the air and soaked into his pores. I kept my eyes on the road but knew from experience that if I were watching, I'd see a faint purple sheen to his skin as the magic was absorbed into his blood stream. Maybe it would mix with his unique silver power and the two magics would dance around each other as they had so many times that wild, unbelievable day.

The purple sheen wouldn't last, and no one would see it except me—and any of the Mooneys who shared my bloodline gift of seeing magic as colours—but it made me happy to know I could give him even temporary relief.

A low moan drifted from his direction, and he flipped his

hand over so his fingers wrapped through mine. My heart leapt and tears pricked my eyes with an infuriating sense of *hope*.

In the next second, the car filled with soft, steady breathing. When I turned to look, I found Trace fast asleep.

Chapter 5
Alyssa

I PULLED UP under a streetlight and turned off the engine. Gramps's voice—and Trace's, I had to admit—was in my head telling me to pull up into the shadows to avoid being seen, but what could I say? The habits of being a woman alone at night were strong. Depending on how tonight went down, I didn't want to get mugged on my way back to the car.

Through the window, the park looked quiet. No group of people standing ominously in a coven circle, no screaming grandfather, no subtle colours suggesting a magical trap had been set. But there also weren't any homeless people sleeping on the benches or young people strolling through after a night out. If I had to guess, I wasn't the only one to have the get-here-early-to-scope-out-the-place plan and whoever else was here had woven a subtle spell around the park to keep people away.

A shiver ran through me, and I pulled my magic into my palms. It wouldn't do to go in unprepared.

Trace shifted in his seat, a low groan of pain escaping him, and his head tipped towards me. I took in his sleeping features, wishing he appeared more at rest instead of an unconscious version of his uncomfortable waking self. In the shadows, the hollows of his cheeks were more pronounced than they had been outside.

The desire to brush a stray hair out of his face was strong—the *need* to touch him almost overwhelming—but I settled for resting my hand on his where it had fallen into his lap.

"Trace?"

He didn't react to either his name or the contact, and although I knew he would be furious at me for leaving him, I didn't have the heart to try again. The man needed to sleep, and Madison would be here soon.

So, armed with my magic and a growing rage at the idea that anyone had laid hands on my grandfather, I got out of the car and walked into the park.

A low hum of magic swept over me. Not enough to be visible, but definitely enough to keep any mundanes from wandering through. I shoved my hands into my pockets, kept my power close to the surface, and scanned the darkness.

Finally, I spotted the van on the far side of the park. It was a black panel van, so it blended in well with the night, but I made out the faint cloaking spell over it as well. Most witches would have cloaked it entirely, but then I would have been able to see the magic. These people had been strong enough to nab Gramps, which meant they had power, so I doubted the less effective spell was a coincidence. The Mooney family's genetic quirk of seeing magic wasn't exactly a secret, but it did mean these witches had studied us.

I pulled my hands out of my pockets and kept them by my sides, playing with the atmospheric energy around me. It prickled my skin and swirled in waving patterns, testing the air, searching for anyone hiding in the shadows. With one good pulse, I could throw any unwanted attackers away from me, but I had to bide my time. No attacking until I saw Gramps. Ideally until I had him safely by my side.

Well, frankly, the ideal would be not having to fight at all, but I strongly suspected that the odds of these people saying *Oops, so sorry about the misunderstanding, we'll just be on our way* were slim.

My heart thrashed against my ribs as I reached the middle of the park. I felt eyes on me but couldn't place them, and the obscurity was messing with my head. I didn't like being on this side of what felt like a one-way mirror. It made me feel vulnerable and small, and there was nothing I hated more.

I pumped more magic into my hands. "I know you're there.

Come out and show yourselves. And give me my grandfather."

"Where is the amulet?"

The voice came from right behind me, but when I whirled around to face the speaker, I found the path empty. They'd used a spell to project their voice. The realization sent creepy-crawlies down my spine, and I forced my body not to shiver.

I hated this. I wished now I'd been less compassionate and tried harder to wake up Trace. I wished I'd arranged with Madison to meet me here earlier than the agreed-upon time. Or that I'd called my brothers after all. At the very least, I wished I had someone else at my back so I didn't have to look everywhere at once.

"I told you on the phone, it broke."

"You're lying."

The voice had moved to my left. Was it following the source? If I sent a blast of magic in that direction, would I send the witch behind the spell sprawling into the glow of the streetlights that barely lit the park?

"I'm not. It was smashed. There's nothing left of it but a really ugly setting. You can have that if you want."

It wasn't smart to goad them. I knew that. But sarcasm was my panic language, so I couldn't bite my tongue. It was either throw them a handful of snark or let my shaking limbs overwhelm me.

"Where is my grandfather?"

The only response was silence. I took a few more steps down the path, once more scanning the park for any sign of other people here with me. I paid particular attention to the van, squinting into the darkness to make out any figures standing beside or sitting in the vehicle, but there was nothing.

And then there was nothing at all. The lights in the park blinked out, leaving me draped in endless night. I could barely make out the porch lights from the houses only a street away.

Then a flash of green elemental magic morphed into a ball of fire as the witches attacked.

Chapter 6
Trace

I WOKE UP feeling more rested than I had in weeks, though the reprieve lasted all of thirty seconds before the souls taking up space inside me slammed against the magical barriers I'd put up. They were so desperate to get out, and I didn't know how much longer I'd be able to contain them.

Still, those thirty seconds of peace had been more than I'd accomplished on my own, even after hours of meditation and dozens of spells to strengthen my hold.

I'd have to send Alyssa a gift basket in gratitude.

Alyssa.

The rest of my night tumbled through my memory. Where the hell was she? I swung my head around to search for her, only realizing belatedly how ridiculous that was. What did I think she was doing? Crouching in the back seat?

The car was parked under a streetlight near the corner. To my left, through the driver's side window, I made out the row of old Victorian houses that lined the street. To my right was the park.

During the day, this park was a hub of activity, with markets and tai chi and folks going for walks. At night… well, it had a reputation in this neighbourhood for a reason. No matter what time anyone walked through, it was best to wear shoes to avoid a hospital visit.

Of course the witches would suggest Alyssa meet them here where it was unlikely anyone would look twice at a group *trading a person* for fuck's sake. What the hell were they thinking?

I wished I'd gotten to the pub earlier. Been there for Alyssa when the witches had called to make their demands. When Chip had called me this evening to tell me the rumours about Alyssa's grandfather, it had taken all my energy to drag myself into the shower and throw on some clothes so I could get to her and find out what the hell was going on.

He'd thought I was ridiculous for making the effort in my condition. Considering I hadn't been able to do anything other than lie in my crappy rental apartment and wrestle my resident spirits into place, he was probably right, but there was no way I'd let Alyssa face this threat alone. Not after everything she'd been through a month ago. Seriously, this woman had the worst luck.

She was holding up well on the surface, but she had to be freaking out. I'd gotten to know her well enough to imagine the million directions her thoughts had taken as soon as she'd received the ransom call. She would have already run through every worst-case scenario and come up with a few even these bastards hadn't thought of. And she was right to be afraid. They'd taken her grandfather. For an amulet that shouldn't have existed.

What were they planning to do with it?

Clyde Corrick had wanted the damned thing bad enough he'd killed at least two fae, syphoned their magic into himself, and framed Alyssa for murder and magic theft just so he could take over the bar, dig up the amulet, and lay claim to the city.

We'd destroyed him *and* his army of witches, demons, and shifters. What did this coven think they could do that Corrick couldn't?

I hoped I was right and their arrogance outweighed their intelligence, but I couldn't bank on it. Not when Alyssa and her family were involved.

For the tenth time tonight, I told myself I shouldn't care so much. Nine years ago, I'd promised myself I would never again let my heart rule my decisions. Hazel had ruined that option for me. Because of her, I'd lost my freedom for three years. I'd lost my dream of being a SMOAC task force soldier. I'd lost my innocence. All because I'd fallen in love and put my faith in someone I cared about.

For nine years, I'd held on to that promise—to so many promises.

How many had I broken for Alyssa already? I'd lost count somewhere around the time I'd taken the released souls into myself to protect her and ensure Corrick didn't get them for himself. I was already dealing with those consequences. How much more was I willing to sacrifice?

The question was still echoing in my head as I dragged myself out of the car and used the door to push myself to full height.

Where the hell was Alyssa?

The streetlights inside the park had gone out, shrouding the space in shadow, and my heart lurched with the realization that the witches she was supposed to meet were already here.

Had I slept through the whole damned thing?

Great job, Trace. Real fucking helpful.

I strained my senses to pick up anything beyond the darkness and the pulse rushing in my ears, but it was the prickle of familiar magic on my skin that guided my steps.

Until I'd spent the day with Alyssa, I'd never been able to recognize individual signatures before, but hers brushed against mine in a way that made me think of soft fingertips brushing over bare skin. It raised goosebumps on my arms and, usually, made my jeans a bit tighter.

Tonight, the way her power rose into a cresting wave set my heartbeat racing, and I upped my pace.

Soon enough, she came into view through the darkness, her concentration focused on holding off a man trying to pin her down. Her atmospheric magic was strong, but whatever bloodline this guy came from challenged that strength. They were caught in a state of attrition, each one working to wear the other down, neither gaining ground.

I summoned my telekinetic power and launched a discarded bottle at the man's head.

He cursed and staggered to the side, leaving Alyssa free to launch a spell and hurl him backwards into three other guys who were running away, dragging an older man between them.

Shit. I'd been so caught by Alyssa's trouble, I'd missed the fact that her grandfather was right there, still in the hands of whoever had abducted him.

Get your head in the game, Wyatt.

Alyssa was already tearing after them, so I joined her on the chase. After ten steps, my body rebelled, but I made up for my lack of speed with a few bursts of magic that knocked one guy on his ass and sent another hurtling forward. Unfortunately, neither of them had hold of Alyssa's grandfather.

A black van came into view through the shadows up ahead, the back doors open, the engine running.

Alyssa threw out her hands and tried to pin down the van with her power while I kept my attention on the kidnappers. I wrapped more magic around the one on the ground to bind him in place and threw out a magical net to grab hold of one of the two dragging the old man.

My magic bounced off, blocked by a strong ward.

I pushed my legs harder, doing my best to close the distance between us. My heart battered against my ribs, my breath came in wheezing gasps, and my steps faltered, but I pressed on… reached out my hand… made contact with the cheap polyester of the asshole's shirt—and got slammed by a hit of magic that threw me back half a dozen feet.

I landed on my shoulder, the air bursting from my lungs, as Alyssa shouted her frustration. The van door rolled shut, the engine revved, and the tires squealed as the vehicle drove away. I twisted towards the guy I'd pinned down, but his buddies must have grabbed him because the park was empty.

The string of curses that left Alyssa's mouth was as endearing as it was impressive, but the fact that she felt the need to get that creative meant I'd let her down. Again.

The crushing weight of that failure left me groaning as I rolled onto my side and pushed myself up. I startled on finding Alyssa crouched beside me.

"You all right?" she asked, her question packed with concern and not a hint of accusation. As though I hadn't ruined her chances of getting her grandfather back.

"I'm fine. What happened? Why didn't you wake me up?"

Well, that came off more than a little accusatory. *Well done, Trace.*

She frowned, as she had every right to, but didn't smack me upside the head, which I would have thoroughly deserved.

"I tried, but whatever you're—you didn't wake up."

The worry that skittered across her beautiful green eyes gave me a pinch of guilt, but for now I pressed it down with the other emotions, trauma, and neuroses I didn't feel like addressing this early in the morning. Soon enough, she and I would have to talk, but right now the priority was that black van and the man those creeps had dragged into it.

"I went into the park to check things out. I knew they were here but couldn't see anything. Somehow they put the lights out when I told them I didn't have the amulet, and then they swarmed me." She shuddered and ran her hands over her arms.

"They touched you?" Red snaked into my vision as I looked her over as best I could in the darkness.

"It's fine. I fought them off well enough. Thanks for helping with that last one. Too bad they grabbed him and threw him in the van before we could question him."

Despite her words, I watched the way she rubbed her wrist, and beneath her sleeve, I made out the shadow of a bruise against her pale skin. The pulse of rage sparked a simmering heat that spread to my fingertips, and I balled my fists to stop myself from chasing after that van and tearing out the throats of every scumbag who'd laid a hand on her.

This wasn't me. I didn't do overpowering anger. I was reason and logic. It was how I'd earned my reputation as the best bounty hunter in Canada. I was Mr. Hands-Off when it came to women. I was the detached professional who always put the job ahead of everything else.

I needed to sort my shit out, because the path I was heading down would not end well for me.

"I'm sorry about your grandfather," I said, and the crease between Alyssa's eyebrows deepened.

"He looked so scared, Trace. But not for himself. That worries me even more."

"Hey." I longed to bundle her against my chest until that worried look in her eyes faded, but I settled for wrapping my fingers around hers. "We'll get him back. We know he's breathing, and by the look of it, he wasn't hurt. They must have bound his magic, but they're keeping him alive. They won't risk losing their leverage over you. It buys us some time."

She replied with an unassured nod and stared off in the direction the van had gone.

As my breathing slowed, my magic settled, and another wave of exhaustion swept over me. Alyssa's car, only a few metres away, looked too far for me to crawl to. Maybe I'd curl up and sleep next to the park bench. I wouldn't be the first person to make myself comfortable here for the night.

"Come on," Alyssa said, her soft voice jerking me out of my doze. "I better give Madi a call and tell her not to bother showing up. Can you make it to the car?"

I grimaced, and her shoulders slumped.

She stood up without letting go of my hand and hauled me to my feet. She was stronger than she looked. Once I was steady, she let go of me and slid her arm under mine. I didn't want to burden her, but after a few steps, I found myself leaning on her, my weight partially offset by her solid form. I hated how *right* it felt to be this close to her. Or maybe how wrong it felt that we weren't closer still. Too many unsaid words and unknown feelings stood between us. And that promise. The one about leaving my heart out of it. Couldn't forget that.

What felt like days later, we reached the car. Alyssa set me against it as she opened the passenger door, and she didn't leave until she'd helped me in and actually lifted my legs over the lip. She closed the door, rounded the car, and slid into the driver's seat.

"Where can I drop you?" she asked.

I started to tell her I had a rental on Metcalfe but quickly stopped myself. I'd seen the hurt in her eyes when she'd asked me why I hadn't been in touch. If she found out I'd been that close the whole time, she'd turn those sad eyes on me again, and I didn't think my heart could take it. Plus my keys were in my car.

"Back at the pub is fine. I can drive myself home."

Was that me? The words sounded slurred.

Alyssa huffed and buckled herself in. "Not a chance in any kind of hell. I guess you're coming home with me."

Chapter 7
Alyssa

I CLOSED MY bedroom door and sank against it, exhaling all the wild emotions from the past hour that had yet to settle.

Trace was already asleep on my couch, having passed out the moment he'd collapsed onto it. Parka still on, boots off—though that had been close. He'd nearly been out before taking the second one off.

Trace Wyatt was asleep on my couch.

A parade of butterflies marched up and down my stomach, and I rested my hand over my lower belly in an effort to get them to shush.

Trace Wyatt was a wreck of a human being right now, and I had far more serious issues to think about.

Reminding myself of my grandfather's situation dropped

a boulder on those butterflies, crushing the delicate wings in puffs of dust.

I pushed myself away from the door, pulled my phone out of my jeans' pocket, and dropped onto the side of the bed. Madison picked up after the third ring.

"Alyssa? Where are you? I'm at the park, are you here?"

I pressed the heel of my palm into my forehead. "Crap, I was hoping to catch you before you left. No, I'm at home."

"It's no problem, I'll head back to the car. What happened? Are you all right? Did they not show up?"

"Oh, they showed up." I winced as I twisted my shoulder to check out the line of nasty bruises forming along the back of my left arm.

"Tell me."

With a groan, I threw myself onto the bed. "I got there half an hour ahead of schedule. I thought I was being so clever. Get an idea of the area, be able to see them drive up."

"Except they had the same idea?" Madison asked, her voice full of sympathy.

"You got it. The van was on the other side of the park, so I didn't notice it right away. As soon as I told them I didn't have the amulet, there they were."

"Did you get a look at them? Maybe I can ask Jet to poke around to see who we're dealing with."

"I really only saw one of them. Short brown hair? Hoodie,

no coat. Beard. Couldn't really make out more than that." My chest grew tight, as though a hand had wrapped around my heart. "Gramps was there. They dragged him out of the van to show him to me, but I never got a chance to talk to him."

Only now that I was home and safe did the pain of what had happened tonight start to sink in. Emotionally and physically, I was destroyed.

"They still have him, but without the amulet…"

"At least you know he's alive," Madison said gently. "They won't injure him if they think they can use him."

A bitter laugh escaped me. "Trace said the same thing."

"Trace? Wyatt?" Her surprise was nearly enough to earn a genuine laugh from me. "You've spoken to him?"

"He's asleep on my couch."

Asleep. Unconscious. Same difference.

A shudder ran through me as I thought of the state he was in. Such a wasted version of himself compared to the man who'd thrown up a magical wall to stop Dara from coming after us. The way he'd slept in my car, the lack of any response to my touch. If he hadn't been breathing, I would have thought my burst of healing magic had killed him.

"That's… Huh. That's a lot to take on in one night," Madison said.

"You're telling me." I kicked my feet against the side of the bed and squeezed my eyes shut.

With luck, when I opened them again, Trace would be awake and well, laughing with Gramps in my living room.

Not for the first time tonight, my positive thinking let me down.

When I opened my eyes, all I got was a buzz in my hand. An incoming text from Simon.

"Do you need me to come over?" Madison asked, pulling my attention back to the active phone call. "I can bring some of Nan's tea. It might help you sleep."

"I wouldn't want you to waste your magical tea on me, Madi. A hot shower, a pillow over my head, and I should pass out easily enough."

The silence on the line told me she believed it as much as I did.

"If you change your mind, I'm only a phone call away."

I thanked her, hung up, and rolled off the bed, barely catching myself from face-planting on the floor. Once I found my feet, I stood up and dragged myself to the bathroom. The ensuite was small but serviceable, with a shared second door to the living room. I'd considered installing a second bathroom for company, but it was so rare anyone stayed over. I'd opted to save my pennies and paint the living room a muted Tardis-blue instead.

I ran the water for the shower, and while it heated up, I rifled through the vanity cabinet for an extra toothbrush.

Unless he planned to slip out before I woke up, Trace would need one in the morning.

Because he was sleeping in my living room.

Trace Wyatt was asleep in my apartment.

A thrill ran through me despite the weight of my shitty night. He was sick—maybe dying. Gramps was in the hands of an enemy that wanted something that didn't exist. My best friend was acting like he'd gotten caught under a thundercloud. So many things that should be holding my focus over a foolish school-girl crush.

At the thought of Simon, I went back to my room to grab my phone. A series of messages from him waited for me.

Simon: How did everything go tonight?

Simon: Are you still there?

Simon: Call me.

Simon: Seriously. Call me.

Simon: I'm coming over

The last text had come in only a few minutes ago, but if he was still at the pub, he would be here soon.

Not wanting him to wake up Trace, I hurried out of the bathroom, through the living room, out of the apartment, and down the stairs. I pulled open the door at the bottom to find my bestie outside, his hand raised to knock.

Instead of relief at the sight of me, his amber eyes glowed a shocking demonic red. "What the fuck, Alyssa? You're home and walking around, and you didn't fucking call me?"

Exhaustion had wiped out my patience for his bullshit. "What the fuck yourself. I've just had a night from hell, and you come here to give me shit?"

He opened his mouth to snap back but caught himself. The glow in his eyes—a disturbing new development—disappeared, and his expression turned down with remorse. "I'm sorry. Infernals, Lys, I am so sorry." He pulled me to him and bundled me into a tight hug. The scent of cedar and hops wrapped around me, as familiar and comforting as an old sweater. "I was just worried, and you weren't answering and—Did you get him? Is Gramps all right?"

The dam I'd been holding back all evening snapped, and I cried against his chest. He held me as I let out my fear and rage and frustration. His strong hands stroked my back. At every moment, I expected Impatient Simon to make another appearance, but he stayed quiet and let me cry until I finally got the leftover panic out of my system.

I pulled away, used the heel of my palm to wipe my face, and sniffled in a way I only allowed my closest friends and family to hear. Good thing I wasn't trying to impress him anymore. "No," I finally said. "I didn't get him."

I gave him the same quick rundown I'd given Madison, and by the time I was done, the red sheen had returned to his eyes. "Wyatt was with you and he didn't step up? After everything you did when—"

"He's sick, Simon. He shouldn't have been with me in the first place. But he did step up. He gave a few of those guys a good walloping, but they were already halfway to the van."

Simon growled. "I should have been with you."

For the first time in my life, I was afraid of what might have happened if he had been—and not for the worry of spontaneous magical combustion.

Enough was enough. There would never be a perfect time to pry, but if I was going to be stressing about Gramps, I didn't have space to worry about my best friend as well.

"Are you… Is everything all right, Simon?"

The red faded again. "I'm fine, Lys. I promise."

I didn't believe him, and I opened my mouth to press a little harder, but I was smacked over the head with an exhaustion so heavy my legs nearly gave out. I didn't have the energy to argue with him or drag confessions out from behind stubborn lips. If he didn't want to tell me, I would respect his secrets. For now. "All right. But you know I'm here to talk if you need me. Any time, day or night."

His smile warmed me straight through. "I know it. I love you."

"I love you, too." I wrapped my arms around him and pulled him in for another hug.

"Need me to come up and keep you company?" he asked,

his chest vibrating under my ear. "We could throw on some stupid old show and chow down on a giant bowl of popcorn."

I chuckled. "Just like the old days, eh?"

"The best days."

They really had been.

"Thanks, but Trace is asleep upstairs. If these guys call again, I won't be alone."

Simon stiffened in my arms and pulled away. I braced for more anger, but there was only a faint hint of concern. "Are you sure that's smart? This is the guy who accepted a bounty on you. I know you two cleared the air a few weeks ago, but you haven't heard from him since. Then he conveniently shows up the same night Gramps gets taken? Do you really trust him enough to let him spend the night?"

I considered how it might look to someone on the outside looking in and had to admit Simon's suspicion made sense. But he didn't know Chip. Trace hadn't mentioned his friend specifically, but if he'd heard rumours about witches abducting my grandfather, there was only one person who could have passed them along. And instead of staying wherever he'd been holed up trying to get more sleep, Trace had come to find me. To help me.

I shoved my hands in my pockets. "You didn't see him tonight, Simon. Something's really not right. Whatever happened during that fight against Corrick—well, I think it's killing him. Even if he came to me with ulterior motives, he's not in any place to make a move against me."

If anything, I was going to have to find a way to help him. I wouldn't be able to live with myself if something he'd done to save me led to his death.

"Is he in any place to help you, then, if these witches come back?"

I pressed my lips together and said nothing, and Simon sighed. "If you're sure you don't need me to help you get your mind off things, I'll head out. Reverie invited me to the opening of her new club. I was going to see if you wanted to join me, but I'm guessing you'll give it a miss?"

"Unfortunately," I said, surprising myself by meaning it. I was more than a little curious to see how the fae-succubus had transformed the demon sex den into an elite underground experience. I owed the woman that much for dealing with Delvin and getting him off both our backs. "Please give her my best and tell her I'm rooting for her. I'll bring Gramps for cocktails as soon as we get him back."

Simon gave a nod and a wry smile, but as he made to leave, I reached out and grabbed his arm. "Thank you for coming tonight. And I really am sorry to miss the grand opening. One day soon, you and I have to catch up. Embrace some of those old days."

"I'd like that." He leaned in and kissed my cheek. "Try to

get some sleep. And if you need to call in tomorrow, just let me know. I'll make sure your shift is covered."

He left, and I dragged my feet back upstairs. Trace was still passed out on the couch, so I left him to it, headed for my still-running shower—the water still, for the time being, blessedly hot—and tried not to think of the fear in Gramps's eyes the moment before they'd thrown him into the van.

His fear for me.

Chapter 8
Alyssa

I DRAGGED MYSELF out of bed at an absurdly late hour the next morning to the smell of fresh brewed coffee.

Confusion warred with terror that someone had broken into my apartment to make me breakfast, but both emotions disappeared as the events of last night came back to me. The call at the pub, the trip to Dundonald Park. Gramps. Trace.

My stomach dropped out from under me, and I collapsed onto the edge of the bed and buried my face in my hands. Gramps was still gone. Now that I'd had time to sleep and process, I could accept just how serious this problem was.

Edwyn Mooney was the head of our coven, which happened to include the entirety of the Mooney clan. He'd led us all for the past few decades, ever since my nana passed away.

Whenever someone in the family had a problem, he was the one we'd call. Now he was missing.

I reached for my phone and checked the notifications, but there were no messages waiting for me from this mystery coven. Just an update from my parents in the family group chat letting us know they were about to board the plane.

My parents. I groaned into my hands as anxiety took another spin around my insides. They wouldn't know what had happened to Gramps, which meant I'd have to tell them, and oh, how I did not look forward to that.

Mustering my courage, I dialled Mom's number. When it went straight to voicemail—the woman was notorious for not charging her phone—I tried Dad. It rang four times before also going to voicemail. Their flight must not have landed yet.

"Hey, it's Aly," I started, but what the hell was I supposed to say? Did I drop this on them via voice message? Did I vague-book it and spike *their* anxiety about what was going on? In the end, I landed on blunt. Tear that Band-Aid right off. "Some-one's abducted Gramps and wants to trade him for the amulet of stolen souls." An amulet they did not know about since Gramps had sworn me to secrecy. Fuck. Family secrets were so overrated. "I think we need a family summit. Until I hear from you, I'm going to reach out to a few people and see what I can find out." I paused. "Hope your trip was amazing—can't wait to hear about it. Love you."

On that incredibly awkward note, I hung up and returned my head to the comfort of my hands as I brainstormed how I could follow through on that whole reaching-out thing.

The sound of someone moving around outside my room redirected my thoughts down a different path. Trace Wyatt was in my apartment.

Gramps was gone, but Trace was back.

Why did it have to be my fate that the one thing I'd hoped for had piggybacked on such a nightmare?

I looked down at my raggedy T-shirt and blue-and-green flannel pyjama pants. I had way bigger problems than what Trace Wyatt thought of my clothes, but dammit, if the rest of my life was falling apart, I could take tiny steps to make it look like I was holding my shit together.

First step: brushing my teeth.

But when I pulled the bathroom door open, it was to find Trace naked—*so* naked—and dripping, rifling through my cabinets.

I squeaked and closed the door. "Sorry! Towels are in the bottom drawer. Help yourself."

He mumbled his thanks, and I squeezed my eyes shut, though I didn't question myself too hard about whether I did it to block out or capture the memory of the sleek planes of his back, the suggestion of sculpted abdominals, or the tight lines of his glutes. It was clear he wasn't in his best shape—all the signs of rapid weight loss that I remembered from my brief healing days—but it was just as clear he was usually a man who took care of his body. In his job, he had to. When he'd run me down after I'd escaped his trunk, I'd probably been slow and clumsy compared to some of the more criminal bounties he hunted.

I swallowed hard and focused on grabbing clothes from my closet, *not* thinking about the rivulets of water trickling between his shoulder blades and down the curve of his—

I cleared my throat and rolled my eyes skyward, praying for strength. I would need to look this man in the eye in a few minutes, and I wouldn't be able to do that if my thoughts were full of everything from the neck down.

A minute later, a light double rap sounded at the bedroom door, which I took to mean the coast was clear. I gave it a moment before easing the bathroom door open and peering around the corner to make sure that was indeed the case. I brushed my teeth, threw my hair into a quick ponytail, then pulled on a clean pair of black jeans, a light blue T-shirt, and my favourite purple hoodie. I needed comfort clothes.

After a few bracing breaths and a pep talk in my bathroom mirror, I stepped into the living room to discover an omelette waiting for me on the kitchen table.

"This smells amazing. Thank you."

I sat down, keeping my gaze firmly on anything except

Trace as he poured me a cup of coffee and added the perfect amount of milk to the rich blackness. It had been five weeks, and the man remembered my coffee preferences. While I took my first sip of caffeine, judging myself for indulging when I knew how likely it was to kick off my anxiety, I snuck a few peeks at Trace's clothed body. Damn, the man cleaned up well. His damp hair hung loose around his face, the strawberry-blond a few shades darker than when it was dry. The strands brushed against the stubble lining his jaw, which was longer than I'd ever seen it, a shade closer to a full beard. It suited him. The dark circles that had swallowed his eyes last night appeared slightly less overpowering, giving his beautiful violet irises more space to stand out. And beneath his grey, long-sleeved tee, the sleeves rolled up to reveal forearms that made my mouth water, his shoulders looked straighter.

Overall, miles beyond how he'd looked yesterday. For the first time since he'd surprised me in the parking lot, I wasn't afraid he was about to keel over.

He caught me looking at him and raised an eyebrow, and I shifted in my seat to cover up my embarrassment. "How are you feeling today? Did you sleep well?"

"Better than I have in weeks. Your couch is even more comfortable than Chip's."

I grinned. "Having also slept on Chip's couch, I won't argue with you."

He sat in the chair across from mine and wrapped his hands around his coffee cup. "Speaking of Chip."

I raised my eyebrow. "I don't know if any good conversation starts with those words."

He chuckled. "I can see why experience might lead you to that conclusion, but you can't deny he's the best at digging up information people want hidden. We should give him a call. He might be able to access the security cameras from around the park last night. Or maybe track the call from the pub. If we know where your grandfather was taken, he might get footage of the people who took him. Just because we didn't win last night doesn't mean we're giving up."

I didn't think my heart could get any bigger for this broken man sitting across from me. "You think he'll be willing to help me out? After last time?"

Trace's eyes sparkled. "Are you kidding? He loves you like a sister. Not that he'll ever admit it—you'll have to take my word for it. He'll want a hand in destroying the bastards who took your grandfather."

At the thought of Gramps in the hands of said bastards, my warming heart turned cold again.

"Gramps," I said.

Trace tilted his head in question.

"He'd want you to call him Gramps. You've already done so much for me—the initial misunderstanding excluded."

His lips twitched. "Misunderstanding?"

I tossed my ponytail over my shoulder. "Of course. You never would have accepted the bounty if you'd known how amazing I am." I winked at him to let him know my ego wasn't actually as big as all that, but my stomach dropped and heat pooled between my legs when his eyes darkened to a deep indigo.

"You're right about that," he said.

His gaze bored into mine for a heartbeat. Two. Three. I broke first, grabbing my empty plate and taking it to the sink. "So. Chip?"

"I'll call him right away. In the meantime, keep your phone on you and the ringer volume up. These guys didn't get what they wanted, so they're going to try again. We need to come up with a plan to draw them in long enough to get Gramps away before they realize we've screwed them."

I chewed on my lip as I scrubbed my plate and set it on the rack to dry. He made everything sound so easy, but this was Gramps's life we were talking about. If the fight in the park last night proved anything, it was that I was in way over my head. With Trace on my team, my odds were better, and if he was right that Chip would get on board, maybe we stood a chance, but I didn't think it would be so straightforward.

I couldn't wait for my parents to get back to me. They'd have their own ideas on how to tackle this, and maybe be less likely to fuck things up. Because what could I contribute? Sure, I'd taken the fight to Clyde Corrick, but look how that had gone. My actions had led to Simon almost dying, Trace having to break his vow of never touching spirit magic again, and the breaking of an amulet that had been safely—okay, maybe not so safely—buried under the pub for forty years. I was a screw-up. I'd tanked my healing career, and it was a miracle Mooney's Pub was doing so well, but that was in large part thanks to Gramps and Simon, and if something happened to Gramps because of my decisions—

"Talk to me."

The simple command in Trace's calm, steady, deep voice broke though my anxious spin, and I realized I'd begun to hyperventilate with my hands stuck under the running water. I shut off the tap, dried my hands on a dish towel, and turned to lean my butt against the counter, crossing my arms in a classic defensive posture.

My throat was thick with emotions, shame being just one, and I concentrated on relaxing the muscles in my neck and shoulders. I could talk to him. I could tell him my concerns without breaking into tears out of fear for a beloved family member.

The words tangled on my tongue, and my vision blurred.

Goddammit.

"Hey." Trace pushed his chair back and strode towards me.

His shirt hung off his shoulders, but instead of making him look small or silly, he looked all the more approachable. Maybe that was why I didn't think before sliding my arms around his waist and resting my head against his chest. His heartbeat sped up under my ear, and I told myself it was because of the stress his body was under and not anything to do with me.

He wrapped his arms around me and set his cheek on top of my head, and for a moment we stood like that, with only my mixing bowl clock and his heartbeat filling the silence.

"We'll get him," he murmured. "Before you know it."

I didn't see how, but for this moment, I chose to believe him.

As the seconds passed, his body hardened, and the heat in my core rose another few degrees. This wasn't the time. This, in fact, was the worst possible moment to be feeling any of the things I was feeling, and yet I didn't want it to go away. Everything else was horrible, but this—this was the first purely happy experience I'd enjoyed in weeks.

This time Trace broke first. He patted me on the back and gently pulled away. "Come on. The sooner we get on this, the sooner we can throw the welcome home party."

I smiled and nodded, swallowing my disappointment and my lingering curiosity of just how much I was reading into what might have been interest on his part, and followed him into the living room where his phone lay on the coffee table.

First we'd call Chip and hear what he had to say. Once we got his opinion on the matter, I'd call my parents again. At least that way my next update would be more than bad news.

Trace unlocked his phone and brought up Chip's number, but his finger hovered over the call button. "Maybe…"

I held up my hands and walked back to the kitchen table to grab my coffee cup. Chip was the most paranoid man I'd ever met in my life. If you complimented the colour of his shirt, he would assume you were speaking in code and passing it along to someone outside his fortified house. He didn't have a door-bell, he had a trapdoor that would drop the unwanted into a vat of boiling oil beneath his porch.

Okay, probably not. But maybe. I couldn't rule it out. Which was why I understood that it would be better for Trace to call him without me sitting at his elbow. Chip would no doubt hear my breathing through his enhanced speaker system, know that Trace wasn't alone, hang up, and never speak to his best friend again.

Better to not take the risk.

Trace made the call and gave me a wink as he dropped onto the couch with the phone pressed to his ear. My stomach launched into Olympic-level flip-flops, and I buried my grin behind my mug.

"Hey," he said after a short time had passed. "Alyssa's place. No. No. Yes. No! What the fuck, man?"

I smothered my laugh with another sip of coffee, guessing where Chip's questions had headed. From the start, he'd made assumptions about the nature of my relationship with Trace, and clearly Trace hadn't been able to convince him otherwise.

I refused to hope that it was because he hadn't tried very hard.

"No. Yes. Yes. A coven abducted her grandfather and is demanding she return the amulet that broke."

Trace seemed to have uttered the magic words, because he set the phone on the table, put it on speaker, and gestured for me to join him on the couch.

"Heya, Chip," I greeted.

"Cheers," he replied, using his term of endearment for me. Or he'd already forgotten my name. Either way, I was pleased he'd decided to acknowledge my existence. "Sorry about Gramps."

I opened my mouth to ask how he knew my name for him, then snapped my jaws shut. Of course he did. The man probably knew how I organized my underwear drawer.

Which was not at all, of course. Who even did that?

"Thanks," I said. "I don't suppose you have any ideas on how we can find him? Or how to get him back?"

"Tell me what you know."

I gave him the rundown, going into more detail for him

than I had for either Madison or Simon, describing the way they'd used their magic, which had mostly been elemental with some spirit power mixed in. I told him about their fighting ability and dropped the few details I'd noticed about the van. I didn't know what information would help Chip, so I gave him everything. Maybe there was something in the way they'd attacked me that would give them away.

"Really?" he asked when I finished. "You've had all these opportunities to learn something useful, and that's all you've got for me?"

I sat up straighter and glared at the phone. "Excuse me, Mr. Conspiracy, but I don't spend my life analyzing every blink or hair toss for a secret message, all right? That's what I saw. Can you help me or not? Because if not, then I have better ways to spend my day."

Like pacing the length of my apartment hoping the kidnappers would call me again. Without Chip, I had nothing.

Trace scooped up my hand and twined his fingers through mine. His silver telekinetic magic hummed against my skin, and I relaxed into the sensation. Without thinking, I let my purple atmospheric magic come out to play, and the two powers swept around each other, creating beautiful unplanned braids that I was sad Trace couldn't see for himself.

"Unbunch your panties," Chip said. "I didn't say I couldn't use what you gave me. And you should absolutely watch out for hair tosses. They always mean something."

I wished I could argue with him, but no. He was right.

The clacking of fingers flying over a keyboard reached us from over the phone line, and a moment later, Chip let out a grunt of satisfaction. "I don't know if these are the people who have your grandfather, but they've been naughty lately. Naughtier than they've been in the past. Their coven has been skirting SMOAC's trackers for years. They disbanded for a while, but about three years ago, they got back together. Though… huh. I think they've been absorbed into a larger group. Over the past few months they've been taking a lot more risks, buying up expensive tomes of dark magic, recruiting, storing power."

They had to be nasty if the government was on their asses. I wondered if Jet or Madison knew who they were.

"Who are these guys?" Trace asked.

"Remember you're the one who asked me for help, all right? I'm just the messenger."

Trace's jaw flexed. "Just hit me with it."

He spoke as though he'd already guessed. I was sitting close enough to him to catch the faint tic at the corner of his mouth. His long eyelashes fluttered as the lines around his eyes hardened.

His reaction undid all the work he'd done to calm me down, and I tightened my grip on his hand, bracing myself for what we were about to learn.

"It's the Bone Casters."

The name meant nothing to me, but Trace bowed his head into his free hand, and his shoulders slumped. "Fuck me."

Chapter 9
Trace

Alyssa stared at me as though I'd grown a second head, but I wasn't ready to explain myself to her. Not until I'd given myself a chance to process the worst news Chip might have dropped on me.

"You're sure?" I asked.

"All the hallmarks are there. Except for the obvious one. Kurt Stippen, Emile Gauvin, Nathalie Muir. All the old gang. They must not know you're back in town. Like I said, I don't think they're leading this, but I can't track down who's giving the orders."

They never would have taken the chance of getting back together if they'd known I was close. Unless they believed their new coven was powerful enough that it didn't matter if I was here or not.

"Can you check in on Hazel for me? Make sure she's where she's supposed to be?"

"I'm on it."

"Thanks, man," I said. "See what else you can find. We'll be in touch."

"Trace." I noted the concern in his voice. Chip didn't do concerned, only brash and sarcastic, so my chest tightened as he said, "Take it easy on this one, okay? You might be facing a long, hard look in the mirror."

I thanked him again, hung up, and sagged into the couch. All the energy I'd recovered from Alyssa's magical touch and her almost-as-magical couch seeped out of me, and I was sure that, given thirty seconds, I could pass out right here. But we didn't have time for that. As Chip said, we didn't know for sure that the Bone Casters had Gramps, but if they were in town and working together as a coven, Ottawa was in for a bad time.

Alyssa pulled her leg onto the couch so she could face me, but although her green eyes remained solidly on my face, she kept her questions to herself. I could have kissed her. Goddess knew I wanted to. It had taken all my restraint in the kitchen not to slide my fingers through her hair and trail my lips down her neck. The woman was driving me wild.

But she deserved answers more than the attentions of a broken, possessed witch.

I scrubbed my hands over my face and opened my eyes to meet her gaze. "They're not actually called the Bone Casters," I started, taking a stab at what the first of her million questions might be. "It's what Chip and I call them. A way to turn the bogeyman into something more approachable."

"I'll admit I'm a little relieved," she said. "By the way you guys talked about them, I get the impression they're into some dark stuff, but with a name like that, who would take them seriously?"

I chuckled, appreciating her attempt to lighten the mood a degree or two, but my amusement dried up quickly. "Unfortunately, all its done is take a ridiculous name and turn it into the monster under the bed." I rolled my neck until it popped a few times, then slid backwards until I hit the arm rest. "You remember what I told you? About my history?"

I wasn't sure if she'd retained much of the spiel I'd dumped on her in my panic-induced confession while I'd raced her to the fae duchess. Not my proudest moment, any of it.

Yet Alyssa's gaze softened, and she leaned her shoulder against the cushion as she pulled her knees to her chest. "You were eighteen and in a relationship with an older woman who pulled you into spirit magic. Hazel."

I nodded. "Hazel." Speaking her name—especially saying it in front of this beautiful, comparatively innocent woman—left a rancid taste in my mouth. And made me feel as though I was asking for the evil bitch to pop back into my life to cause more trouble.

"She convinced you to dabble in absorbing souls," Alyssa continued. "You backed out. She sent SMOAC after you, and you went on the run for three years before you finally worked with the federal officers who sent her north to Moongrave Prison. I think that was all the highlights?"

I didn't think twice before reaching out and taking her hand, once more wrapping my fingers through hers. She was amazing. "That's the important stuff. The Bone Casters—or the Anima Venatores, the Soul Hunters—was her coven."

Alyssa's eyes widened as she leaned towards me. "You mean…"

I nodded. "They're my old crew."

She slumped back against the cushion. "Well, shit," she breathed. "Is that why you asked Chip to look into her? You think she might be behind them coming back?"

"I think it would be an oversight not to consider it—an oversight we can't afford."

Alyssa caught her bottom lip between her teeth and threw her gaze to the side, as though she was considering something. I watched that lip and swallowed hard. After a moment, she shook off wherever her thoughts had gone and met my eye. "Chip's right. This won't be easy for you. If you bowed out right now, I'd understand it. No hard feelings, no blame."

I wondered what she'd been thinking before and suspected it hadn't simply been about me walking away, but let it be for now. Instead, I tightened my grip on her fingers and, with as much firmness as I could wrangle, said, "I'm not going anywhere."

She stroked her thumb across the back of my hand, sending sparks racing under my skin. "Trace, these are the people who betrayed you. Who stole everything from you."

The worry in her eyes—concern on my behalf—melted my self-control. I tugged her towards me, taking my free hand to brush a loose strand of hair behind her ear. "I told you I would help you get Gramps back. I won't let my past mistakes get in the way of doing that, all right?" I found myself staring at her mouth and licked my lips in response. "I've met your demons. Now we'll go play with mine. It's about time I figured out a way to banish them for good."

Chapter 10
Alyssa

I'D FORGOTTEN HOW to breathe.

Trace was so close, and his hands were so warm, and he smelled so good, and I wanted to lose myself in him and never let him go. Especially when letting him go would mean walking out of this apartment directly into my problems and the past he had spent so many years running from.

He had become Canada's most famous supernatural bounty hunter in an effort to put these bastards behind him. Hazel had accused him of her own crimes, and it was only because one fed had been willing to listen to the truth that Trace wasn't the one wasting away in the supernatural prison up north. Probably in one of the higher security facilities because of the magic he was supposedly capable of casting.

Okay, more than supposedly.

The fact that he was currently playing host to hundreds of stolen souls was proof enough that he was most certainly capable of working the magic he'd been accused of. But let's face it, it was the intention not the type of magic that made someone evil or not. Trace had absorbed those souls to prevent Clyde Corrick from using them in ways they wouldn't have wanted. And he was trying to figure out a way to release them safely without them winding up in anyone else's hands or wreaking uncontained havoc throughout the city.

He had used illegal magic to save the day.

As far as I was concerned, that got him a pass.

But I couldn't expect him to face his old coven for me. Especially while he was carrying said souls. That was torture no one should have to endure.

I also didn't know how to tell him that I'd also asked Jet to look into Hazel's current status. My reasons had been out of curiosity and no small amount of suspicion, but I had to consider the possibility that he would see it as me poking my nose in where it didn't belong.

I felt wedged into a corner, sure of making all the wrong decisions, forced to watch everything around me fall apart while everyone else scrambled to pick up what I'd let fall.

"Alyssa?" Trace's voice dragged my attention out of its tailspin back into the room and his beautiful, deep, violet eyes.

"Are you hearing what I'm saying?"

I swallowed to try to work some moisture back into my mouth. "That you're not leaving me to do this alone."

"That's right. We're in this together, just as we were with Dara. Okay? You and me."

I shouldn't accept. I should ask him to do me a favour and keep his distance until he was sure he was up for it. But even as my selfless side urged me to utter the words, the rest of me held back. He was a grown man, and these were his demons. He had a right to make up his own mind how he wanted to tackle them. I would help him through it as he helped me. We'd proved we could be a good team. Now we'd prove it again.

I tightened my grip on him. "You and me."

He heaved a breath and squeezed his eyes shut. I didn't know if he was bracing himself for what came next or fighting a bout of pain from the restless souls, but I took the words we'd spoken to heart. He wasn't about to let me deal with Gramps's kidnappers by myself, and I wasn't about to let him suffer alone.

I ran my fingers through his strawberry-blond hair, the strands still loose and damp from his shower. It was the first time I'd seen him with his hair down. Normally he kept it tied back and out of his eyes. This look suited him. His locks were thick and lush, catching red and gold in the overhead lights. And so soft.

He tilted his head into my palm, and as my pulse leapt, my magic surged. Sprinkles of purple poured out of me and tangled with the shimmer of yellow-tinged silver encircling him. The weaves of our magic tangled together, seemingly playing in the air as though they were friends who'd missed each other's company.

When my attention shifted from the dancing magic back to Trace, I found him staring at me. So much closer than I'd realized before. My breath caught, my heart stuttered, and I couldn't look away.

I swore I remained still, but by some gravitational force, Trace grew closer. His warm breath fanned across my cheek, the heat of his skin stroked mine. For a moment, we were back on the wintry street outside the demon sex club, hearts racing, lust woken thanks to the demonic pheromones floating through the air of the club. Except here there was no supernatural excuse. Despite the layers of chaos and disaster waiting for us beyond this house, my body was responding to him all on its own, and I was surprised by how strong a response it was.

By the way his pupils dilated, turning almost full black in my cozily lit living room, there was no misreading his desire. My attraction wasn't one sided.

His phone buzzed on the table, making us jump.

He reached for it and frowned. "Chip just sent over the address the Casters are working from. It's not far, but we'll probably want to drive." He hesitated. "Think we could pick up my car? I'd rather have them recognize mine than yours."

I pushed myself to my feet and walked to the counter to get my keys, wanting to put my back to him until I'd composed myself. "Of course. We may as well head out now. The sooner we track them down and get Gramps back, the happier I'll be."

Because right. Priorities. Normally I was better at keeping them straight.

"Alyssa?"

At the sound of his quiet voice, I made myself turn around. He'd stood up and was shoving his phone into the extra-large pocket of his man pants. But what caught my attention more than the unfair fashion discrepancy was the heat in his eyes.

He stalked towards me and stopped only when his tall frame towered over me. "I'd like to finish that conversation once we've taken care of everything else. If you're interested."

"Oh, I'm definitely interested," I replied. Or I attempted to. I had no idea if the words that tumbled from my mouth were coherent.

His smile nearly made my legs give out, but it vanished too soon as he reached for his coat. "First let's get this next part out of the way."

"Where are we headed?" I asked as I followed his example and grabbed my coat and slid my feet into my winter boots.

He grimaced. "The old power station."

Chapter 11
Alyssa

I HAD ALWAYS believed the building on the corner of Bronson and Glebe Avenues with the boarded-up windows and loading dock was an actual power station. Turned out, I'd been living in a mundane dreamworld. According to Trace, it was a well-known supernatural community centre.

I was no stranger to the effects of the perception filter on the mundane mind—the magical barrier that prevented non-supernaturals from seeing the truth about the world they lived in. This barrier protected supernaturals from their secrets being outed, and it protected the mundanes from having their sanity suctioned out through their eyeballs. Win-win.

That didn't mean I wasn't caught off guard the odd time I had my eyes opened to a new truth about this city. Usually I loved the surprise. It was a chance to see the familiar in a new way. But today, given everything we faced, I would have liked to walk on solid ground and not have my expectations ripped out from under me.

"So the coven is working here?" I asked Trace as we sat in his SUV across the street from the building. Now that the blinders were off, I could see the truth for myself. It was a nice enough two-storey building, bright with windows on all sides facing quiet Glebe and busy Bronson. The double doors in the front were closed but covered with bright papers inviting people to participate in the drop-in courses on offer.

"According to Chip, this is where they've been meeting a few times a week."

"If they're up to something illegal, why not meet somewhere more private? Surely one of them has a place here in Ottawa."

He frowned. "They might not. They're all Alberta-based. The reason Chip and I call them the Bone Casters is because they—we—used to perform most of our rituals out in the Badlands where we wouldn't be seen or interrupted. I don't know what might have brought them here. It's possible they're staying with someone who doesn't know what they're up to, so they're taking their plans off-site. Or they have a home base but if they're recruiting, they don't want to bring people there until they're in deep enough not to pull away."

I chewed on my lip, considering the possibility that the reason they were here had something to do with the man beside me. The odds were too great to ignore, and I was certain Trace had thought about it as well.

He shifted in his seat and played with the vent. "Whatever their intentions are, they're not being subtle about what they're up to. Chip tells me rumours are bouncing across the city that these guys are taking a tour of the magical hot spots, performing rituals to strengthen their power—mostly in shady ways. The owner of the centre is about to cancel their rental contract because of it."

"What kind of shady ways?"

Trace tapped his fingers on the steering wheel, a gesture I remembered from our time together. The guy was stressing. For his sake, I hoped he didn't go full panic attack at the memories that had to be bombarding him right now, but I wouldn't blame him if he did. "None of the others have my ability to harness the souls they absorb." His brow furrowed, the harsh lines adding years to his face. "My telekinetic magic—I told you—it… I can create a sort of cage around them, bind them in. Every form of magic can do something that comes close, but not for as long or with as much stability." He shrugged and shifted again, and my heart broke at the depth of his shame over what his magic could do. "So they can't harness what they take, but if the souls are weak enough, they can absorb them.

Or store them in artifacts, like the amulet. All they need is a strong enough magic source to do it. Like a hot spot."

Magical hot spots were common enough. Little pockets of space where power gathered until something caught it and channelled it—a bush that stayed in bloom longer than made sense for the season, a spontaneous localized storm. Or an asshole with an amulet and a mean streak.

"So you think they're harnessing souls?" I asked as horror settled in my gut. "Like, killing people?"

I didn't know why I was so shocked. Corrick had made it clear he had no qualms about spilling blood to get what he wanted, and I doubted Hazel had limited her ambitions to robbing graves of the lingering spirits within. But I did my best to believe in the goodness of people, dammit, and these folks were making that a real challenge.

Trace's expression didn't lose its grimness. "I doubt they're going around committing murder—yet. But I wouldn't put it past them to encourage people to go down dark, life-threatening paths, and then lie in wait to take what they can get. A drug-loaded person might not have the strongest spirit, but it's still more powerful than no spirit at all."

I hated the thought of some poor kid sitting around debating his life choices and these witches coming along and acting like the devil on his shoulder to push him over the edge.

"I wonder if it has anything to do with the rise in ghost

sales in the area," Trace added, seemingly to himself. But I couldn't help but hear him, and once I heard it, I couldn't help but gawk at him.

"You think this coven is pushing ghost?"

Ghost was a supernatural-created drug that temporarily heightened the abilities of supes or cleared the perception filter for mundanes. It was incredibly dangerous. A smidge over the limit, and you were looking at an early grave. Jet had been chasing the Ghostmaker, the mystery person behind the drug, for months and hadn't gotten any closer while the overdoses in the city piled up.

Trace shot me a glance, and the corner of his mouth quirked upwards. "For someone who owns a pub, you are incredibly sweet."

I crossed my arms. "I'm not naive. I know what goes on in this city, and I know not all witches are bright, sunny angels looking to help everyone. But to encourage broken people to cross that line just so they can absorb their souls? That's... dark."

Trace's smile disappeared. "It is. It's darker than what we used to get up to, but Chip's kept his eye on the coven since we parted ways, and they've clearly sprinted away from any lingering morals they might have once held."

I peered out the window at the community centre. "You think that's why they want the amulet, then? Because they believe it has more souls that will fuel whatever it is they're trying to achieve?"

He nodded. "The amulet isn't the end goal, but with the amount of power it contained, they'd be a lot closer to whatever that end goal is."

Everything inside me tightened up as I forced myself to look at him. "What will they do when they learn the spirits are now in you instead?"

His throat bobbed as he stared out the window.

If we were right, then as soon as these Bone Casters—or whoever was leading them now—found out about Trace, he would be a target. He wasn't safe anywhere near these people.

"I'm still not leaving," he growled, arguing as if I'd once more suggested it. "If they want to come after me, they're welcome to try, but I won't make it easy for them. They have no idea what I'm capable of. Especially now."

As far as I could tell, the thing he was most capable of right now was blowing over in a strong breeze, but I wasn't about to say that either. He'd proved me wrong many times since we'd met, and I was more than willing to let him prove me wrong again.

"So what's the plan, Mr. Bounty Hunter?" I asked. "Go inside and pick up a flyer? See what the coven's initiation fees are?"

"Sorry to break it to you, princess, but right now our job

is eighty per cent of a bounty hunter's gig. Sitting and waiting."

"Great." I pulled my phone out of the small purse I'd brought with me. "I'll catch up on my emails, then. You let me know when there's anything interesting to—"

"There's Emile."

I dropped my phone back into the pocket. "That was fast."

Trace pointed out the balding man in his early forties walking down the street away from the community centre. His black parka gave the impression of a portly frame, but a portly frame ready to face the elements. Boots on, scarf tight around his neck. Everything except the hat.

Mr. Witch was too cool for hats, apparently.

"Do we follow?" I asked.

"Let's give him a minute. We'll see which way he goes or if any of the others come out. I doubt they'd have made us already, so I'm curious to see if they lead us anywhere interesting."

My hopes leapt. "To Gramps?"

"Someone has to be watching over him, so it's not impossible. If they don't take us to him, maybe we'll get an idea of what they're really after."

We kept our sights on Emile as he made his way up the street towards Bank, but no one else came out of the building. Trace only turned off the car engine once our target was a block away, and we got out to follow him on foot. The pace we kept to go after him was fast enough not to lose sight of him but well enough back that it was unlikely we'd be noticed.

We might be walking towards my grandfather. The thought was enough to send my system into a state of chaotic anticipation. I still hadn't heard from my parents, and I thought of how incredible it would be if Trace and I were able to save Gramps and bring him home before Mom and Dad had time to panic. Instead of a family summit to rescue the head of our coven, we would summon one to stand against these witches creating mayhem in our city. It was a much better, safer, less personal approach. Because the alternative was that I would have to watch my family scramble to fill the void Gramps left in his wake. Someone would need to take his place—only until we got him back, I assured myself—and come up with a plan of attack.

And what would happen if we never got him back? What if we failed, and this coven killed him and ran Trace down and—

Trace grabbed my hand and slid it under his arm, pulling me closer. I shot him a surprised look, reeling after being torn from my thoughts, and he grinned at me with his violet eyes brimming with understanding.

"It's a beautiful day," he said. "The weather is changing, we're out for a walk in a beautiful neighbourhood. We'll draw less attention if we're happy and carefree and discussing our options for what dog we want to adopt."

I couldn't help but laugh, too shocked to hang on to my bleak spiral. "Dog?"

"You don't like dogs?"

"More of a cat person."

"Really? This surprises me. I could see you going for a run with your canine companion in the morning."

"Me? Go for a run? I guess you're right that I should start given recent experiences." I pulled back enough to look him over and nodded. "But yeah, I should have guessed. I totally see you as a throwing-balls-in-the-dog-park kinda guy."

"What can I say? I'm a sucker for a pair of big, beautiful eyes."

The way he stared into mine made my cheeks grow warm, and he nudged my shoulder with his as we crossed the street and continued after Emile.

His flirtatious—was he flirting?—banter had distracted me away from my worries for a few seconds, but they returned in a wave when Emile turned onto Bank Street and we lost sight of him. But I should have had more faith in Trace's experience. He turned us left at the corner, and sure enough, there was our quarry heading into the liquor store.

What an anticlimactic turn of events.

"What do you think?" I asked. "Picking up some beer for this evening's shenanigans or is there a secret spell circle under the store?"

"Definitely the beer," Trace said, looking both ways before he jaywalked us to the café across the street. "He always preferred to finish a spell with a drink. Says every magical casting deserves a celebration. He also tends to go to sleep early and wake up late."

"That tracks."

Trace kept an eye on the window while I ordered us some coffees to go—and a muffin because I was starving—and by the time our order was up, we were on the move again. Emile wasn't carrying anything visible, so I guessed he'd only grabbed a can or two for the evening and stuffed them in his pockets. It left his hands exposed, and before long he was rubbing them together, uncomfortable as the wind picked up and the sky grew darker.

"Where to next, do you think?" I asked.

Trace frowned. "He might go back to the community centre if this was just a booze run. We might be back to the sitting-around-waiting part." He cast me a sympathetic look. "Sorry to have gotten your hopes up for a quick and easy resolution."

I struggled to find my smile as my visions of revealing a rescued Gramps to my parents slipped away. "At least we got some exercise."

But where we would have expected Emile to turn right to return to the centre, he struck left, heading towards Elgin. We kept him in our sights as we crossed Centretown and hoofed it all the way to the park outside the Natural History Museum.

"What's he want with the castle?" I asked, using the name people across the city called the museum, an old stone building with its aesthetic parapets and less attractive but kinda cool giant glass cube at the front.

"Couldn't begin to—" Trace started, then cut himself off as the guy ducked behind some trees near the parking lot. "Ah."

"Ah?"

"I'm going to guess there's a magical hot spot hiding in there. They're up to their old tricks, stashing their stuff ahead of time to keep everyone else away. I shouldn't be surprised. Witches are creatures of habit."

"We are not."

"No? When's the last time you went out and did something spontaneous?"

"Five weeks ago, I was abducted from my apartment and stuffed in the trunk of a car. Does that count?"

Trace grinned. "I'm never going to live that down, am I?"

"You're really not."

Despite the time of day, Emile seemed quite comfortable wandering through the greenery doing… whatever he was doing. Prepping for some spell tonight, maybe? He was out of sight for a while, which left my attention free to wander while I ate my muffin, and my gaze fell on the apartment building across the street.

"That could be handy."

Trace looked at me, and I nodded towards the apartments.

"Isn't that where your friend lives?" he asked. "The fed?"

"The one and only. I wonder if she'd let us hang out in her living room tonight. Maybe to watch the park for any strange behaviour? Like a spell being cast outside the castle?"

"Couldn't hurt to ask. Better than sitting in the car all night. At least we'd have a bathroom."

My hopes had been on a wild ride today, but they were in full gear now. If we played this right, we could have a lead to finding Gramps. We could only take this one step at a time, and now we were one step closer to putting my family back to rights.

Chapter 12
Alyssa

WE WALKED BACK to get Trace's car, and while he called Chip to have him put eyes on the castle, I set to work on contacting my family.

Though I put it off another few minutes by texting Simon.

Me: How is everything at the pub?

Simon: Going fine. Pulled in Becca to cover some tables.

Me: Sorry for being so last minute. We're hunting Gramps's kidnappers. Might have figured out who they are. Stakeout tonight.

I left out the part about them being Trace's old coven. Given Simon's unpredictable nature right now, I didn't think it was in anyone's best interests for him to know.

Simon: Stay safe. Call me when you need me to crush some skulls.

He ended with a brain emoji, and I couldn't help but think he was imagining smearing said brain matter across the asphalt, which worried me. Simon was a chaos demon. He'd never been one for violence. At most, a little bit of mischief. And even then, it was mostly his magic that created the wild and unexpected. He'd spent his life trying to curb his demonic nature. But for the past two weeks—especially with that red glow in his eyes—it seemed like he'd suddenly embraced it.

Again, my thoughts turned to Reverie, the half-succubus with the heart of champagne. Was she corrupting my beautiful friend with her… ways? Because if she was, she would have me to deal with.

Still, I had to ask.

Me: How was the opening last night? Rev happy?

Simon: It was perfect. She was glorious. Everything about that woman is beauty itself.

I rolled my eyes. I'd also never known him to wax poetic, especially over a woman. But, hey, new love and all that. I'd give it a pass. Unless it turned out she was ruining him.

Me: Glad to hear it. Can't wait to see for myself. Will keep you posted about tonight.

Still procrastinating on dealing with my family, I shot a quick text to Jet.

Me: Hey, beautiful. I don't suppose Trace and I could take over your living room window tonight? We're planning a stakeout of the museum.

Jet: If you have sex, keep it down. I have a meeting tomorrow morning. I'll leave the door unlocked.

My cheeks warmed, but all I said to Trace was "Jet says we're good for tonight."

He nodded. "Excellent. We'll stock up on snacks."

Finally, having no other reason to avoid it, I readied myself to ruin my family's day. I really didn't want to do it over group text, but it was the easiest way to tell all my siblings at once.

Me: We have a problem.

To my lack of surprise, my sister Valery replied first.

Val: What? Why didn't you call me? What's going on?

Me: I didn't want to wake up the kids last night and then I was out trying to look into something this morning, and… where are the men? We need a group call pronto.

Brody: Just waking up. Gimme a sec.

Val: It's 1:30 in the afternoon, Brody. What is wrong with you?

Brody: Spending twenty-five years around your micromanaging ass. I'm still recovering.

Dylan: OMG will you all shut up. It's so early.

I banged my head against the window.

"You all right?" Trace asked.

"My family being my family." I shot him a look. "You'll understand soon enough."

Me: Family emergency. Code word.

My video call came up immediately at the family password for Serious Trouble, and as soon as I accepted the call, my three siblings appeared.

"What's going on, Aly?" Brody asked, his blue eyes narrowed in concern. "You all right? You're not being accused of murder again, are you?"

"It's Gramps. Someone's abducted him. I got the call last night at the bar."

Oh my goddess, it felt good to get those words out to someone who shared a genetic connection. Trace and the others had been a huge part of why I hadn't lost my mind last night, but the stress over telling my family had been eating at me.

"*What?*" Val shouted, and the three of us flinched. Even Trace made a noise of discomfort, and I wrinkled my nose in apology. "Who are you looking at? Who's with you? Is it the cops? The feds? The witches' council?"

I shifted the phone to give them a quick glimpse of Trace. "I'm with Trace. He's helping me figure this out."

"*Trace fucking Wyatt?*" my sister screeched.

"Seriously, Val, dear goddess," Dylan groaned. "Do you think you can drop it a few decibels? My head is killing me."

"Will you two shut up?" Brody snapped. "Aly, what's going

on?"

"A coven wants the amulet—the one Corrick was after."

"What amulet?" Val asked, and I cursed myself that I'd forgotten again. Gramps had ordered me to keep it between him, me, and Simon. Purely need to know. That was clearly no longer an option.

I gave them the quickest summary I could manage—the whole hard-to-swallow family secret that everything the Mooney name had been built on had come from illegal magic—then jumped back into the current crisis. "I don't know how word got out about it, but they know and they snatched Gramps. He's still alive. I think. I'm pretty sure." I chewed on my lip and tried not to consider any other possibility. I filled them in on what had happened in the park and watched my brothers' faces grow redder and more closed off.

"Why the fuck didn't you call us?" Dylan asked. "We would have been there with you, and we could have taken them and gotten Gramps back. What the fuck, Aly?"

Brody nodded. "He's right. You shouldn't have gone out there by yourself. You should have called us right away."

"I made the best decision I could with what I had," I said, even as I accepted that he was right.

"It wasn't your decision to make," Val said. "Aunt Courtney is next in charge if Gramps is out of commission. You should have called her. Also what the fuck with keeping that much of a family secret to yourself?"

I squeezed my hand on my lap, and Trace reached over to wrap his fingers around mine in support. I sank into his warmth—even if I noticed he was running a little *too* warm. "You can keep giving me shit for things we can't change, or we can look to the future to find a solution. Trace and I have a lead on the people who've taken Gramps. Trace knows what these people can do, so there's no one I trust more to guide me through this." I snuck a glance at him and was amused by the glimmer of smugness peeking out along with his dimples. I turned my attention back to my family. "What I need from you is to gather the rest of our coven and be ready to move when we have something to go on."

The other three grumbled, and I knew they wanted to argue with me or call me out on taking the lead when I was only the middle child. But in the end, the twins nodded and Val sighed.

"Fine," she said. "We'll call the family meeting and let everyone know what's happening. But you better keep us updated, Aly. No more going off on your own. Gramps is important to all of us."

Guilt speared me. She was right. It had been selfish of me not to sound the alarm last night even if it had meant waking up the entire Mooney clan.

"I'm sorry," I said. "I promise I'll keep you in the loop from here on out. Regular updates in the group chat."

Brody nodded. "And Wyatt?"

I shifted the phone again so my brother could see Trace.

Trace glanced at the screen to acknowledge him.

"You keep my sister safe. If I hear anything to the contrary, these witches won't be the only ones getting buried."

Trace didn't balk, nor did he look at all offended. He only met Brody's eye through the screen for a poignant beat before returning his attention to the road. "You have my word. I won't let anything happen to her."

My heart fluttered, but beneath the butterflies, something far more uncomfortable and dark woke up. Trace had already sacrificed his ethics, his vow to himself never to touch spirit magic, and his body to save me from Corrick. I feared what else he was ready to give up to keep his promise to my brother.

Chapter 13
Alyssa

THE MUSEUM WAS quiet when Trace and I made ourselves comfortable by Jet's window, which overlooked our target. We'd stayed close to the community centre all day, the two of us taking turns buying supplies for tonight as an excuse to get out of the car and walk around. Trace hadn't recognized anyone else coming out of the building, and according to Chip, who'd already hacked his way into the security camera around the museum, no one else had approached the bushes where Emile had spent those few minutes.

I had a cup of coffee and a box of cookies in front of me. Trace had a coffee but was showing the self-control of a minor deity by ignoring the treats. My memory threw me visions of the muscle definition of his naked body, and I felt a moment's envy. Then I took another bite of cookie.

"Do you think we'll be lucky enough for them to show up tonight?" I asked. "For all we know, your old covenmate popped in there to relieve his bladder out of view of the tour groups. What if we're on the wrong track?"

It wasn't the first time I'd asked these questions today, but Trace showed no sign of impatience at my growing anxiety.

"Chip confirmed there's a magical hot spot behind those trees right now. From what his sensors were able to pick up, it's a pretty strong one. This coven would be foolish to waste the opportunity or let someone else get to it before they do. I suspect that right now they're somewhere in the city finding someone to harvest, and they're going to come here afterwards to absorb the soul."

The whole subject turned my stomach, but I knew better than to suggest we get out there and stop them from doing the harvesting in the first place. There was no way we'd track them down in time. It was better to make sure this was their last hurrah.

"Should we be calling in the witches' council on this?" I asked.

Trace raised his eyebrow, and I got his point. The Ontario Witches' Council wasn't known for their swift, decisive action. It would probably be better to call in SMOAC—or wake up the task force captain in the next room—but our problem was the same: bringing in the feds would put Gramps in their cross-hairs.

So all right. We would handle this ourselves. I hmphed and sipped my coffee, cringing at the thick, bitter brew. Jet obviously preferred nothing short of diesel oil to get her going in the morning. Considering the nature of her job, I got it, but I didn't get it.

I followed the coffee up with another bite of cookie.

Jet's snoring soon spilled out of her bedroom, and Trace and I exchanged a smile. In another breath, though, the air between us crackled as it sank in that we were once again sitting alone in the quiet, with time to kill and no excuse not to discuss what had sparked between us earlier.

I cleared my throat and took another sip of coffee before remembering it was awful and setting it aside.

"Alyssa…"

"You can call me Aly. If you want. Or Lys."

He arched an eyebrow. "I don't want to chance your bartender going all demon on me for stealing his nickname for you."

I opened my mouth to assure him he wouldn't, then remembered all the ways Simon's demon had been coming out to play lately and firmly pressed my lips together. Trace chuckled. "Besides, I think I'd prefer to stick with princess."

The word trickled over his tongue and raised the hair on

my arms as my blood warmed. He'd thrown the word at me long before we'd discovered it was technically true—for all intents and purposes, Mooney's Pub was its own principality, and I was its ruler—but never had it made my soul sing before.

Oh boy, was I in trouble.

"Anyway," I said. "You were going to say?"

He took a breath, his free hand reached for mine, then he froze and twisted towards the window, and not for the first time today, I cursed our horrible timing.

"We've got movement."

I turned my attention to the museum, and my eye fell on three figures dressed in black creeping towards the trees. Subtle.

"Were you so melodramatic when you were one of them?" I asked. Trace's grimace was answer enough, and I grinned.

"I was eighteen," he reminded me. "If they'd given me a cloak, I probably would have thrown it on and called myself a rebel. Don't hold it against my youthful nature."

My grin remained, now directed at myself. Leaning towards him, I dropped my voice and said, "I held girl band concerts for my stuffed animals when I was sixteen. I would never mock you for a cloak."

"You didn't."

"Tell anyone, and I'll curse you."

His eyes twinkled, and my heart melted a little more.

Deep trouble.

As the minutes ticked by and Trace made no move to get up and leave, my confusion grew. "What's the plan? Are we going out there and confronting them before they finish what they're doing?"

He pushed out an exhale, and I realized the only reason we were still here was because his past had bound him to his chair. I rested my hand on his arm. "Do you want to stay and have my back from here?"

The lines around his eyes hardened. "Not a chance in hell. Come on. Let's get this over with."

I grabbed one more cookie for the road, and we left Jet's apartment. Down the stairs, out the front door, and into the chilly midnight air we went. As we crossed the street, the power emanating from the magical hot spot drifted over me, and I soaked it in. If we were up against three powerful witches, it only seemed smart to give myself a boost at the same time. I looked at Trace and deduced he was doing the same as his eyes glinted with silver-yellow magic.

My stomach swam with unease, and it took me a second to figure out what made me so uncomfortable. What concerned me wasn't the strange hue of his eyes, but what burned within them, especially against the determined set of his jaw. I'd never seen that look on his face before, and the expression only grew more thunderous as we got closer to the witches hiding in the shadows.

He raised his hand, and silver magic sparked over his fingers as the trees bent out of the way to reveal the trio huddled over a salt circle on the ground. In the middle of the circle lay an old amulet, as tarnished and ugly as the one that had broken, if significantly smaller. I also didn't sense nearly the same amount of power as what had poured out of the Mooney family heirloom—a small mercy. Being able to say the situation was less shit than I'd feared, however, didn't make my feelings about this encounter any lighter.

The three lurched to their feet in silence, and I caught the familiar yellow of spirit magic spinning around all of them, brightest around the woman who stood in the centre.

"Who the fuck are you?" she asked.

Trace didn't bother with introductions. Instead, he used his magic to snap a branch off the tree and smack the woman across the chest. She flew to the ground with a grunt. The other two wheeled back to us, and the magic around their hands grew stronger. Trace's focus was still on the woman, so he didn't notice the coming attack. I shoved him out of the way as the man on the left—I thought I recognized Emile's portly frame hidden beneath the dark clothes—shot out a rippling spell.

It hit the ground instead of Trace, and the snow-spattered grass turned into a rotting, festering mess. My stomach lurched, and my heart thrashed against my ribs. All right, these guys weren't playing nice. Good to know.

I summoned my atmospheric magic and let it loose at Emile and the other man, who I guessed was Kurt based on Chip's quick introduction. It bound them together and their heads collided, making a shockingly hollow sound, before they fell apart blinking the stars out of their eyes.

The woman—Nathalie, I supposed—found her feet and unleashed another spell, but Trace was ready to deflect it before it hit me. His yellow-touched telekinesis wrapped around whatever attack she'd tried to throw, and the intention went back the way it came. Nathalie must have sensed the incoming magic, because she lurched out of the way, and the spell hit the tree behind her, taking the entire trunk to the ground.

The witch's eyes flared with fear, and she thrust her hand to the side. Kurt grabbed hold of it, and they summoned their power between them, heightening the strength of both. They wanted to play that game? I drew my purple-tinged magic into my palm and looked to Trace. He shot me a sideways glance, nodded, and tossed me a thread of his silver power. I wove them together and hurled them like a net at the pair up ahead. By bad luck, they'd launched their spell at the same time. Their magic punched a hole through our net, but enough of our spell survived to drape over them and bind their hands to their sides.

While they struggled to free themselves, we turned our attention to Emile. His eyes widened, and he scrambled to draw on his power, but Trace and I were too quick for him.

Trace launched the silver bubble I recognized from the night we met, when he'd so unceremoniously destroyed my pub. It settled over Emile and stuck to him like plastic wrap, rendering him immobile as he crashed to the ground.

I approached the other two, magic ready between my hands if they tried to attack, and stood over Nathalie. "Are you the people who have my grandfather?"

She blinked her large eyes up at me. "I don't even know who you are. You come here and assault us when we're just trying to cast some magic. What is wrong with you?"

"Always playing the innocent, aren't you, Nat?" Trace asked, coming up to stand over her. His eyes were shining again, this time enough that they were almost glowing. The silver was barely noticeable as the yellow overpowered it. It leached out from his eyes and veined across his face, as though the souls within him were taking over. I couldn't look away from him, every instinct telling me to run while my concern for him—and no small amount of curiosity—kept me rooted to the spot.

Nathalie sucked in a breath. "Drew? Is that you?" She barked a laugh. "Son of a bitch, you're a fucking hypocrite, aren't you? Hazel's spent how long rotting in Moongrave, and you're doing exactly what you swore you wouldn't do. I should have known."

"You're playing with power you shouldn't touch," Trace said without acknowledging her accusations. Except it wasn't

Trace's voice coming through his lips. Not exactly. His words were layered, as though hundreds of other people spoke along with him. "You were warned, but you insist on drawing on those who wish only to rest."

She laughed again. "You're one to talk. Look at you. You're drunk on power."

The streaks of yellow spread down his cheeks, over his neck, and under his collar, then appeared across the backs of his hands.

"Trace…" I said softly. I didn't know if *drunk* was the right word. This was beyond overindulging on his magic. He was being consumed by it.

Nathalie shot me a look. "And who is this? Your new recruit? Passing along everything Hazel taught you to some new slut? Tough nuts, cupcake. The power in this city—it's ours."

Magic trickled over her fingers, growing stronger, more intense. Whatever spell she was about to throw, I didn't know if my ward would be strong enough to stop it.

"No," Trace said, stepping between us. "It's ours."

He gathered his magic into a large ball that flashed and lurched like a solar flare, and let it fly.

Nathalie's screams filled the night, and I jumped on Trace's arm to pull him away before he unleashed another flare on Kurt. Horror left me speechless—not so much at what Trace had done as at what the spirits inside him had driven him to do. This wasn't the man who'd taken down criminals across the country for the better part of ten years. This wasn't the man who'd stood up for me in front of Clyde Corrick. This was the spirits within him fighting for dominance, and the farther he slipped, the harder it would be for him to come back.

I could only stand and stare, forcing myself to stay put and not to bolt as far from him as I could, as Trace turned his attention to the other two witches.

Nathalie's screams subsided, her body little more than ash where she'd knelt. Kurt was on his feet, ready to run, but I threw out another blast of magic that knocked him onto his stomach. I didn't want to give Trace's guests the opportunity to crispy fry anyone else.

I released Trace's arm, grateful for the excuse to put distance between us and to give my stomach a chance to settle, and crouched next to Kurt. "Now that we have your attention," I said, as though the nightmare of the last few minutes had been entirely planned, "I don't suppose you want to answer our questions?"

"I-I'll tell you anything you want to know. Yes, we have the old man. I don't know where, though. We weren't part of that loop. Nathalie got a text a few weeks ago ordering us to come out this way and start harvesting. We were told there was a lot of power to be found in the city, but only if we did as we were told."

"Told by who?" Trace demanded as more magic flurried

over his fingers, this time silver as much as yellow. Some of the bright veins had receded from his neck, but I shot him a warning look nonetheless. He dropped his hand, but the magic stayed at the ready.

"I don't know," Kurt said. "Nathalie was the point of contact. She communicated with this person via text message."

On a phone that was little more than cinders. Just great.

"I'm going to strongly suggest you and your friend leave town," I said. "And if it turns out you know more than you've told me, there's nowhere in this world you can hide that this man won't find you."

I let that threat sit with Kurt for a minute, giving him the opportunity to spill the rest if there was any rest to spill.

He nodded and scrambled to his feet. Trace waved his fingers, and the binding spell around Emile evaporated. He joined Kurt, glanced at the amulet, whose souls must have been purged by Nathalie as she prepared her final failed attack, and the two of them disappeared into the shadows.

As soon as they were gone, I turned to Trace. His empty, glowing eyes stared after them until finally some buried part of himself broke through. He clasped his hands to his head and fell to his knees in the melted snow, gasping for breath as tears streamed down his cheeks.

Maybe I should have held my place until I was sure he wasn't going to lash out at me. Maybe I should have questioned my sanity for having stuck around here at all the moment Trace cast that spell. I did neither of those things.

I rushed to his side and sank to my knees beside him, throwing my arms around him and holding him close until his breathing slowed. I didn't say anything, not sure what to say or what he needed to hear. For now, all I could do was let him know I wasn't going anywhere.

Finally, he slumped against me, too tired to hold himself up. I slung his arm around my shoulders and eased him to his feet, throwing one last look at Nathalie's charred corpse next to the toppled tree. "Come on. Let's get you home."

Chapter 14
Trace

I couldn't stop shivering.

Alyssa had loaded me into the passenger seat of my SUV and left the engine idling with the heat on as she ran back to Jet's apartment to gather our stuff and leave a note for her friend telling her all was well.

But it wasn't. Not even close.

After Alyssa came back down, she drove me to her house. Tonight, she didn't even bother asking if I wanted to go back to wherever I was staying. She—rightfully—assumed I didn't want to be alone.

I didn't—I really didn't—but how could I be sure I wasn't putting her in danger by staying near her?

I was losing control. The souls inside me had taken over

my mind before I'd realized they were doing it. Their response to the spirit magic being cast, spells that went against the will of the spirits in use, had been immediate and brutal. I'd been a bystander in my own body, aware of every moment, every detail, as Nathalie had screamed through her immolation.

With a groan, I buried my face in my hands. Another tremor wracked my body, and I was sure I was going to throw up. If I'd been anywhere other than Alyssa's living room, on Alyssa's couch, over Alyssa's rug, I would have. But as it was, my desire not to make a mess of her comfortable home forced me to breathe through the churning, overwhelming nausea.

And the deeper I breathed, the more I caught her faint scent of aloe vera, and it soothed me more than anything else could have. Like a hit of nostalgia even though I'd only experienced it for the first time for a single day five weeks ago. The scent permeated the blue fabric of the couch, the throw pillows, the blanket draped over the back. It trickled into my lungs and spread through my veins. A narcotic with no side effects beyond increasing the gratitude I already felt for the beautiful woman currently puttering around her kitchen to fix me a cup of peppermint tea.

She had no idea that her proximity was more helpful than any herbal remedy.

"Here," she said, coming over with a mug and a plate with two chocolate cookies. "I wish the cookies were homemade but… yeah, no, you don't want to taste my baking. Store-bought is for the best. But I thought the sugar might help calm your nerves."

I didn't have the heart to tell her I was more a cinnamon than a chocolate guy. I bit into the cookie and washed it down with a sip of steaming tea—also not my favourite, but tonight I was willing to drink anything if it eased my chills.

As though she knew a drink wouldn't be enough, she grabbed the blanket from the couch and wrapped it around my shoulders. When she made to walk away, I set my mug on the coffee table and grabbed her wrist to stop her.

At the flash of discomfort in her eyes, the barest hint of fear, I released her. Regret pulsed through me along with a wave of self-disgust that anything I'd done should have caused that expression on her face.

I thought we'd finished with me scaring her. I'd hoped that part of what existed between us was lost to the past. I'd fucked up enough times during our wild journey together, and I never wanted to make mistakes like that again. Now, thanks to the souls trapped inside me, I'd pushed away the one person who'd made me feel like maybe I could finally, after nine fucking years, stop running.

Someone who had almost convinced me that letting someone into my life might not be the worst fate. Or that maybe I wasn't as undeserving of that sort of connection as I'd come to believe.

But clearly I'd been right to keep my distance. It would be best if I left. As soon as my legs were steady enough to carry my weight, I'd walk out of here, leave Alyssa to take care of the Gramps situation with her family, and deal with this coven on my own. It would be safer for everyone.

The couch cushion dipped beside me as Alyssa sat down, jarring me out of my plans. I looked up at her, braced to see more of that fear—or worse, sympathy—before she told me she'd prefer if I left. Shaking legs be damned, I didn't want to put that pressure on her.

Taking the initiative, I stood up, and her soft expression changed to one of confusion.

"Where are you going?"

"I—"

I had no idea. There was no way I'd be safe behind the wheel of my car. I could walk back to my rental from here, but the thought of sitting alone in the dark was almost enough to make my resident souls come out to play again. If I had to, I would start walking and see where I wound up by the time the sun rose. Maybe in the light of day, I'd be able to faceplant into my bed and sleep until this agony of guilt and horror went away. So, forever.

"Trace, please sit down." Her green eyes were downturned with concern, her voice so soft, so kind, that I couldn't disobey her. Despite everything I'd just decided would be better for both of us, I lowered myself back onto the couch, and my breath caught when she took my hand.

"Talk to me."

The command was spoken in the same gentle tone as the previous one but was so much more difficult to heed. My throat closed, panic gripped me, and a moment later, Alyssa's hand was on my back while I struggled to breathe.

"It's all right," she murmured. "You're not alone in this. I'm right here. You can get through this, just find your breath."

She guided me through my panic attack, and by the time my heart rate settled, I felt as wrung out as a dirty towel. It was only then I noticed that at some point she'd pulled me down so my head rested on her lap. Her feet were propped up on the edge of the coffee table, her fingers stroking my hair, and I was on my back, staring up at her ceiling.

I waited for the shame to hit. For mortification to push me into another attack, but it never came. On the contrary, I felt safer than I had since my anxiety had first sprung up in high school. Alyssa's lack of judgement removed the necessity of judging myself, and once the adrenaline subsided, we were both able to move on from it.

I swallowed the lump in my throat, closed my eyes, and took a few seconds to relish the feel of her fingers combing through my hair, massaging my scalp, sending tiny prickles of magic through me. Not enough to have a strong effect—just enough to raise pleasant goosebumps on my arms. I doubted she was aware she was doing it. Her magic seemed to enjoy playing with mine as a reflex, though at the moment my natural magic was dormant.

"I don't know what happened," I finally said. "One second I was with you, and we were charging the coven. I sensed the effects of the hot spot on my power and was revving up for a fight, and then… I don't know. I sensed the spirit magic Nathalie and the others were trying to wrangle, and it felt so dark, so *wrong*, and something in me snapped. The souls slipped their bindings and choked my magic. They overwhelmed me and took over. I didn't mean to kill her. I swear to the goddess, princess, I didn't mean to do it."

My trembling started again, and Alyssa pulled the blanket tighter around me before continuing to stroke my hair.

"I know," she said. "I saw everything. I know you would never have killed her if you'd been in control. I'm sorry I flinched when you grabbed me. I'll admit, the sight of you with your eyes glowing and magic seeping through your veins—it was intense. But I never got the sense you were going to hurt me. I trust you, Trace. After everything we've been through together, you've proved that I can."

I heaved out a shuddering breath, and a few muscles in my back released their steel grip on my bones.

"That being said," she added, and I tensed again. "Drew?"

The faintly teasing note succeeded in making me laugh, something I hadn't been sure I could do again so soon. "You got me. I didn't have the fancy nickname when I joined the coven. Back then, I was just Andrew Wyatt, shithead university dropout who believed he could do whatever he wanted and be accountable to no one. That guy died after what happened with Hazel, and Trace was born."

"So why Trace?"

I grimaced. "Promise not to laugh?"

"No."

I bit down on a smile. "My middle name is Tracy. After my grandfather. Trace wasn't such a leap."

She hmphed. "That's not nearly as bad as you set it up to be."

"Want me to try again? I could probably come up with a really good story that would live up to your expectations."

"Nah, I prefer the truth. I like learning these things about you. Things the fawning world doesn't know about their national hero."

I ran my fingers up and down her arm where it wrapped around me. "I like you knowing them."

A light flush spread across her cheeks and the bridge of her nose, highlighting her freckles.

"My middle name is Winnifred," she said after a moment

had passed. "After my grandmother. But if I ever ask you to start calling me Winnie, please know it's a code for something having gone terribly wrong."

I stared into her catlike eyes, and she smiled down at me. Without giving myself time to worry about the consequences, I cupped her cheek. Only when she didn't flinch again could I admit how much I'd been afraid she would. "I'm sorry I scared you."

Her smile flickered out as she leaned into my palm. "What scares me is whatever's going on with these souls. I hate that they seem to be using your power against you. I wish we'd already found a way to evict them."

"Me too, but given the nature of the magic, I'm on my own with figuring it out. The two easiest options are to simply let them go or to store them in another gem. But the consequences of either choice make them not worth considering."

She groaned. "No, they're not. Let them go, and they'll create chaos across the city until someone else manages to bind them. Stuff them in a gem, and we're no better off now than we were before—hundreds of illegal souls who were promised freedom trapped in a stone that's nearly impossible to break."

"Exactly. I haven't given up, though. There has to be a safe place to release them. Some way we can get them where they're supposed to be without anyone else having the chance to snatch them up."

Alyssa bit her bottom lip, and my tired blood heated at the gesture. "Do you think SMOAC might…"

She trailed off, but the suggestion was enough to cool whatever desire had woken within me. "I know you have friends in the department, but I wouldn't trust the feds not to be as corrupt with this magic as the Bone Casters. They just have official sanction to do whatever they want."

I expected Alyssa to be offended, but she grimaced. "I don't want to think you're right, but since I can't say for sure, I'll go with your gut on this one." Her jaw tightened. "What about the other thing? The part about Nathalie being given orders by some unknown texter? Do you think Kurt was telling the truth?"

With a sigh, I pushed myself up, already regretting leaving the comfort and warmth of her lap. The blanket fell over my shoulder, and as I adjusted it, I wrapped it around Alyssa as well, bringing her closer to me.

"I don't know. I didn't get the sense he was, but that doesn't mean anything. At the very least, we can't ignore the possible lead." I shifted in my seat to pull out my phone and, for the second time that day, dialled Chip's number.

"Dude," he said on answering, "I know I'm good, but I'm not a god, all right? It takes time to get the kind of information we need." He cleared his throat. "Though, uh, do we need to talk about what happened outside the museum tonight? I didn't see much in the trees, but I can count. Three witches went in, two came out. Anything I need to know?"

Alyssa and I exchanged a look, worry back in her eyes, and I squeezed her hand. "Not a thing."

"Great," Chip said. "I hate knowing things. I'll send a cleanup crew to take care of whatever mess you left behind, though. No questions asked."

An unfortunate occasional requirement of my job on a good day. Not my favourite part, but at least we had a system that kept the mundanes from learning things they shouldn't.

"Thanks. We did learn something that might be useful. Can you find your way into Nathalie's text messages? Supposedly she's been the one communicating with the top dogs of this mystery coven. We're hoping you can get us a name."

"You can't just look at her phone?"

"Her phone is ash."

"How—Know what? Never mind. Don't want to know. Give me until tomorrow. Somewhere between now and then I need to sleep before I start drooling and destroy a perfectly good keyboard."

He hung up on me, and Alyssa rose to her feet, still gripping my hand. "He's right, you know."

"Oh?"

"We should sleep. It's been a while, and you—well, to put it nicely—you look like shit."

I tried to smile but suspected I missed the mark. "I'll set up on the couch again, if that's okay? I'd go home, but…"

She tugged on my hand. "I thought… Maybe… It's just—" She heaved a sigh and, sounding far more sure of herself, finished, "I don't want to be by myself tonight. Not after everything."

Understanding dawned on me, and I didn't think I could have stood up faster if the couch had been electrified. "Whatever you need."

She smiled and led the way to her bedroom.

Chapter 15
Alyssa

I WOKE UP the next morning feeling more rested than I had in a long time. Warm, cozy… and completely wrapped up in Trace's arms.

For weeks, despite my best efforts to believe my association with him was over and done, I'd wondered what it would feel like to be curled up around him, and I had to say, reality surpassed the dream. The big difference, of course, being that we were still clothed. I'd changed into my usual ratty pyjamas, having been too exhausted to dig out anything fancier, and Trace had only removed his belt so he could get comfortable.

Now that I'd slept, I was disappointed in us for being so responsible. The moment had passed, however, and the weight of my troubles once again pressed me into my mattress.

Gramps was still missing, Trace's control was slipping, and some new witchy superpower was gaining a foothold in my city and ordering dark-leaning witches to go out and gather more spirits. If said superpower was the same person who had Gramps, then at least two of our problems could be resolved with one massive boulder. The Trace problem, on the other hand… Well, I tried my best not to think too hard about that one. I didn't want to consider what would happen if we didn't get those souls out of him not only safely, but soon.

I rolled onto my side to look at him. Even in sleep, Trace appeared troubled. The creases on his brow hadn't released their hold, and his lips were twisted into a grimace as he twitched with dreams. Unpleasant dreams, by the looks of him.

I stroked my fingers over his temple, down to his jaw, and like magic, his face relaxed. His lips parted with a soft sigh, and his breathing evened. I wished I could have woken up hours ago and offered some comfort early enough for it to have made a real difference, given him a chance for the rest he so desperately needed. As it was, I would have to wake him up so he could see if Chip had updated us on anything while we slept.

For now, though, I was happy to indulge in these few moments of peace. In the strength of Trace's arms where they coiled around me, keeping me against his chest. The patter of his heart where it beat against my arm.

The hardness of him pressing against my hip.

My cheeks flushed, and I was relieved he wasn't awake. He would have been embarrassed that I was embarrassed, and then things would be awkward. All for nothing. A perfectly normal phenomenon for a guy needing to pee.

Though when he shifted in his sleep and nuzzled my neck, I had to wonder just what direction his dreams had taken.

"Thank you," he murmured in my ear, making me jump.

I waited until I was certain my heart wouldn't pound out of my chest before asking, "For what?"

"For not running away from me. For letting me stay here with you."

He blinked his violet eyes open, and his expression was filled with such tenderness, I wanted nothing more than to bundle him up and never let him go. It broke my heart that the people in his life had made him believe he wasn't worth sticking around for.

"It would take a pretty big reason for me to run you off," I said. "After what we survived together, I don't think my life would be the same without you in it."

Some people might believe such confessions were best saved for darkness, but I was of the opinion that if you had the words and the courage to say them, they could be thrown around at any time. And the emotion that swam in Trace's eyes afterwards made my bravery all the more rewarding.

"I feel the same way," he said, and I smiled. Then he

moaned and twisted in on himself, pulling his arms away from me to wrap them around his middle. In another moment, he was out of bed and hurtling towards the bathroom. The door slammed shut and the retching began.

I got up and went into the kitchen to start the kettle for another round of peppermint tea. While the water boiled, I did my best not to let my anxiety get the better of me. Trace had experienced a massive power surge last night. Of course he wouldn't be at his best today. The nausea wasn't because of his gradual deterioration or loss of self. It wasn't a sign that he was wasting away and if we didn't get these souls out ASAP, I would lose him. This was just a side effect of too much magic. He would recover. He would be fine.

I waited until I could show him my calm face before delivering his phone and a cup of water to the bathroom. Trace was hunched next to the toilet, his face flushed red, his hand shaking as he dragged the back of it across his mouth. My anxiety threatened to return, but I shushed it for now and did my best to be what he needed in this moment: relaxed, compassionate, and slightly detached. All the bedside manner I'd learned as a healer.

"Can I get you anything else?" I asked as I handed him the water.

He shook his head and took a sip. "I'm fine now. This is… kind of a daily thing."

Totally normal, then. I was right to tell my threatening spiral there was no need for it to spin out of control. What was a little bit of daily vomiting in the scheme of things? He would be fine.

"Congratulations on your bundle of unwanted souls," I offered.

He barked a laugh and tilted his head back to lean against the wall.

"Is it getting worse?" I ventured to ask, not wanting to know the answer, but needing to at the same time.

He stared at me for a moment as though he was debating how honest he should be. "A little bit. Not quickly, though. You don't have to worry I'll disappear on you just yet."

My throat tightened. It had to be the air in this apartment. I was due my vents being cleared out. Maybe next time I got one of those spam calls, I'd take them up on their offer.

"You promise you'll tell me if that changes?"

I caught the faint swimming of yellow and silver in his eyes before it melted back into the violet. "I promise."

The vow didn't make me feel much better, strangely, and I shifted my gaze to the door, not wanting him to have to see all the emotions waging war in my chest.

"Give me a minute to clean up, and we can plan our day," he said, nudging my thoughts back into the room.

I left him with the water and his phone, got dressed in a

clean pair of jeans and a heavy green sweater, then returned to the kitchen to prepare two bowls of cereal to go with our tea. I doubted Trace would want anything heavier, but I was starving.

While I waited, I checked my phone, unsurprised to find a flurry of messages from my siblings, my cousins, my parents, my aunts and uncles. Most of them were coming through the larger family chat, but a few of them had reached out to me directly. I'd been too exhausted last night to go through them all, and now, in the light of the morning, I didn't feel that much more prepared.

But it needed to be done, so I focused my efforts on the group chat, telling them most of what had happened last night. I left out the role Trace's souls had played, not wanting Gramps to feel any guiltier when we finally got him away from these witches, but I did tell them about Kurt's confession.

Me: We have someone looking into one of the witches' phones to find out who's giving the orders.

Hacking into people's phones? my aunt Courtney replied. **Is that really what we need here? What about SMOAC? Or the council? If we're dealing with a kidnapping, we should bring them in.**

Three dots appeared next to Mom's name, then: **We can't. If SMOAC or the council learns about the amulet, they'll send Dad to Moongrave.**

**Courtney: I hate that you're right. I hate that he never

told us. We could have prepared for this.

Avery: Prepared for someone to kidnap him and interrupt Aly's night at the pub? No way.

My cousin had a point. Nothing we could have done would have readied us for this to happen.

Courtney: Aly, since you already have a grasp on what's happening here, you take the lead and keep us informed.

Mary: How can we help?

I read my mom's message and tried not to cry. It felt so good to have her back, and I wished I could hand the whole thing off to her and Aunt Courtney. But my aunt was right. I had Trace and Chip, and we had already made more progress on this than my family could have. It only made sense for me to carry on.

Me: Keep your ear out for any rumours about soul harvesters in the city. We don't know why this coven is out for power yet, but if we find out, we'll be in a better place to get in their way.

Mary: You got it. Be safe and remember to eat something. You and Trace need to keep your energy up.

Avery: [snicker emoji] Yeah they do.

Courtney: Avery!

Their exchange nearly made me smile, but I didn't have the heart for it. I rubbed my eyes, blinked blearily at my phone, then read Simon's messages from last night. He wanted to know how the stakeout had gone and what we'd learned. His last text around three o'clock in the morning told me he was on his way to Illusion, Reverie's club, and he'd check in tomorrow.

I glanced at the time and figured it was late enough to leave him a message. Not like there was any rush for him to answer. I filled him in about the Bone Casters and tasked him with the same job as the rest of my family. If anyone who came into the pub was throwing gossip around that we could use, Simon was in a prime position to pick up on it.

Me: And I'm sorry I won't be in again today.

Simon: No worries, Lys. I'm on it. You do what you need to do. And remember: skulls.

Again with that brain emoji. Was he turning into a zombie and I hadn't noticed?

Trace came out of the bedroom a few minutes later looking scrubbed and put-together, his belt on and his shirt hanging loose on his shoulders. "Chip has something. He says to give him a call when we stop being so lazy."

I gestured to the food and tea waiting for Trace on the counter. "That will be a big fat never. Given the opportunity, I would spend every day on the couch with a sitcom and a box of cookies, please and thank you. But sure, now's as good a time as any."

Trace sat across from me at the table, poured milk into his cereal, then called Chip.

"Do you know how long I've been waiting for you two to stop whatever you're doing? And no, I don't want to know what that something might be. I do not need those visuals in my head. Not the point. I have the texts from Nathalie's phone, and I have some security footage from Dundonald Park the other night. The good news is Emile and Kurt were among the assholes who dragged Gramps into the van. The bad news is that I don't have a name for Nathalie's boss. What I do have, however, is their phone number. Likely a burner phone, but the same number's been used for the past couple months, and I was able to follow it. Nathalie wasn't their only point of contact. Sloppy work, really. If you're going to use a burner phone, why would you use the same one? Why not change it up every month to keep people like me from figuring out what you're up to? You're lucky, Trace. Not everyone has someone in their back pocket making sure they don't fuck up every step of the way."

I stared at the phone with my jaw on the table. How was this guy still talking?

"You didn't even say hi," I said. "You just… started. How could you be sure we were listening? What if we'd butt-dialled you?"

"Then you'd be out all this great intel, Cheers, because I'm not repeating it. I hope you have a pen handy to write down the number."

I scrambled to get my phone out of my pocket as he rattled off the nine digits.

"You two can figure out what to do with the number," he said. "That's not my line of work. But off the top of my head, based on the messages they received from their other contacts, it might not be a bad idea if you messaged them asking for a job. It seems lots of people got referred to them via phone. As for Hazel, I'm still digging. So cool, we done? I can go back to not dragging my way through phone logs? Excellent. Call me if you have anything interesting for me to do."

He hung up, and Trace and I stared at each other.

"It's lucky for him he's the best," he finally said.

I dropped my gaze to the phone number in my notes app. "What do you think? Does he have the right of it? Message this person about a job and see where it gets us?"

"Not on your phone. We'll take a walk and grab ourselves a clean one, then we'll send our text messages. We don't need anything to come back to either of us. If this person knew Nathalie, they might know about me. If they have Gramps, they definitely know about you. We'll come up with a new identity and run with that."

My stomach squirmed with apprehension. All this cloak-and-dagger stuff was outside my knowledge base. Give me craft beer and cocktail menus, and I was in my element. Burner phones and anonymous texts? How was that my life now?

"Should I be worried that we didn't hear from them yesterday? About Gramps, I mean? You don't think he's—They wouldn't have…"

Trace reached across the table to loop his fingers through mine and gave them a soft squeeze. "I think if anything had happened to him, you'd know by now. They still have him. If we haven't heard yet, it's probably because they're trying to figure out another way to use him. It won't be long now before they try a different approach."

I didn't know how much of what he said was from experience or how much was him talking out of his ass to make me feel better, but I was grateful for it nonetheless.

"Well then," I said. "Eat up and let's get going. It's time for me to turn into Jason Bourne."

Chapter 16
Alyssa

A LITTLE OVER an hour later, I was the proud owner of a new, unregistered phone. Trace had crafted a text message telling our mysterious leader that we'd learned about him through the Ottawa coven network and were interested in knowing if they had any jobs for us.

With what we knew about the kinds of jobs this person asked their minions to do, I wasn't feeling good about making contact. If it got us closer to Gramps, I was willing to play along, but I had to wonder how far this particular road would take us.

"What are we supposed to do in the meantime?" I asked.

"Try to relax. You could probably go to work if you wanted."

I knew I should. The sounds and smells kept me grounded when everything else was chaos. But at the thought of putting on my professional smile and wading through the crowds, delivering food and drinks and small talk, my energy evaporated. "I think it's probably best if I leave the pub in Simon's capable hands until I know what's going on here. The last thing my patrons need is for me to lose my crap on them."

"You? Be anything less than professional? I'll believe it when I see it."

I grinned. "Remind me to tell you what happened my second night running Mooney's. You want unprofessional? That story will have you questioning my managerial skills for sure. And my impulse control."

Trace threw his arm around my shoulders as we walked back to my house. "We have time to spare right now."

I shrugged him off with a laugh, though the ease with which he'd pulled me closer had set off those pesky butterflies again. "Maybe after we get this sorted. I don't need you doubting my ability to play it cool."

As we crossed the street, the hairs on the back of my neck rose. I kept my smile firmly in place and didn't look around. Trying not to move my lips too much, I said, "I think someone's watching us."

Trace's breath tickled my ear. "Try to be more obvious about it, princess."

I turned to look at him and only now did I notice the line of tension between his shoulders. Subtle, not enough that anyone else would have spotted it, but I'd spent the morning watching the man sleep. I knew what he looked like when he wasn't *on*. "How long have you known?"

Trace's arm returned around my shoulders. "Since we hit Bank Street on our way back. There's two of them trailing us. Badly."

And I'd only sensed them now. Clearly they weren't the only ones doing badly.

"Do you know them?" I asked as I leaned into him, playing along.

"Nope. If I had to guess, they're with the group looking to get the amulet from you. Probably hoping they'll catch you walking around wearing it."

I snorted. "Do they have any idea what that thing looked like? Not exactly an easy accessory to pair."

The amulet had been large and clunky with a bright yellow tourmaline set into the centre. I supposed it might have gone well with the sweater I was wearing now if I were one for big, ugly, vintage jewellery, but these people didn't know me at all. Obviously. If they did, they would know the amulet no longer existed and we wouldn't be in this mess. Gramps would be at home in his favourite armchair watching hockey.

As he would be again. Soon.

"What do we do next?" I asked.

"We could find out what they want."

My stomach lurched at the idea of getting closer to the people who wanted to harm us. I wasn't usually the sort to walk into trouble. I was the sort to de-escalate the situation. To cut people off or switch them to a half-pint while they waited for their designated driver to come get them. Taking a more aggressive approach went against my training and my personality, and, frankly, I usually lacked the courage to do it.

But with Trace at my side, I felt capable of anything. Even besting the sort of people who followed a couple down the street in the middle of the afternoon.

"I'll follow your lead, Mr. Bounty Hunter."

He looped his fingers through mine and carried us along the street. When we got to my house, he pulled us past it instead of taking us inside, and in another few minutes, we were walking towards the park behind the mundane community centre, this one not hidden behind any kind of perception filter. At this time of day, it was busy enough that we would have witnesses, which I hoped increased the odds of us getting out of here safely.

I expected Trace to take us deeper into the crowds to try to lose our tail, but instead he subverted my expectations for a second time and jerked me into the shadows around the corner of the building. We watched our stalkers approach the park and look around, then backtrack and head up the street towards the intersection. Before they could get far, Trace tugged on my hand and led me after them. We were now the hunters, and I marvelled at how easily he'd played them.

They jaywalked across Gladstone—because I guess when you're used to breaking other, bigger laws, you don't care too much about causing potential car accidents—and before I knew it, I was also dodging traffic to keep up with them.

A few blocks up, they went into an old house on MacLaren that had been converted into office buildings. Another instance of rental space being used to house a dark coven like the power station-slash-supernatural community centre, or was the whole building a front?

Trace seemed to have the same thought because he snapped a photo on his phone and sent it to Chip.

I read the sign on the door. "They could be lawyers. That would explain a lot. Dark covens, attorneys at law. Are they really so different?"

"I know some great lawyers," Trace said. "I don't know any great dark witches."

"Oh, I don't know about that. I'm sure some of them are a riot at parties."

"No, they *cause* riots at parties. That's the difference."

"See, this is why I keep you around, to explain the error of my ways."

He shot me a grin, but it didn't quite reach his eyes.

"So?" I asked. "Do we knock on the door, or do you want to sit here and wait for Chip to work his magic?"

"I don't know. I was hoping they'd go somewhere public so we could pin them down and have a word with them, but I don't want to take the chance that there actually is a whole coven in there."

My heart pattered. "Do you think Gramps could be inside?"

We weren't far from Dundonald Park. It almost made sense they would keep him somewhere close.

"It's possible," Trace admitted. "That's another reason I don't want to storm the gates just yet. At least we know where they're hiding. We should head back to your place and come back later when it's dark. Maybe with a team."

My phone buzzed, and I pulled the new one out of my purse. No messages. I dropped it back into the void of my bag and fished my actual phone out of the front pocket. Aside from a hundred messages from the family group chat demanding updates, a single text message waited for me from an unknown number. Dread coiled through my intestines, threatening to squeeze.

If you have the amulet, you can come in and get your grandfather. If you don't, he won't survive the night.

I swallowed hard and passed my phone to Trace. "I guess we've been made."

Made and owned. We had until tonight to figure out a way to trade Gramps for something that didn't exist. I hoped Trace had an idea, because as of now, I was fresh out.

Chapter 17
Trace

INEEDED TO get my head on straight. I'd walked us all the way here, and now it seemed we'd set the timer going on Alyssa's grandfather's life.

Maybe this coven would have sent the message anyway, but I couldn't help but feel I'd royally fucked up. Here I thought we'd been so clever, but those witches had no doubt been leading us back here, knowing full well we were behind them.

It was like I'd lost my skills, gone back to being a mediocre rookie in the bounty hunter business. I could blame the souls riding around inside me, I could blame Alyssa for being the most beautiful distraction, but the truth was that after all my years and all my experience, I'd gotten cocky. I had to remember I wasn't at my best, and I was up against people who'd proved they were quick and well prepared.

That was on me.

Now I had to hurry to clean up this mess before it spread.

I held out my hand for Alyssa's phone. "Do you mind?"

She set the phone in my palm, showing the utmost trust that I knew what I was doing. I had to bite my tongue to stop myself from admitting I didn't have the first clue. She didn't need to hear that. She needed to believe I had everything under control and that before the night was over, Gramps would be walking out of this house under his own steam.

The amulet is toast. It no longer exists. Let Gramps go, and we can talk options.

They were looking for power tools. As long as we promised them something in exchange, they might be happy with it. Once Gramps was safe at home, I could deal with the dark witches prowling the city with toys they didn't deserve to have.

The phone buzzed. **Your lies won't save him. The amulet for his life.**

I ground my teeth. Were these people that stubborn or just ignorant?

The amulet shattered. The souls are gone. Ask Clyde Corrick.

Not that they could ask Corrick, of course. By now he was dead—the fae duchess would have seen to that. But if these people were interested in soul-filled gems, it was likely they already knew what had happened to poor Clyde.

Buzz. **Guess he dies then.**

"Shit!" I hissed, then rapidly typed out another message. **Fine. It won't be the same amulet, but we'll have something. Lay a finger on him, and you'll never see it.**

Buzz. **10 p.m.**

I returned the phone to Alyssa, and she gave the messages a quick read before she slid the phone back in her purse. Her face was pale, almost gaunt, and I worried she was going to pass out right here on the street.

"Come on." I wrapped my arm around her waist to hold her steady, a marked reversal of roles compared to the past day and a half. "Let's get home and figure this out."

She was silent the entire walk to her house. She unlocked the door, led us upstairs, tossed her purse onto the kitchen counter, and flopped onto the couch still wearing her boots and coat.

While she stared blankly into the dark TV screen, I sat on the coffee table in front of her and set to work pulling off her boots before too much melting snow ruined her rug.

"They're going to kill him," she said. "The amulet broke, and they're going to kill him, because there's no way we can find a second two-hundred-year-old gem filled with stolen souls. They're not exactly lying around the city waiting for someone to find them." She snorted. "Then again, maybe they are. After all, that's what mine was, wasn't it? Just some hidden heirloom tucked under a safe in my office, and I never knew it even after six years of owning the pub." She let out a frustrated scream and buried her face in her hands. "Goddammit, Gramps, how could you keep this from me? We could have handled the stupid amulet years ago before it started shedding power and bringing in all kinds of nasty people." She dragged her fingers down her cheeks and peered at me between them. "What are we going to do, Trace?"

I took both her hands in mine and caught her eye. "First we're going to breathe." I waited until she managed to take a single deep breath. "Then we're going to talk to Chip and find out everything we can about that building. We have nine hours to figure this out. We've done crazier things with less time to spare."

Her gaze darkened. "Sure. I walked into a nightclub and had it out with Clyde Corrick. You ended up absorbing hundreds of souls and are still trying to keep them from killing you. I don't know if comparing our current situation to our last crisis is the best way to boost my confidence."

I'd also betrayed her, forced her to steer my car into a ditch and move ahead without me. A mistake I would not make this time around.

I nudged her with my knee. "We survived that one, didn't we? And we'll survive this one. All of us."

It was my turn for my phone to buzz, and I put Chip on speaker between us. "What do you know about the house?" I asked in greeting.

"It's a nice place," Chip said. "Lovely family home converted to office space about three years ago. But while there are a bunch of signs on the doors, it seems like only one business is actually set up to work there. Supposedly a law firm, but something about it gives me weird vibes. That could be because they're lawyers."

Alyssa and I made noises of understanding, and Chip continued. "What I find most interesting, however, is not the house itself but what lies under it."

"Under it?" Alyssa asked.

"Your hearing checks out, Cheers. You'd think there would be a basement, some cold storage. Maybe even, if you're wild and crazy, some kind of panic room, right? How about an entire tunnel system. It leads to the Labyrinth eventually, but there appears to be a smaller network of offices and tunnels designed as a sub-basement. Please don't ask how I learned this. I would have to kill you, and that would get messy."

"Your sources are safe," I assured him. I really didn't care where he got his information as long as he passed it along.

"The Labyrinth?" Alyssa asked. "I thought SMOAC sealed off most of the entrances."

"They couldn't if they tried," Chip said. "The feds have

claimed some of the main routes, but the rest have been commandeered by groups whose activities would keep you up at night. SMOAC uses the tunnels to get around the city quickly without their targets knowing they're coming for them, and the rest are used by people on the run from SMOAC. It's like one of those old *Benny Hill* sketches. With more violence."

I knew a little about the tunnels. Had even been down there a few times, though they weren't somewhere I enjoyed hanging out. Ottawa had a whole network of out-of-service sewers that had been converted into underground roads for supernaturals ages ago. The tunnels were lost to mundane blueprints, keeping them one of the best-kept supernatural secrets in the city. They stretched from one end of the capital to the other, with access points randomly located in almost every neighbourhood.

"That's our way in," I said. "We can get to the house via the tunnels instead of trying to go through the front door. If we're lucky, they're keeping Gramps somewhere under the building to make him harder to find, but that would work to our advantage as well."

Best-case scenario, we could break in, grab him, and leave before anyone was the wiser. There was no way in hell we'd get the best-case scenario, but I enjoyed imagining it anyway. It gave me some goalposts to reach for.

"They're expecting us for ten o'clock," I continued, "so we'll take them off guard and go in before nine. Even if they're looking for us to come early, they'll be watching the front door."

Alyssa didn't look certain, but the trust in her eyes made my heart clench. I would make this plan work. We had time to workshop it until it was airtight. I wouldn't let her down.

I didn't think I could bear disappointing her again.

Chapter 18
Alyssa

IDID MY best to sit quietly and let the experienced Cloak-and-Daggerites talk shop, but as Trace and Chip put their plan together, my mind whirred in other directions. SMOAC oversaw some of these tunnels, so my immediate thought was that now would be a good time to bring in Jet. If these dark witches had been harvesting souls in the city, the odds were good the feds already had their sights on them. But there was also the possibility that this coven had larger reach than we knew of if they'd been able to work so long without anyone catching on. Even if Jet's team gave Gramps a pass, if there was a mole in the department and we called them in, the odds of him winding up dead were too high.

But that didn't mean we had to go in alone. Surely Jet had

maps of the Labyrinth. Maps she might not mind sharing if she knew it would get Gramps out of this trap. With my family ready to stand as reinforcements, we stood a good chance of taking down this coven before anyone found out their reason for coming after us.

"What if we split their attention?" I asked, and by the way the room hushed, it was as if I'd suggested I go into the house naked. Or maybe I was projecting my discomfort at the sudden shift in attention my way. I cleared my throat and rubbed my palms on my thighs. "I think it's a good idea for us to go in early, but as we said before, they'll be prepared for that. They might not be prepared for us to go through the tunnels if we also hit the front door."

"You have a cloning device I haven't heard about, Cheers?" Chip asked.

"I have a family coven that's been hounding me for a role to play. There are about thirty of us in the city, and at least twelve of those thirty are available and would love to get their hands dirty."

Trace nodded. "It could work. It could also backfire. If this coven has any idea that we know about the tunnels, the second their defences go up, it could make it harder for us to access the basement."

He had a point. Stealth would be the better option... until it wasn't.

"So we delay the reinforcements," I suggested. "You and I go in via the tunnels, give a buffer of twenty minutes or so, then have my family ring their doorbell."

"Won't they be expecting your face on the other side of that doorbell?" Chip asked. I was surprised not to hear a note of derision in the question. The demon hadn't exactly shown a respect for my ideas in the past. Memories of his creative list of ways I might die came to mind.

"It'll be dark, right? My cousin Avery looks a bit like me. We have the same hair, the same facial structure. She could take point. We only need to fool them until the door opens and we can take our shot."

If we got that far into this plan before the coven acted. Even if they attacked first, I'd be glad to have support outside the house.

Trace looked to the phone as though he and Chip could confer in silence through the plastic and metal.

"I like it," Trace said. "It spreads the risk and raises the odds that we take these assholes down tonight. Rescue Gramps and destroy the coven in one fell swoop."

Relief warmed me through, and I reached for my phone so I could let the family know it was time. "Excellent. I can message Jet to get blueprints of the tunnels, then—"

"Already done," Chip said. "No need to bring the feds in and worry about paperwork slowing us down."

I raised an eyebrow. "What'd you do? Hack into SMOAC's network?"

"Do you really want to know?"

Trace shook his head, so I answered, "No. No, I do not."

"Didn't think so," said Chip. "I'll send over the blueprints I have. I suggest you use the access point near the university, then follow it underground until you reach the turn that'll take you to the office building. It should take you about forty-five minutes to walk from point A to B… barring any delays by the fiends that call the Labyrinth home, of course."

I shot Trace's phone a dirty look. "You really know how to sell your plans, you know that, Chippy?"

"Hey, I tell it like it is. You don't have to follow through with them. You could level up your computer skills past the basics, get yourself some sweet digs with a master setup, and do all the research while people like Trace do the legwork. Oh wait, you can't, because no one is as awesome as I am."

I stuck my tongue out at the phone, and Trace shot me a grin that spiked my body temperature from cheek to… other cheek.

"Trace, man, do you need any protection?"

Chip's question, so on the heels of my rising desire, made me jump, flush, then die of embarrassment. My death was made so much worse when Trace's grin widened and he replied, "Probably for the best. We're dealing with spirit magic here, so any extra defences will be helpful. Have any spell blockers handy?"

Magical protection. They were talking about *magical* protection.

Bastards.

"Not enough for everyone, but I'll see what I can scrounge up and have them couriered over. We'll be in touch."

Chip hung up, and my embarrassment remained as I tucked my hair behind my ear. "So," I said, choosing to pretend I was still a living person who hadn't expired from a blush so intense my skin would never be pale again, "let's call the family next and come up with a plan."

Perhaps understandably, my parents were not thrilled with the idea of Trace and I leading this rescue mission.

"You should be at the front door," Dad said from my phone screen where I was hosting the video call. Eight other Mooney witches were on the call with us, and so far I'd received zero positive feedback from any of them. "Let Mom and Courtney use the tunnels to get Gramps."

The grownups, he meant. As though I were still a little girl skinning my knees chasing after my brothers or spilling juice out of the fridge.

"With all due respect, Mr. Mooney," Trace said.

"Henry," Dad corrected, shoving his glasses up his nose. "You're helping us rescue my father-in-law, so I'd say there's no point in formalities, wouldn't you?"

"Henry," Trace said with a nod. "I have experience getting through all manner of locks and security systems. We don't know what we'll be facing down there, so it makes sense for me to take the lead."

"Then Mary can go with you while Alyssa stays up top with the others."

I lowered my eyes so Dad wouldn't notice my worry. Yes, Trace was the most experienced out of all of us in doing these high-risk jobs, but he was also suffering from a possession gone wrong. I'd seen what could happen if he lost control. I didn't want any of my family to see him like that and think… Well, I didn't want them to think the worst of him.

There was also the matter of my not wanting to leave his side. My anxiety was already fighting to rise to the surface, and only with Trace did I feel confident enough in our success to keep it at bay.

"I want to go with him," I said, raising my gaze to the phone. "There are going to be risks either way, and honestly, Avery is the better warder. If the people at the front door end up taking more of the assault, she's the better option to keep them busy while we get Gramps."

"We'll be with Avery," Dylan said, his face coming up on the screen. His blue eyes were hard, and I caught the fire burning within them. Oh yes, my brother was ready for a fight.

"So will we." As my cousin Grayson spoke up, his face—next to his brother Kyle's—replaced Dylan's. "That's five fighters ready to lure them out of the house, giving Aly and Wyatt the opening they need to get out."

Dad sighed, and Mom rested her hand on his shoulder. "I don't like it any more than you do, but Aly's right. There is no safe option. If she's more comfortable with Trace, we'll trust our girl."

My heart filled with gratitude for her, and I wished she were closer so I could give her a hug.

"I'll guard her with my life," Trace said, warming me even further.

"Aww," Val spoke up from behind Mom. "Sweet as well as hot? I can't even deal."

I rolled my eyes and made a note to read out sections of her diary later.

"We'll have more than five on the street, but we won't be able to engage until we get inside the house. Someone else should go with you two as well," Aunt Courtney pushed. "What if you meet resistance in the basement?"

"I considered that," Trace said, "but it makes more sense to go in quiet. The tunnels can get narrow, so having too many people risks clogging our exit. Having a few reinforcements stationed at the edge of the tunnel might be smart, though. That way if we're followed out, some of us can focus on getting Gramps to safety while the others stay and fight."

A shudder ran through me. Once again, I was preparing for battle. For the second time in two months. For the third time in four years. I hadn't realized growing up how common this sort of confrontation would be, and suddenly it made a lot of sense why Mooney parents insisted on teaching the younger generations how to wield our magic to the best of our abilities.

"I'll go with you," Mom said. "That way I can start to heal Dad as quickly as possible, get him back on his feet to escape on his own.

"Jennifer and I will be with you too," Courtney declared.

"We will," Jennifer said over her wife's shoulder. "I'd say Hilary and Tony might be talked into it as well, but they won't want to be left out of the main fight."

She knew her sister and brother-in-law well.

Dad frowned. "I'll join the second wave, and we'll keep our distance until we're needed."

Trace rubbed a hand over his face. "All right, we'll let you guys sort out who's going where and send you the tunnel blue-prints so you can study them as well."

We arranged to meet those who would be joining us in the tunnels at the University of Ottawa entrance at eight o'clock, which would give us an hour to make our way to the basement under the MacLaren house. The others would wait until nine-twenty to knock on the door. It meant Trace and I would have to be as quick and quiet as possible to avoid bringing the fight downstairs before my family got into place, but I trusted him and Chip to consider every eventuality.

Once we were sure everyone was on the same page, I ended the call and stared at the blueprints spread across my coffee table. I'd printed them off to make our planning easier, and as I followed the various twists and turns and the sheer space they took up, I couldn't help but be amazed that they were still secret.

"Do you think these tunnels run under the pub?" I asked.

"They must," Trace said. "It wouldn't surprise me if there was a whole network set up under the building. Mooney's is old enough, and from the time it was built, it's always been owned by supernaturals. There's probably an evacuation route available if the mundanes ever turn on us."

What surprised me most was how elaborate the setup under the MacLaren house was. When Trace and Chip had mentioned tunnels, I'd expected just that—dirty underground passageways. But the space under the office building seemed to have rooms branching off the main tunnel. Someone had transformed these secret roads into extra living space, and I wondered what the original purpose had been. Had the intention always been to shield nasty people's nasty deeds?

Sometimes I wished supernaturals kept a better history of our doings. We usually didn't in case some mundane ever came across them and saw through the perception filter, but the secrecy meant that so much of what we'd learned and built was lost to the ages. Unless some wise person had taken the histories across the unseen wall to the magical realm beyond. I'd never been across myself, too human to have merited an invitation, but I imagined how many libraries existed over there full to the brim with our supernatural stories.

By the time seven o'clock rolled around, we'd come up with—I felt—a strong plan. We would go in via the access point Chip had recommended and walk through the tunnels until we arrived under the house, which we would recognize thanks to Chip's map. There we would leave Mom, Jennifer, and Courtney and, armed with the spell-blocking amulets, go through the underground rooms until we found Gramps, who was hopefully holed up somewhere under the house so we could free him and go back the way we came. Worst case, we would need to fight our way out. With the time we had, Trace and I practiced a few moves with our magic, playing with the various ways they might intertwine and how we could combine spells for maximum effect.

We'd had some practice against Corrick, but that had been on the fly. Today, without death immediately bearing down on us, we were able to discover some new combos that I almost hoped we had an opportunity to try out.

If we did have to enter the higher levels of the house, our options grew a little more strained, but we weren't without defences.

By the time we finished making our preparations, my greatest fears revolved around Trace losing control of his spirits and causing more harm to himself or our surroundings than necessary, the coven proving stronger than we anticipated and members of my family getting hurt, and us being too late to save Gramps.

I wished I could ask Simon to get someone else to cover the pub so he could come with us. Heck, I would have felt even better if he and Reverie both tagged along. But I accepted that wasn't an option. His chaos magic was already on the fritz. It would be unfair to put him in a position where he was pushed to lose control. Trace's unpredictable magic would be challenge enough to manoeuvre around.

But even if I couldn't ask him to serve as backup, Simon deserved to know the plan so he could prepare for any… eventualities. To that end, while Trace attempted to take a quick nap on my amazing couch, I disappeared into my bedroom to call my bestie.

"Everything okay?" Simon asked when he answered. "Any word from Gramps yet?"

"We think we found where they're keeping him," I said, and a thought occurred to me. "You haven't heard any rumours about someone calling the shots on a bunch of spirit witches lately, have you?"

"Can't say I have," he growled. "Believe me, if I'd known there were spirit witches walking around, I wouldn't have let you go to the park by yourself the other night. Are they the people who have Gramps? Tell me you're reporting them to SMOAC."

His worry for me warmed the chill of apprehension slowly icing over my veins. "Eventually, absolutely. But first we're going to get Gramps away from them."

"You're what? Lys, what the hell are you doing?"

"Following the Labyrinth to a series of mysterious rooms under a law firm in Centretown?"

"Lys…"

I pictured him pinching the bridge of his nose and didn't blame him. Having spelled it out like that, I was amazed I'd made it this far without being stunned by my own ridiculousness. What the hell were we thinking?

"I know," I said. "Does it make you feel any better to know my family will be joining us, and Trace and I will both have magic-blocking amulets? His buddy sent them over, and they're a lot snazzier than the soul amulet."

I played with the tiny pendant at the end of the slim golden chain. It was an amethyst, able to absorb some basic spells, and pretty to boot. By the magic wafting off it, I suspected it was enchanted to the brim and therefore incredibly expensive, but I didn't care. If Chip didn't ask for it back once this mission was over, I wasn't going to return it. I deserved it for putting up with him.

"No," Simon said. "That doesn't make me feel better. Not even a little bit."

Something smashed behind him, shouts rang out from the pub, and Simon cursed under his breath.

"What was that?" I asked.

"A shelf just collapsed and we lost a whole fucking row of glasses. What the fuck was that?"

I opened my mouth to ask if his chaos magic had slipped but thought it best not to antagonize him when our conversation was going so well.

"I have to go clean this up before we get sued," he said, "but Lys, please, rethink this rescue mission. I'm glad your family's involved, but I'd feel better if I was there too. I can shut down here. Wait for me."

I wished that were possible. Despite how confident I was in Trace's abilities, I always felt better with Simon nearby. But unfortunately, I didn't trust anything that might upset our only advantage: stealth.

"If anyone is watching the pub, you closing up early will

give away that something's up."

He sighed. "Just be careful, all right? I love you too much to lose you to some spirit witches."

"I love you too, Simon. Go see about those glasses."

He grumbled and hung up, and I rubbed my face. I was making the right call here. I had to be. Gramps deserved my best, and Trace, even in his current condition, was my best. And no one in this city—heck, in the province—compared to the Mooney family. We would find a way to make this work. By the time midnight came, Gramps would be with us, and we would turn the whole spirit witch nonsense over to SMOAC.

So mote it be.

Chapter 19
Alyssa

IT FELT LIKE no time at all before Trace and I stood in front of the service door in the university underpass. I must have passed this door a hundred times, but I'd never looked at it twice.

In fact, as I stood there watching students and other commuters pass by, I realized that no one looked at it twice. As though to them it wasn't there at all. Maybe it was the nature of service doors in general, but I suspected it was the perception filter at work again. People didn't see it because they didn't expect to see it. If they did notice it, it would be nothing more than a door they didn't have access to, and they would carry on with their day.

At the moment, we were waiting for the underpass to clear

so we had an opportunity to go in.

Mom, Courtney, and Jennifer stood down the way, making it seem as though they weren't with us. They had their phones out and were… Were they pretending to chase Pokémon?

I turned my back on them and shifted from one foot to the other, torn between anxiety and eagerness. I wanted to get this over with so I could put it all behind me. At the very least, I wanted to get started. Once we were on the move, there would be no turning back. Until we took those first steps, I still had the opportunity to run.

And goddess how I wanted to run. I wanted to head back to my apartment, call Jet, and let someone else take the terrifying leap against a coven of dark witches who'd somehow gotten the upper hand on Gramps. I did not want to go in there myself.

Beside me, Trace looked calm. He leaned against the wall, one foot crossed over the other, scrolling on his phone. His strawberry-blond hair was neatly brushed and pulled back out of his face, his cheeks and jaw were lined with stubble, and his violet eyes were sharp. The black parka, worn open to reveal a dark blue sweater over a pair of black jeans that he'd grabbed from a bag in his car, and a scuffed-up pair of boots completed his look. Everything about him said *I'm supposed to be here, and I'm too awesome to pay attention to any of you.*

Everything about me, on the other hand, probably said *Oh*

my goddess, I'm about to throw up all the cereal I crammed in my face an hour ago.

What the hell did Trace see in me?

No, that wasn't right. I was a badass, business-owning witch who was kind to her friends, decent in an emergency, and made an all right cup of tea. I was a catch.

I was not, however, the first person a bounty hunter would choose to bring on a job.

But not once did Trace suggest I stay at home, and I didn't know if it was because he actually had faith that I could help or if he believed he lacked the strength or control to handle this on his own. Because if he were at the top of his game, he would have been able to. Trace Wyatt, Bounty Hunter, was the stuff of legend. A little rescue mission like this was probably a party game for him when he wasn't also wrestling the hundreds of angry spirits writhing inside him.

Or maybe my thoughts were rambling.

He pushed himself away from the wall and slipped his phone into his pocket. "All right, we're good. As soon as we go underground, we won't have cell reception, so stay close. You ready?"

I looked around, surprised to discover we were alone. I hadn't even noticed. So no, clearly I was not ready. "You betcha," I said anyway, then turned my back and reached for the door before he could watch the embarrassment overwhelm me at my overly perfect, corny response. What was wrong with me?

Mom, Courtney, and Jennifer followed us in, but they kept their distance, and as soon as we'd outstripped them, Trace took my hand and pulled me close to his side. At first I thought it was to warn me of something up ahead, but when he didn't loosen his grip or whisper any explanations, I realized it was simply to hold my hand. As though this was his idea of a first date.

For all I knew, inviting women to help collect a bounty was his love language. I'd have to find a way to reciprocate. Maybe with a generous pour of his favourite craft beer or the offering of a warm, oversized sweater.

I shook off those thoughts and took in my surroundings as we went down the graded incline deeper under the city. My sense of direction was usually good, so I knew we were heading west towards Centretown, but that was all I was able to gather. The tunnels were lit by evenly spaced light bulbs stuck within metal cages and caked with so much dirt and so many bugs I was astounded any light made it through. The walls were damp with leaking water, and I splashed through more than one puddle as we walked. I didn't want to think too hard about what those puddles might be composed of.

"This is not how I expected to spend my first days back home," Mom grumbled behind us, her voice carrying along the tunnel.

"Admit it, Mary, this is way more fun than sitting on some ship watching the sights go by," Aunt Courtney teased.

"Fine. But I could do with fewer spiders."

For the most part the tunnels were quiet—seemingly empty—but Trace never dropped his guard. Oh, he appeared relaxed enough, but I noticed the way he held his free hand out of his pocket and slightly away from his side, ready to summon his magic at the first hint of a threat.

Following his lead, I kept my magic close to the surface, tamped enough that no one would sense it easily if they searched for it. I didn't want to be taken unawares. From what Chip had insinuated, all kinds of people used these tunnels, many who I wouldn't want to run into at night. Or, frankly, during the day. The lighting down here really was garbage.

We didn't say much as we walked. Thanks to my mom and aunt, we knew how well sound bounced off these stone walls, and, knowing my luck, anything I said would echo all the way to the house on MacLaren and give us away before we got within spitting distance of the right door.

"How are you holding up?" Trace asked in a low voice, his lips so close to my ear his breath raised goosebumps along my neck.

"Well enough. Staying positive. Focusing on the goal. How about you? Your guests causing you any trouble?"

I hadn't wanted to ask earlier in case he said yes. Now that we'd passed that handy Point of No Return, it wouldn't matter. We would have to make do with what we had. Selfish of me? Maybe, but I knew my own limitations, and going in to rescue Gramps by myself wasn't an option.

"I'll be fine. Probably."

It was the first sign of uncertainty he'd shown, and guilt that I hadn't asked him before pinched my heart. Point of no return or not, I tightened my grip on his hand to pull him to a stop. But he shook his head without looking me in the eye and tugged me along, making it clear there was no more room for conversation. He was going ahead with this regardless of his fears about himself, and I would have to suck it up and run with it.

I glowered at his back as I hastened my step to keep up with him. Oh, I'd suck it up, all right. I'd suck it up and spew it out when we reached safety. If he thought we were in for trouble and hadn't bothered to warn me? He'd never hear the end of it.

He looked over his shoulder to give me a reassuring smile, but the gesture only mollified me so far since he still didn't make eye contact. There was something he wasn't telling me, and I had a suspicion I wouldn't know what it was until we were thrown into a situation where it mattered.

At that thought, I pulled my magic even more closely

around me. I needed to be prepared for anything. I had once sworn to do no harm, but we were getting out of these tunnels tonight even if I had to take a life or two to do it.

The realization of how possible that was twisted my guts, and I breathed through the nausea. The people we were going up against were not kind or nice or even vaguely pleasant. They'd harmed others. They'd dealt in magics that were forbidden on both sides of the unseen wall. This coven was messing with the souls of those who deserved to rest in peace. Whatever we brought down on them would be on their own heads, not mine. I was trying to rescue a man who hadn't done anything except train me for everything this world offered.

I wiped my free palm against my thigh to dry it off and sent a silent apology to Trace for the sweatiness of my other. More sweat dripped down the small of my back, and I regretted my heavy coat. How much would I miss it if I stripped it off and left it here in the tunnels? Maybe I could ask Mom to carry it for me.

Deciding I would rather not get rid of an expensive item of clothing simply because my anxiety was getting the better of me, or revert to toddlerhood by leaving Mom to pick it up, I settled for unbuttoning it and flapping the lapel to stir up a cool breeze on the back of my neck. Trace shot me another look, but I ignored him. He didn't need to know what dark paths my thoughts had gone down.

The closer we got to Centretown, the more supernaturals we passed in the tunnels. Some were heading back the way we'd come, some were cutting towards downtown or Old Ottawa South. A few were going our way, but they kept to themselves, showing no interest in our being here. I'd had no idea the Labyrinth was so widely known, but what I noticed was that most of the supernaturals using it were those who would have struggled to blend in on the surface. Creatures whose physical traits couldn't be hidden easily behind the perception filter, with too many tentacles or horns or feathers. Once I realized that, the purpose and usefulness of the tunnels became so much clearer. Yes, Chip was probably right that some people used them for dark deals, but they also kept us safe. They were a place to disappear if the balance of the world ever shifted and our secrets came out. They were a way for supernaturals who couldn't fit in to get around and create some kind of life for themselves without constantly hiding behind a glamour.

As I sat with that idea, the more determined I became to find out if Mooney's Pub attached to the Labyrinth. If we could allow more people access to a good drink and some company, then I owed it to my community to see it done.

I made a mental note to raise the idea with Simon, then focused once more on where we were going.

Trace's expression darkened, and he drew me to the side as we approached a turn. My mouth dry, my stomach a mess of knots, I peered around the corner to find another doorway, this one marked *Private*.

I met Trace's eye, and he nodded. This was it.

My heart galloped in my chest, and I drew in a series of deep breaths to gain some control over it. Anxiety was temporary. I was in control of my reactions. Thank you, brain, for warning me of everything that might go wrong. I was aware of the risks I was taking, but values over fears.

So what if I was about to walk in on a dark coven armed with souls that might turn me to ash with a single well-timed spell? So what if I might watch my grandfather be murdered in front of me because we miscalculated and they knew we were coming and we had nothing to trade with them? So what if—

Trace grabbed my shoulders, turned me towards him, and kissed me.

My thoughts went quiet.

My heartbeat raced for a different reason.

My toes curled.

It was a chaste kiss—nothing close to what I'd imagined our first kiss would be like—but even so, the softness of his lips, the pressure, the firmness—it was perfection. He pulled away, and his eyes were full of questions with a hint of concern. Was I all right? Was *that* all right? Was I going to lose my mind? Had he distracted me well enough?

I answered them all with a smile and rose on tiptoe to

return his kiss, a promise that when we finished here, I wanted to explore far more of his kisses and whatever else he wanted to surprise me with.

Trace grinned at me as though he'd read my thoughts, but before I could kiss him a third time, Mom, Courtney, and Jennifer rounded the corner, and he stepped back. Mom caught my eye and gave me a questioning thumbs-up. I returned the gesture, letting her know I was good. We were good. Everything would be good.

Now I had to prove it.

I took one more breath, then looked to Trace, and when he winked, my legs threatened to turn to jelly. I might be terrified, but he'd given me all the motivation I needed to take down as many of these bastards as I could. To hell with ethics or morals. Burn the place down, get Gramps, lets go. I had a post-rescue-mission date with a bounty hunter to get to.

Chapter 20
Trace

MY BLOOD HUMMED in my veins, adrenaline coursing through me even as the minutes ticked away from that kiss. I couldn't believe I'd worked up the courage to do it, but Alyssa had been so nervous, so fixated on all the ways things might go wrong tonight, that I hadn't been able to help myself.

I also couldn't deny the buzz of fear layered under the thrill. I'd lived through enough situations like this to know what to expect, but Alyssa was new to my world. Before two months ago, as she was the first to admit, her life had been governed by routine and predictability.

Nothing about tonight would be predictable. We had no idea how many witches were inside or what level of power they might hold. We knew they worked in spirit magic, but that only increased the unknowns. How would the spirits using me as their personal party bus respond to this coven's spells?

We didn't know where Gramps was being kept or what kind of defences might be around him. The biggest unknown factor, however, was that we had no idea who sat at the head of this coven. Who had decided Gramps should be taken and ransomed for the amulet? Who had known about the amulet?

With all those questions running through my mind, I worried we were about to find ourselves in over our heads. Alyssa was a strong witch—one of the strongest I'd ever met, even if she didn't realize it—but up against an entire coven, I didn't know if she had it in her to be that aggressive.

I could only cross my fingers that her sense of self-preservation outweighed her sense of ethics.

And beneath all of that was a lurking suspicion I hadn't been able to shake since I'd heard the Bone Casters were involved. It wasn't based on anything more than the coincidence of my old coven being in town, but I hated coincidences. They always suggested that either our fates were out of our hands, which I wasn't sure I believed, or that something bigger was at play.

And if my suspicions were right—that I was somehow more connected to this mystery coven's plot than I realized—then I vowed to myself I would do everything in my power to make sure Alyssa wasn't hurt by their plans.

I squeezed her hand one last time and looked behind us to

confirm Mary, Courtney, and Jennifer were in place in case we ran into trouble. Once I was certain we were as prepared as we could be, I wove my magic through the lock, opened the door that led us to the space underneath the office building, and stepped through.

The first thing that struck me was the decor. This was no unfinished basement. Someone had redecorated this section of the Labyrinth to be an extension of the house above. Soft light glowed from the sconces on the wall, which were more up to date than the metal cages we'd passed in the rest of the Labyrinth. The light washed over the austere beige walls and the soft blue-and-grey corporate carpeting that covered the concrete floor. Four doors lined each side of the hallway, and each door bore a plaque with a name on it. Assigned office space.

I didn't recognize any of the names, and when I glanced at Alyssa, she shook her head. Were these members of the coven, or were these offices part of the law firm?

The idea of having an actual office down here, of having to descend into the depths day after day with no windows and no fresh air beyond what was piped through the vents… I shuddered. Give me long drives across the country and chasing people through the snow. I might have begun my path into bounty hunting on a whim, but I'd embraced it over the years. Regular jobs in cramped, unwelcoming spaces were not for me.

No sound reached us from beyond any of the doors. Taking a chance, I tried one of them and eased it open only to find a dark room. Light spilled in from the hallway to reveal a desk, a bookcase, a computer, and some chairs, but nothing that indicated a dark witch worked within. And no Gramps.

A pinch of worry nagged at me as more questions whirled through my skull. Our entire plan was based on assumptions. What if we'd been wrong about everything? Had we given ourselves away by coming here? If this was where we'd find the leader but not Gramps, we'd walked into the lion's den and Alyssa's grandfather was a dead man.

I hesitated at the end of the hallway and looked back the way we'd come. The door at the end remained open. If we wanted to, we could turn around and leave right now. No one would be the wiser. We could do a bit more recon and find out for sure where they were holding Gramps.

Except by then, he might already be dead because we had nothing to trade for him.

Alyssa rested her hand on my arm to get my attention, and when I looked down at her, I found her green eyes filled with confusion and concern. I squeezed her fingers to assure her all was well, then turned and continued towards the other end of the hallway. For better or worse, this was the best chance we had, and I wasn't about to let it go to waste.

Before we reached the door that would take us up to the

house, however, a low thump caught my ear. Again I paused, this time tilting my head in the direction I thought the sound had come from. A few seconds later, it came again, and Alyssa sucked in a breath as she headed towards the door to our right. I tensed, ready to pull her away from it in case she stepped into a trap, but the tickle of her magic caressed my skin as she channelled it into her hands. My clever witch. She might not be experienced with breaking and entering, but she was no stranger to keeping herself safe. I didn't want to take all the credit for that, but I was sure my grabbing her from outside her house and stuffing her in the trunk of my car hadn't hurt.

Alyssa turned the handle, but it caught. Locked. Her lips pressed together in a frustrated grimace, and I nudged her out of the way to send some of my magic into the lock. It clicked over, and I stepped back to let her open the door while I scanned our surroundings for any hint of a warding spell guarding the door. Although I detected nothing, I had to wonder what protections did exist down here. There hadn't been any on the door we'd come through, and so far I hadn't picked up anything along this hallway. I'd checked the ceiling for cameras as we'd walked and hadn't spotted any.

Either these people had the utmost faith that anyone of any importance would come through the front door, or their defences were higher tier than anything I'd encountered before. Given what we'd seen so far, I was tempted to believe the latter.

The minions were mediocre, but the setup had been professional. If I was right, it meant we had to move quickly before someone came down to investigate.

Alyssa hissed as the door opened to reveal another dark office and the single person inside. Gramps was tied to the chair behind the desk, mouth gagged with a cloth handkerchief and hands bound with magic-suppressing cuffs. His eyes widened, filling with so much alarm that I was ready for our unknown enemy to pop up behind us.

Alyssa gasped and rushed over to him while I watched the hallway. For now, we were alone.

She pulled down his gag and threw her arms around his neck. "I'm so glad you're okay."

"What are you doing here, Pip?" he whispered. "You shouldn't be here. These people, they're… I don't even know what they are. They're harvesting souls, using them to kill people. I think they're building up to something bigger, but I haven't learned what. The only reason I'm alive is because I convinced them the amulet still exists."

Alyssa's jaw dropped. "You what? But Gramps—"

"I know, but you didn't hear them. They would have killed me that first night. We've got to get out before they know you're here. If they find out the amulet's broken, they'll kill all three of us. Spells won't work on these cuffs, so you'll need the key. It's in one of the offices. I don't know which one."

"We can get the cuffs off later," I said. "We should get out—"

"I need my magic. I can't breathe with it cut off."

He also wouldn't be able to help defend himself if he needed to.

I cursed under my breath and left Alyssa to undo what bindings she could while I hunted for the key to the cuffs. Someone had been clever in not keeping them too close to the prisoner. I wondered if they were experienced enough to have thought of it on their own or if Gramps had given them reason to level up quickly.

I found the key in the third office, and when I returned, Alyssa had managed to get all the non-magical bindings released. Gramps was on his feet away from the chair with only the magic-suppressing cuffs remaining. He wasn't anything like I pictured when Alyssa had described her favourite family member. I'd pictured a Santa Claus–type figure with a portly belly and a thick white beard. The sort of jolly face you'd like to see working behind the bar. Instead, he was on the heavy side of fit—definitely showing the effects of many long years slinging pints—but the belly was offset by broad shoulders, and enough muscle definition showed in his bared forearms that I wouldn't have wanted to try messing with him. He did have a white beard, but it was trimmed close to his cheeks, and when he pulled his lips back to sneer at the cuffs, I caught a glint of a silver tooth in the soft light.

Clearly Alyssa came from wilder stock than I'd thought.

I tossed her the keys, not wanting to give up my spot as sentry while she released him, and she set to work.

The moment the cuffs were off, Gramps rolled his neck until it loosened with a series of pops, and magic prickled the back of my neck. If I'd believed Alyssa was powerful, her strength was nothing compared to the punch her grandfather packed.

"How the hell did they grab you?" I asked.

Gramps grinned at me, his green eyes—so like Alyssa's—dark with rage. "A story for another time. We have to move."

"Mom is just outside to patch you up," Alyssa said. "The rest of the family is waiting out front. If we get out of here fast enough, maybe we can call them off before they knock."

Together we hit the hallway and started back the way we'd come. The door we'd entered through was now closed. Dread dropped like a weight in my stomach, and I summoned my magic into my hands.

Alyssa crept closer, willing to try the door regardless, but I swept my magic ahead of her and grabbed hold of her arm before she could make contact. Testing my suspicion, I released a small burst of telekinetic power to shake the handle, and sparks flashed across the door. Someone had electrified the damned thing when we weren't looking.

Alyssa whipped around on her feet, and my skin hummed under the intensity of both her and Gramps's powers. If I spent much time around these two, I would need to work on blocking my magic sensitivity or my teeth would start to ache.

"There's no way this didn't trigger something upstairs," I said. "If we stay down here, we'll be sitting ducks the moment that door opens."

"The only other way out is up," Gramps said grimly. "Hope you kids are ready for a fight."

He took a step, but I put my arm out to stop him. He raised an eyebrow, a look that might have quelled a less stubborn man, but I wasn't fazed. "If things go south up there, the priority is getting Alyssa home."

I didn't want to say anything else, not wanting her to panic or argue with me, but the longer we stayed here, the louder that nagging voice in the back of my mind became. These people were out for souls, and I was bringing them a whole host. If they realized it—if they recognized it—there was no way they'd let me walk out the front door.

Gramps eyed me for a long moment, then understanding flashed across his expression, and he nodded. "Of course."

"Excuse me?" Alyssa hissed behind us. "What is this? Some honourable pact? I'm capable of getting myself out, thank you very much. Besides, we're all leaving."

"Come on, Pip," Gramps said, ignoring her lecture. "Let's

hope the family's in position."

Her jaw dropped, and she shot me a dirty look before following him. I didn't care. We'd come here for her grandfather, and we'd achieved our aim. Depending on what we faced upstairs, my only concern now was keeping the two of them safe. From there, they could go to Jet, and SMOAC could raid the house. Ideally fast enough that the coven didn't have time to clear out.

First things first, though, we had to get upstairs.

I drew a breath and braced myself for mayhem.

Chapter 21
Alyssa

I WAS SEETHING as we edged our way up the stairs.

We'd come this far. We'd achieved our goal. Now Trace was preparing for us to fail? I wanted to throttle the man. And for him and Gramps to have some kind of secret discussion about my safety when I was standing right in front of them? No way was that going to fly. After we got out of here, there would be words. Very strong words.

But first, we had to make it to the front door, and despite my anger that Trace and Gramps had decided my life was worth more than theirs, I was ready to concede that the next few minutes weren't going to be fun. A glance at the time confirmed my family should be almost in place, and I debated the wisdom of heading up now instead of waiting. But we couldn't take the risk that Trace was right and the back door closing had signalled our presence to the people upstairs. We wouldn't want to be trapped down here in this narrow hallway if anyone came to look around.

Magic rippled over my skin, my pores filling with a light purple glow as I kept my power steady and available. Although I appreciated Simon's strong, level-headed presence in a crisis, I had to admit I was relieved he hadn't come with us tonight. If he had, our magic would have been bouncing off the walls right now, his demonic chaos power reacting who knew how with mine or Gramps's or Trace's. At least with only the three of us, I was able to keep my power at a comfortable simmer, ready to be used.

Which I had an opportunity to do before we reached the top of the stairs.

The door swung open, and a blast of magic shot down at us from someone above. Gramps called out and threw up his hands to form a ward, but I was already on it with a thick purple net that wove across the stairwell and repelled the magic as it flew our way. Yellow mingled with purple before the spirit spell bounced back towards the witch, and screams filled my ears as he tumbled backwards and crashed to the floor in apparent agony.

"Fast work, Pip," Gramps said, clapping me on the shoulder.

"I could say the same to you, old man."

It had been four years since I'd seen my grandfather in action, and I'd forgotten just how much power he could wield.

"Whatever their original magical energy was, they're all dealing in spirit magic now," Trace growled behind me. "This isn't going to go well for them."

I didn't look back at him. I didn't have to look to know what I'd see. This fight might not go well for the spirit witches, but it wouldn't go well for Trace either if the souls inside him came out to play.

"You should get to the front door," I said to him. "Let me and Gramps deal with these guys."

"We're not leaving here until we put them down," he said. "If the souls they're using can't be freed, then at least they won't be put to work against their nature. We won't stand for it."

I squeezed my eyes shut and gave myself permission to believe he was referring to the three of us with that *we* and not using it to represent the audience inside him. But my denial could only take me so far. We—as in Gramps and I—had to get Trace out of here before he brought the house down on our heads.

Drawing in a breath to find my courage, I led the way up the final few stairs. The witch that had attacked us lay still, his eyes open and half his face decomposed, and I carefully stepped over him. Gramps grabbed my arm, pulled me to the ground, and released a pulse of atmospheric magic that sent three more witches sliding backwards. We'd exited the stairs into a hall-way that split forward and to the right, and these witches had come from our right. By the spell that surged from one of their hands as she tottered backwards, she would have done a lot of damage to my torso if Gramps hadn't caught her first.

I had to get my head in the game. This was the fight with Corrick's lieutenants all over again. The first time I'd faced them, it had been me and Simon. We'd done our best and failed, but we'd managed to take a few down before they got us. This time I had a retired mercenary and a magically trained bounty hunter possessed by a vengeful horde, not to mention the fighters of my coven waiting outside. We could take on a few witches.

Another three came up from the hallway straight ahead, blocking our way to the door. I threw up a net to catch their attacks, and Gramps launched a pulse over top of it. In his efforts to avoid blasting a hole through my ward, his aim was off and the impact only knocked the hat off the middle witch, but the speed with which she darted back to grab it made the effort worthwhile. Her poor prioritization caused the other two witches to turn around to check out the crisis, and in their moment of distraction, I pulled down the net and released another pulse of my own.

Trace followed up my attack with a yellow-and-silver bubble that popped when it hit them and bound them together as though it had been made of super glue. They thrashed against it, but the bubble had nullified their magic. I knew that spell well. Not the spirit-touched version of it, which appeared to be more uncomfortable than the basic silver version, but nonetheless, it wasn't fun to have your magic stripped from you.

He pushed past me, and sure enough, his eyes were glowing and tendrils of yellow had spread down his cheeks. The witches started screaming when he raised his hands and summoned rings of yellow magic into his palms.

"Trace, stop!" I threw myself at him before he could cast. "You don't want to do this. You know you don't. Remember how you felt after killing Nathalie? These people aren't worth that."

He bared his teeth and craned his neck to face me, and chills ran down my spine at the inhuman look in his eyes. But there—a flash of desperate violet as my Trace struggled to regain control.

With a cry, he stretched out his hand, and the whole corridor lit up with yellow magic that rose out of the witches' pores, from their eyes and their open mouths, and entered Trace. His skin took on a glow to match his eyes, his hair rising as though he were filled with static, and I stepped away from the blaze of power emanating from him.

The witch with the hat raised her hands to ready a spell, but nothing happened. Her eyes widened with horror, but her shock couldn't be greater than mine was. I sensed no magic from her whatsoever.

When I looked back at Trace, his lips were curved in a cruel smile. He pulled another spell into his hands and hurled three ropes that lashed the witches together before he magically dumped them on the ground in the room to our left. "Stay there until we're finished."

He slammed the door closed on them, and I pressed my back against the wall to put more distance between him and me. I didn't think he would harm me on purpose, but with that much power oozing out of him, I wasn't sure he could control it.

"You stole their magic?" I asked.

He turned on me. Despite everything, I tensed, and my fear pained me. This was Trace Wyatt, the man who'd promised never to hurt me again. On a rational level, I believed it, but right now, looking at him losing the battle against the spirits within him, I couldn't deny that the possibility was there.

"I stole the souls fuelling their magic." This time his voice was closer to his own. Exhausted but untouched by his hundred-plus spirits. Who knew how many more had joined the others now that he'd absorbed the souls those witches had stolen. "Their natural magic should come back in a few days. Probably."

He wavered on his feet, and Gramps grabbed his arm. My

grandfather didn't show any of the fears I held. He showed no revulsion or concern in laying hands on a possessed man and guiding him down the hallway. "Come on, my boy, let's get you out of here before you collapse. I don't think I have it in me to carry you."

I took a few steps towards the front door, keeping my back to the wall and checking the open doorways to the offices we passed, but before I could cross the foyer, a weave of yellow-touched elemental magic shot past me and struck the welcome mat in front of the entrance. My spell-blocking amulet repelled the drifting cords of power but couldn't prevent the fire that sprang up from the mat and spread across the tiles. Magical fire—not strong enough to burn down the house, but enough to burn anyone who crossed it. Which meant unless we could douse the flames or work around them, our reinforcements would be stuck outside.

Gramps let go of Trace to summon a spell, but a second burst of magic came from an office to my left and struck him in the back. As he stumbled into the wall, I cried out and retaliated with a spell of my own. The atmospheric magic hit the hinges next to Office Witch's head. The door swung to the side, hitting the witch and taking both woman and door to the ground. Not willing to leave it at that, I released another net and threw it at her. She rolled to the side to avoid it, but that gave Gramps a chance to recover. He launched his atmospheric power at her throat, and her face purpled with lack of air before the light drained from her eyes.

Trace had spun around and was facing another witch whose green elemental magic was coming in bursts from another office opposite the first. Trace's telekinetic power grabbed hold of the series of law degrees nailed to the wall, and he launched them at the man standing in the doorway. Glass shattered across the floor tiles, but the witch never flinched. With his gaunt face and pale skin, he reminded me of a corpse, his balding head giving the appearance of someone whose follicles were fleeing rather than receding. His smile, all straight white teeth, raised the hairs on the back of my neck, and I found myself wanting to join his hairline in running as fast as I possibly could. Even more than Corrick, he carried himself as though he owned the room. We were inconvenient, a night's amusement, but he would crush us without breaking a sweat.

I was determined to wring at least one bead from his pasty forehead.

While Gramps stayed on guard for any other witches lurking in the offices, I gathered a spell between my palms, steadied my feet, and released a pulse that shook the airwaves between me and the ghoulish man. It pushed him back a step, but he was ready with a counterattack—another blast of magical fire aimed straight for me. I raised my hands, certain I wouldn't have enough time to block it, but Trace was there with a ward of his own. The magic struck it and spread out, the flames petering to nothing. The amulet around my neck warmed as it repelled more stray tendrils of power.

"Get to the door," Trace said, and his eyes were yellow again with the strength of his deeper magic.

No way in hell was I about to leave him like this, especially not when two more witches had appeared in the hallway we'd just left. They must have stepped out of an office we'd passed along the way. Had all these witches been waiting for us? Had they known we were coming, or was this an unpleasant surprise for everyone involved?

We needed to open the door and let my family in. If any more dark witches joined this fight, there was no way the three of us could fend them off.

Gramps grabbed my arm and edged us closer to the door, but there was only so far we could go. The magical fire blocked our way.

The ghoulish witch stepped forward, the green magic hovering over his hands casting an unpleasant, fiendish glow over his unpleasant, fiendish face.

"I'm glad you were able to make it, Miss Mooney, though I'm guessing by your choice of entrance, you don't have the amulet we requested."

"How many times do I have to tell you people it no longer exists? It broke, okay? Corrick smashed it to pieces. This whole game of yours has been a fuck-up from start to finish." My anger was getting the better of me, but I didn't care. I didn't want to be in this fight. I wanted to be at home, rolling around naked with non-glowing Trace. Instead, we were here, flinging magic and trying to get away from these assholes who believed souls were like Mom's Pokémon and they had to catch 'em all.

The witch's smile widened, and still no gums made an appearance. The guy was all teeth, and it was terrifying. His gaze, tinged green by the magic in his hands, slid to Trace. "Oh, I believe you, Miss Mooney. I never doubted you for a second. We know all about what happened in The Scorpio Lounge. Everything. Even the parts you left out of the official version."

His expression filled with avarice, and horror coiled inside me, grabbing hold of my guts and squeezing.

They'd never wanted the amulet.

They'd grabbed Gramps to make me vulnerable, believing Trace would come out of hiding to help me.

Had they leaked the rumours to Chip? Or did Chip know what this coven's goal really was?

If he did, I was going to kill the son of a bitch.

Trace hunched forward and brought more magic into his hands. He released it in a burst that tore through the wall beside Mr. Elemental, but the witch sidestepped the blow, moving faster than any human should have been able to, and remained untouched.

More witches appeared in the doorways around the foyer, having held back from the initial fight. At least seven in total, all of them with yellow in their hands. Trace spun in a circle with a yell, releasing spell after spell. I jumped in with him, and Gramps stuck to my side, but they were ready for us. They created a cage that blocked Gramps and I but kept Trace inside with them. He threw himself against it to reach me, but the ward sparked and forced him back. I braced my feet to hurl my weight into the barrier, but Gramps grabbed my arm and hauled me away.

The elemental witch revealed yet more teeth with a laugh as ghoulish as the rest of him. "I'd thank you, Miss Mooney, but I don't think you'd appreciate the gift I have to offer. Instead, we'll just kill you and leave with our prize."

Yellow seeped into his green magic, the man showing far more control over his absorbed spirits than the other witches present, but Gramps shouted a word as he threw a purple blast his way. It struck the elemental witch in the chest, and he staggered back in shock, his concentration broken. I summoned enough magic to ward myself and again tried to get to Trace, but I never had a chance.

His violet gaze locked on mine, devoid of any hint of the souls within. He raised his hands.

I knew what he was going to do before he did it, and I shouted at him to stop.

The anguish in his eyes, the apology, the regret—they were all I was able to take with me as he threw a final blast of magic before the cage shrank around him. The spell caught Gramps and I and hurled us through the front door of the house and onto the path outside.

Chapter 22
Alyssa

Someone's arms clamped around me, dragged me to my feet, hauled me away from the house.

I fought against them, needing to get back to Trace, but their grip was strong, amplified by waves of purple magic to hold me in place.

"Dammit, Aly, stop fighting. I'm trying to help you up," Brody said.

I wrenched out of his grip and spun around to face my grandfather, who stood next to Dylan and Kyle. Grayson and Avery stood nearby, magic ready as they watched the door, waiting to see if anyone followed us out.

"We have to go back in," I said. "They have Trace. We have to save him."

"No, we have to get moving, Pip." Gramps sounded nothing like the man who had trained me in both magic and pub ownership my entire life. He sounded like a soldier, and it startled me so much that I dropped my hands at my sides, my fingers as numb as my thoughts had suddenly gone.

"I can't leave," I said, stunned that he would even suggest it. "Trace came with me to save you, and now they have him. They *planned* to get him. You heard what that man said. He was their target all along, not the stupid amulet."

Gramps heaved a sigh. "I know."

I froze, and my eyes narrowed. "You *know*? As in *you know* you know? Did you know before we got here that they were after him?"

Brody sucked a breath in between his teeth and stepped away, as though he sensed a fight brewing. The others did the same, shifting their attention to the house, even though there was no sign of anyone coming. In fact, the windows were quiet, not a single light on. A glamour to hide tonight's activities from the neighbours.

Gramps's face grew pinched. "Of course not, Alyssa, don't be paranoid. They didn't sit me down and tell me their evil plans like it was some action film. I know because I was there when that elemental witch said it. I know because it makes sense. If they learned enough about the amulet to grab me, then of course they dug deeper into it and realized you had it when you went to meet Corrick and didn't have it when you left." He rubbed his hand over his short hair. "I should have destroyed it, Pip. I'm sorry I didn't. I'm sorry your friend is now caught up in this."

My heart rebelled against the word "friend," but if we didn't save Trace, he wouldn't be my anything.

"He doesn't have to be. We can go back in there *now* and get him."

Gramps nodded at Brody, who caught my arm in his strong grip.

I jerked to free myself, protesting the manhandling. "What the fuck, Brody, get off me. Trace already sacrificed himself for me once. I'm not going to walk away!"

Gramps closed the distance between us, his expression firm, unwavering, but his eyes filled with compassion. "He sent you away, Pip. Remember that. I don't know if the lad knew what was waiting for him in there, but at the very least he suspected something like this might happen. He wanted you to be safe. The only safe place for you is at home—where we can come up with a plan together. Grayson, stay here and keep an eye on the house. From a distance, mind. Call me if they move. Henry?"

My dad stepped forward.

"Go collect Mary, Court, and Jen from the tunnel. We won't be able to text them, and they might not know to come back."

"Of course."

Something eased within me when I realized Gramps wasn't suggesting we abandon Trace and go on with our lives. I wasn't sure I would have been able to look at him the same way if he had.

I turned towards the house but this time didn't resist Brody's pull on my arm. We headed down the street towards the intersection that would take us to my place. My haven. Only a few blocks from where Trace was now the captive of a coven of spirit witches, but it may as well have been half a country away. What were they doing with him? What did they want with him?

More important, how the hell was I going to get him out of there?

"Why do you think they didn't come after us?" I asked as I pulled my keys out of my jacket pocket.

My hands were shaking too badly to let us in, so Brody plucked the keys from my fingers and unlocked the door.

"Too out in the open," Gramps said, following me inside and up the stairs to my apartment. The others trailed behind us, silent and focused on what our returned coven leader was saying. "If you'd arrived when you were supposed to, when the streets were quieter, they probably would have been less worried about being noticed by some wandering witch or a human ready to see through the perception filter. But you were early."

I snorted and kicked off my boots. "I'm surprised they care about being seen. They have enough power to fry anyone walking past. Hey, Dyl, boots off. Don't track that muck through my kitchen."

Habit drove me to call him out more than any actual caring. Trace was in danger. I'd rescued my grandfather but lost my partner. Goddess help me, I hadn't gone in there tonight to trade.

Dad, Kyle, and Avery dropped onto my couch, Avery already on her phone to—I assumed—update everyone not out with us tonight, while Dylan and Brody puttered around the kitchen grabbing snacks for everyone.

Gramps took my hand and pulled me into a hug. "They do have power, Pip. A lot of it. And that's why we need to move carefully. We're loose ends, and they don't strike me as the type to like loose ends. They'll try to get whatever they want out of Wyatt, but once they have it, you're next on their list. I won't let them get close."

And here I'd thought his willingness to save Trace had been out of gratitude for the rescue.

I thought of the look on Trace's face before he'd sent us out the door. He'd known that move would save our lives. He'd known it would mean I'd be leaving him behind. But he'd done it anyway so I would have a chance.

But a chance to do what? Like I'd told him before, I was no good at this stuff. He was the brains behind the cloak-and-dagger. I was the march-in-with-half-a-plan-and-pray-it-worked kind of person. Case in point: walking into The Scorpio Lounge with only a chaos demon at my back. I was more likely to wind up dead than I was to defeat this coven.

My heart ached. Pain and fear made my throat grow tight, and I blinked the unwanted tears from my eyes. "So what's next? You've got to help me, Gramps, because I'm out of my depth here. How do I get him back?"

Lines of sympathy creased his face, and he tucked a loose strand of hair behind my ear. "It won't be easy, kiddo, but you're lucky."

"Oh?" At the moment, I didn't feel all that lucky.

"You belong to the most powerful coven in the city. These fuckers might have spirit magic, but we can still make them bleed."

Gramps was right about the power the Mooney family brought to the table. It was why I'd called them in to make our stand against this coven tonight. As well as that had gone. But we had a better idea of what we were dealing with now. We knew what this dark coven was capable of. And that we'd need to level up a few times over if we wanted to take them down without losses.

The Mooneys were an old witch family. One of the strongest in the province, with a lineage dating back long before Canada was a country. We'd mastered atmospheric magic, and our ancestors had married into other strong families to keep the line at its best. The result was a coven of our own, with many of us sitting as representatives on the Ontario Witches' Council and many others in strategic places across the city.

As a rule, we did our best to give back to our community, not lord over it. We protected those weaker than ourselves, kept smaller covens in line, and tried to solve problems before they had to be escalated to the council or SMOAC.

Whoever this ghoulish elemental witch was, he and his spirit witches were in for a bad time.

Especially since my family wasn't the only resource we had.

While Gramps hopped on the phone with the rest of the coven who'd stayed home tonight, I pulled out my phone and drew up the number I'd once promised never to use. Too bad for him, I hadn't said I'd remove him from my saved contacts.

Chip answered after the fifth ring. "If I'd known you were this bad at keeping promises, Cheers, I'd have changed my phone number."

"They have Trace."

"Who does?" His feigned irritation vanished in an instant, and now he was all business, something that made me feel better than I could ever say.

"The Bone Casters—or whoever they're working for. They were waiting for us. We'd known they would be, but they were *strong*. And there was this guy. He looked kind of like a horror movie villain from the sixties. He pretty much told us they'd known the amulet was toast and it was Trace they wanted all along."

"Fuck."

"They penned him in, but Trace threw me and Gramps out of the house."

"Gramps is with you?"

I put the phone on speaker and set it on the kitchen table. "He is. So are my brothers and cousins."

"Nice to meet you, Gramps," Chip said to the room, sounding more respectful than he ever had to me. "I've read your record. It's impressive."

"Thank you," Gramps said, not seeming the least surprised that this stranger on the phone should know more about his history than his granddaughter did. "We're about to find out how much those years were worth."

"We'll put them to use," Chip promised. "What can you tell me about the house or the people who have Wyatt?"

Gramps and I gave him a description of the layout of the house, the offices in the basement, and the nature of the witches' magic, including the rough numbers and apparent hierarchy.

"The corpsy guy was definitely their leader," I said.

Gramps nodded. "He was always there when they questioned me about how I got the amulet. They wanted to know what souls were trapped inside it, how many, how long. They knew more about it than they said. It was more like they wanted me to confirm what they already knew rather than mining me for information."

"What are they after?" I wondered aloud. "The same thing Corrick was? Power?"

Corrick had been looking to gain it the easy way. Because the amulet was as old as it was, whoever wore it would have been able to compel those around them. It was how the Mooney family had claimed their wealth in the first place—something I was so incredibly proud of. Not.

Even Gramps had used it to buy the pub, including the property, outright from the city for a pittance. He'd tried to destroy the amulet for decades, but no matter what he or Nana did, they couldn't get rid of it. Magic, physical destruction—it had all bounced off the damned thing. Only when the souls had been activated and the magic around the gem weakened had it finally shattered.

Now that the souls were in Trace, did they still have the ability to compel someone? Would these witches be able to use Trace somehow to get what they wanted, or were they simply trying to hoard more souls to level up their power for something bigger?

None of it boded well. I didn't want Trace there another hour if I could help it.

"They're on the move," Chip said. "I brought up some of the security cameras around the area, and they just shoved Trace into the back of that black van they carried you around in, Gramps. Didn't look like our boy was conscious."

A whimper escaped me, and I dropped into the kitchen chair before my legs gave out. Dylan sat in the chair beside me and wrapped me up in a hug, while the others pretended not to be listening from the living room. Gramps patted the back of my hand before returning his attention to the phone. "Are you able to follow the car?"

The sound of fingers flying over a keyboard filled my quiet kitchen. "I'll do what I can, but the odds aren't amazing. They're moving fast towards Bronson Avenue."

They could wind up anywhere in the city, and I'd be at square one.

"You try to keep track of that van," Gramps said, not caring that he was giving orders to a stranger. "In the meantime, I'll call in more of the family. Wyatt won't be alone with them for long."

Chip hung up without a goodbye, and I buried my head in my hands. I couldn't sit around here waiting for him to call back. Even if his surveillance led us right to where this coven was heading, we couldn't do anything without solid reinforcements and a plan.

A plan solid enough that Trace wouldn't die if we failed.

I thought of our kiss, of how much I'd wanted so much more than that first taste of him. I would get it, regardless of what it took.

I let out a shuddering breath. "Goddess, give me strength."

Chapter 23
Trace

ICAME TO in a dark room. My muscles ached, my head throbbed, the souls inside me were rowdy and restless, but despite all the discomfort, I was satisfied.

More than one of the witches in that office building had been aiming for Alyssa with their next spells. Now at least she and Gramps were safe. I had no doubt she would make plans for some brave rescue attempt, but I hoped her grandfather would talk her out of it. They should focus on protecting themselves from whoever the elemental witch was. In the meantime, I would try to find my own way out.

Starting with how to escape the magic-nullifying cuffs.

My hands were bound to the armrests of a metal chair, and a hefty one at that. The back of the chair dug uncomfortably into my middle back. My spell-blocking amulet was gone. More straps held my legs, and a wider one wrapped around my chest. Someone really didn't want me getting up.

I tried moving one of my hands, but they'd left me no wiggle room. Concerning, but I'd escaped similar situations more than once in my nine years going after Canada's worst supernatural criminals. It might take me a while and use all my concentration, but it was doable. Probably.

While I had a single moment to myself, I made what progress I could, starting with my left leg, where the straps had a smidge more give than on any other limb. I wiggled my knee back and forth, slowly rolling my calf from one edge of the chair leg to the other. The strap seemed to be leather of some sort, so if I stretched it enough, I might be able to slide my foot out once I kicked off my boot.

I wasn't sure how long I kept at it, but I'd made some progress by the time someone came into the room and switched on the lights. After ages in the dark, the bright LEDs washed out my vision, and I spent the next few seconds blinking away the afterimages.

When the glow cleared, I found myself staring at the corpse-like elemental witch. He wasn't any more appealing in this lighting. His receding hair was slicked back with high shine oil, and the bags under his eyes made him look like his skin was sloughing off. I guessed he was in his mid-seventies, but the lack of jowls or knobbly fingers suggested he was significantly younger.

His teeth were definitely dentures or caps. They had to be. They were three sizes too big for his mouth, and the result gave the impression of a Halloween decoration. It was especially noticeable when he grinned at me from the chair across from mine. His seat was the same sturdy, metal structure but lacked the straps. Shame. They really added something to the ambiance. A sort of… *Fifty Shades* aesthetic.

But maybe that wasn't what he was going for.

I bit down on my stream of consciousness banter, making a note to save it for this asshole instead of keeping it all to myself.

"Nice place you got here," I said.

His grin widened, and I wished I'd kept my mouth shut. The effect of his smile was bone chilling. The pouches under his eyes grew deeper, making his dark irises seem almost black. If the guy started spewing ooze from his mouth, I wouldn't have been shocked.

While he sat back and appreciated my wit, I took the opportunity now that the lights were on to check out my new digs.

The room did not inspire a lot of confidence. The floor was white, the walls were white, and there was nothing I might knock over and use as a weapon if I got my foot free. My chair was bolted to the floor, so no chance of me knocking it over and gaining leverage on the bindings that way, and the door must have been somewhere behind me, because the only thing in front was Creepazoid.

"Have you taken the time to get settled?" he asked.

His voice was less haunting than I'd expected. I thought to hear some kind of Christopher Lee-type intonations, but he spoke softly and at a much higher timbre. I could imagine him doing well voicing a commercial for a furniture store or a gardening centre.

I was doing it again, using up all my one-liners in my own head. Silently freaking out. Because despite my optimistic self-talk, I had no idea what was happening or how to save myself. I couldn't escape, my magic was nulled, and this talking corpse was smiling as though he were about to carve a Christmas turkey.

Well, fuck it. I was not going to be that turkey.

I did my best to keep my movements subtle and get back to work on stretching the strap around my left leg. At the same time, I did what I could with the minimal movement of my right wrist, making the attempt more obvious. By the twinkle in Corpsy's dark eyes, he noticed. I just had to hope he overlooked my actual goal.

"Who are you?" I demanded. "You obviously know who I am, and what I'm carrying around with me, but I want to know how. No one else was in The Scorpio when the amulet broke."

The man leaned back in his chair and crossed one leg over the other. "You can call me David, though I suspect that before long you won't be calling me much of anything. Of course we know who you are, Mr. Wyatt. A man of your reputation doesn't slide under the radar in our circles. Though I believe many of my coven would simply call you Drew."

I shuddered at the name—not only at the nasty memories it brought up of my younger years but the newer memories of Nathalie roasting in the park. When I got out of this, *Andrew Wyatt* was going away for good.

"As for the amulet," David continued, "I had no idea the thing smashed. I believed it was still existing comfortably under Miss Mooney's pub. It wasn't until your run-in with your old coven mates that I realized what had happened. After that, my task became far more… interesting."

That grin was back, turning my insides to water. The hair on the back of my neck danced on the nonexistent breeze, and my heart made a valiant effort to burst through my ribs.

"All right, so," I said, impressed that my voice sounded as level as it did. I gave my wrist another wiggle and winced as the metal cuff dug into my skin. "Now that you have me, what's the plan? Let's stop with the mind games and get to the physical torture, shall we? I don't have time for this bullshit."

Now David straight-up laughed, and the sound was worse than the grin. Every minute spent in this man's company increased my disgust. He should be grateful I wasn't vomiting on his shoes.

"I was told you'd be good for some entertainment if I got my hands on you."

The way he said it dumped a pail of ice water over my head. "Oh yeah? By who?"

He shook his head and clucked his tongue. "I think you're done asking questions. You want to know what I plan to do with you? We wanted the amulet to remove the souls from the gem. The souls are now in you. You can put that big brain of yours to work to figure out the logical conclusion."

With the cuffs on, my magical connection to the souls I carried was cut off, but that didn't mean I didn't sense their panic at those words.

I scowled at him. "You're welcome to try, but I think they're happy where they are."

David rose from his seat and brushed down his slacks. "Then I guess we'll have to give them a more tempting home, won't we? This will go easier if you hand them over voluntarily, but if we have to force them out, then so be it."

He pressed a button on the side of the chair, and the band across my chest snapped open. Before I could hope he was going to move me to an even more uncomfortable seat, he flicked his fingers, and green fire swept over my cotton-blend sweater, scorching through the fabric and singeing my chest hair. The fire spread to my back and a chill set in as more of my skin was exposed.

I clenched my teeth so I wouldn't give him the satisfaction of hearing my pain and was relieved when the fire petered out as soon as my shirt was in tatters.

The relief was short lived as Corpsy disappeared behind me. A beep echoed through the room, and the previously white walls shifted, revealing a dozen tiny mirrors all aimed at random angles. My heart thrashed in my chest and my breaths were irregular as my brain whirled in a million directions about where this might be heading. Corpsy's soft voice uttered an incantation, and the mirrors shone brighter under the LEDs, as though something unseen had lit the room.

Or was bouncing off the mirrors.

Heat from multiple sources hit me like white-hot pokers searing my flesh. Except I didn't smell any burning, and the heat didn't stay superficial. It was some kind of spell burrowing into me, and the effect was agonizing.

"We can't cast the spell directly or you'd die too quickly," Corpsy said. "Originally, we set up this solution to safely extract the souls from the amulet. We're hoping it will be just as effective on you."

He stepped back into view, his hands in his pockets, his posture casual. I glared at him, my jaw so tightly clenched I couldn't even throw out a clever quip. I was too far past being able to pretend indifference. The souls inside me were writhing, trying to escape the battering spell, and it was all I could do to keep them in place. If they retaliated, they would be taken.

Corpsy tilted his head. "Your control over them is remarkable, but there's only so long you can hold them back. Why not do yourself a favour and give them up? We'll make far greater use of them than you would."

He stood staring at me. Waiting for me to speak? Wanting to watch me suffer?

After who knew how long, he shrugged and stepped away from me. "I'll be back in a while. We'll give you a chance to reassess your position."

With another wide grin, he walked by me and disappeared from sight. In another moment, the lights went out again, but this time the room didn't go dark. The mirrors still caught the glow of the unseen magic, leaving me to stare at my own tormented reflection as the spell pressed its way into my muscle and blood.

I sucked in a breath and bit down hard as the heat flayed me from within. The souls squirmed, desperate to break out and preserve themselves but trapped by the cuffs.

Even as I held back the first screams, I understood that whatever happened, there was no way I could hold on forever.

Chapter 24
Alyssa

L et me get this straight," Valery said as she leaned back in her home office chair and crossed her arms. Her hair was perfectly styled despite the time of night, the dyed blond curls bouncing over her shoulders and tumbling over her silk camisole. The soft lighting in her office was designed to make her look incredible on the video call. Turned out even kindergarten teachers could be vain.

Not that I was jealous of my sister's put-togetherness. Not even a little bit. Just because, even after a shower and a change of clothes, I felt like I'd been dragged through the mud, attacked by a raccoon, and vomited on by an angry cat was no reason for me to compare myself to Miss Perfect In the Middle of the Night.

"I still can't believe you hooked up with Trace. Wyatt," she said. It was like we'd picked up exactly where we'd left off on our last call. Had she been stewing about this the whole time? "Trace Fucking Wyatt, and you didn't call me immediately to tell me every single detail? What kind of sister are you? I would have been on the phone so damn fast."

In the direness of our situation, I couldn't help but take Val's reaction as the giant hug it was meant to be. A minor distraction.

There was also a not small amount of embarrassment about my younger sister implying in front of my parents that I'd had sex with a supernatural celebrity.

"We didn't hook up," I said. "It's a long story, but there was no hooking up involved." I left off the *yet* for my own sanity's sake. I couldn't handle the thought that we wouldn't get Trace back in time for him and me to explore that particular adverb.

Valery huffed. "Sure. Whatever. So now he's been kidnapped by the coven of soul witches who snatched up Gramps, and you need help getting him out, is that the basic summary?"

"Pretty much, yeah."

Mom rested her hand on my back from where she stood behind the couch and rubbed in a circular pattern between my shoulder blades. It was the same place she had whenever I got sick or wound up in a panic attack. The gesture was soothing, but I worried if she kept it up, I'd fall asleep. We didn't have time for me to sleep, never mind that I was wrung out and exhausted.

"Great," my sister said. "We'll add that to my budget of therapy I'll need to deal with all this shit."

Mom frowned at the screen. "Val, perhaps a little less sarcasm?"

"Who's being sarcastic? I'm being one hundred per cent genuine. I'm still over here trying to deal with the fact that my sister was accused of murder and never even bothered to *call me*."

I flinched under her accusation. She had a point, but this was hardly the time to talk about it. "I'm sorry, okay? Next time I get dragged before a fae duchess, I'll be sure to let you know so you can bail me out. Can we get back to the key point here?"

Dad pinched the bridge of his nose, too used to dealing with the nonsense between me and Val.

Mom looked at Gramps. "You sure you're all right, Dad?"

He waved a hand to dismiss her worries. "Never better. Pip and Wyatt had everything under control. I never doubted it for a second." He slung his arm around my shoulders, and my throat tightened. Fear for Trace, retroactive terror for Gramps, and uncertainty of how to move forward nearly brought me to my knees.

The only relief I had was that I'd received no judgement or shock or alarm or anger from anyone in my family when I'd filled them in on the details I'd left out about the fight with Corrick. Even after learning how Trace had worked some massively illegal magic to save my life, none of them had seemed ready to turn their back on him and let him face the consequences alone.

As always, my family was here to support me, and I couldn't be more grateful that I wasn't by myself.

"I don't know what to do." I hated how my lips wobbled, making it difficult to speak clearly. "Trace was already in rough shape because of those souls. The spirits keep trying to take him over every time they're exposed to someone else's spirit magic. I don't know how—" I couldn't bring myself to finish my thought—that I didn't know if he would be able to hold himself together.

"What do you think they want with him?" Val asked.

Dylan snorted as he propped his socked feet on my coffee table. "Isn't it obvious? They want the souls."

From his chair behind the couch, Brody agreed. "Seems likely. They wanted the amulet and couldn't get it, so Wyatt's the next best thing."

Val rolled her eyes. "Well, obviously. What I meant was what do you think they want the souls for? Just to have them? To show off that their collection of spirits is bigger than some other coven's? Is this a pissing contest or are they after something bigger?"

"Definitely something bigger," Gramps said. "Again, I don't know what, but they've got something in the works."

"A takeover?" Aunt Courtney asked. She was rubbing Avery's back much like Mom was rubbing mine. It seemed parental instincts were on full alert tonight.

Gramps shook his head slowly. "I don't think so. They didn't talk like they were preparing for war. More… gaining access to something? I really don't know." He grimaced. "I wish I'd been able to learn more."

"Does it matter what they want?" I asked, chafing my arms to chase away the deepening psychological chill. "Trace won't hand them over."

Dylan's expression turned sympathetic. "I doubt they plan to ask nicely, Aly."

My throat tightened. I didn't want to think about what he was enduring while we sat here casually discussing his fate. "Okay, so, how do we get him out?"

"Do you know where they took him?" Dad asked, ever the practical one.

"Chip is looking into it." I picked up my phone and checked it for the hundredth time this past hour. "Still nothing. If I don't hear back in another twenty, I'll call and—" My phone rang. "Speak of the devil. Hey, Chip, what'd you find?"

"Who else is with you?" he demanded.

"No one, why?"

"Because I'm not on speaker phone. If it was just you and Gramps and your family, you'd have me on speaker. Who else is around who might hear what I have to say?"

"Um, more of my family?" Again with his tendency to make me question statements I knew to be true. I cleared my throat. "The rest of my siblings, a few more cousins. Some of them are on video call."

"Nice that you actually called your sister," he said.

I blinked. I didn't remember mentioning Valery to him. "Have you been spying on my call history?"

"Of course. I need to know who I'm dealing with. Which is how I know I don't care if your family is there. They can hear this. The more help we get, the better."

With his permission, I put the phone on speaker and turned up the volume so hopefully everyone on my laptop screen would hear him as well.

"The van went east," he said. "Rockland."

Dad's eyebrows shot up. "That's not a cheap area."

"It's not," Chip said. "Especially not a ranch-style McMansion right on the water. Whoever these witches are, they've got money as well as power. I don't want to know what they plan to do with more."

Neither did I.

"Were you able to pull up anything else on the house? Some of those handy underground blueprints?" I asked.

Brody's jaw fell open, and I could tell he was impressed with the paranoid genius on the phone. Fair. I would have been too if I hadn't met him in person.

"Not yet," Chip grumbled, clearly unhappy with his lack of progress. "Everything about the house has been blocked or blanked out. I can't find any information on the deed, there's no mortgage I can track down, no internet or phone bills connected to the property. It's like the place doesn't exist, but I'm looking right fucking at it. Apologies, Mrs. Mooney."

Now it was Mom's turn to look surprised. "No trouble, Chip. I've heard worse."

She'd said worse. My mother had quite the mouth on her.

"I'm not giving up," he said. "In fact, I'm even more determined to tear through their protections. Whatever they're trying to hide, they won't for long. Let me keep working on it."

"Give me the address anyway," I said. "Maybe there's something we can do while we wait."

"Don't do anything stupid, Cheers. Trace will be royally PO'd if you get killed trying to rescue him."

A low moan escaped Mom as she bent her head into her hand, and Dad crossed the room to put his arms around her. I wished Chip hadn't mentioned the possibility of me dying quite so breezily. My parents didn't need that thought in their heads when they went to bed tonight, no matter how likely it might be.

Chip gave me the address, then hung up. As soon as he was off the phone, I plugged the address into my internet browser and brought up some photos of the exterior. It was a clean bungalow, with beige siding, a big porch, and a double garage. Although there were neighbours, the houses were spaced out enough that it would have been easy to sneak someone inside with no one noticing.

"I wonder why they didn't bring you there," I said to Gramps. "Why did you get the urban treatment, while Trace gets the rural experience?"

Gramps shrugged. "Ease of transfer. They planned to give me back." The expression on my face must have made him realize what he'd said because he reached for my hand as Mom slipped her arm around my shoulders. "Just because they don't plan on returning him doesn't mean we won't take him, Pip. Stay strong here. He'll need it."

"Yeah, Aly," Dylan said, nudging me on my other side. "Don't give up before we get started."

Grayson leaned forward across the table, resting his elbows on the surface. He'd arrived a little over an hour ago after Chip had let us know he had eyes on the house. The dark circles under my cousin's half-lidded eyes revealed the depth of his fatigue. "These people don't know who they've crossed. They can't know Wyatt's connection to our family. If you're with him, he's one of us now, and we don't let anything happen to family."

Kyle nodded. "They might not have planned for war, but they've got one."

My family's encouragement did more for me than any kind of self-directed pep talk I might have mustered. I wasn't sure how long my confidence would last, but for Trace's sake, I was determined to work on it.

"Right," Mom said, clapping her hands together. "Here's what I think. We all need some sleep. It's almost the middle of the night, some of us have… *a lot* of information to process, and we'll all be useless if we're not rested. Tomorrow morning, everyone should meet here at Aly's for an early breakfast. I'll have waffles and lattes ready for seven a.m. We can make our plan then."

The tone of her voice left no room for arguments, though I wanted to scream at her that seven a.m. was seven hours away. Anything could happen to Trace in seven hours.

But she was right. I was exhausted, my muscles ached, my heart bled, and I really wanted to close my eyes and pretend my world wasn't falling apart for just a little while.

"Fine," I said. "But I want everyone to come to the table with an idea we can use. I don't care how stupid you think it is. And whatever plan we agree on, we carry it out tomorrow. I'm not letting those witches play with Trace a minute longer than necessary."

My family agreed with gentle murmurs, and I shut down the meeting. Dad and my brothers, my aunts, and the cousins all left, but Mom and Gramps stuck around.

"Gramps, you take the bed," I said. "After all you've been through, you deserve a night on a good mattress."

He leaned back into his hands until his spine cracked. "I hate to steal it from you, but you're right. I can't handle couches anymore."

"The couch is yours, Mom. There's an air mattress in the storage room I can sleep on."

She kissed my forehead. "Don't be silly. After the day you've had, you take the couch. I'll give you a shot of healing energy to help you sleep, and then I'll set up camp on the air mattress."

Gramps headed for my bedroom but paused on the threshold. "I meant what I said, Pip. Keep heart. Wyatt wouldn't have been able to carry those souls around as long as he has if he didn't have the strength to do it. He can withstand whatever they throw at him."

I chewed on my lip, not wanting to ask the question that had been burning inside me since the events outside the museum, but needing to know. "What happens if he can't? I don't mean if these witches get the souls out of him, but what if the souls manage to take him over?"

Mom and Gramps exchanged a look that dropped my

stomach into my toes. Then Gramps heaved a breath and met my eye. "I won't lie, kiddo, it's not pretty. If the intentions of the witch don't match those of the souls or, more likely, if the host's mind and body aren't strong enough, the host may as well no longer exist. Sanity gone, self gone. They become nothing more than a vessel, and they burn up. Trace is a good man or the souls would never have accepted him. He's strong or the souls would have eaten through his barriers. He'll be okay."

He closed himself in my room and left me to collapse on the couch. I dragged the blanket over myself, inhaling deeply when I caught Trace's scent in the fibres, and sank into its warmth as my thoughts travelled to our last night here, snuggled up together. Of the way he'd kissed me in the Labyrinth. How I wished I'd kissed him when I'd wanted to last night.

While Mom brushed a hand over my head, sending a gentle burst of healing energy through me, Gramps's words drifted through my mind. Although I knew he'd wanted to reassure me, all I could think about was the way Trace's eyes glowed yellow whenever the souls grew angry enough. If this coven pushed his limits too far, how much could he take before his body gave out? How much longer before his mind snapped and the man I'd come to care about was gone?

Chapter 25
Alyssa

DYLAN WAS THE last person to arrive for breakfast, but he brought doughnuts with him, so I couldn't be too angry. My waffles were already heaped with strawberries, yogurt, and syrup, but right now a sour cream glazed sounded like the perfect side dish.

"I think we should storm the place," he said as he sat down on my couch next to Aunt Hilary.

Over a dozen other Mooneys were spread throughout my kitchen and living room, with Val, Brody, Dad, Gramps, and me around the kitchen table, Grayson, Kyle, Aunts Courtney and Jennifer on the floor around the coffee table, and Avery and Uncle Tony on the couch with Dylan. Only half of them appeared awake enough to be having this conversation, while the others stuffed their faces with food in an effort to catch up.

I worried we'd be zombies with indigestion when we attempted our rescue mission, but it would still be better than doing nothing.

Mom groaned and turned her back to the room to pour herself a coffee and hide her reaction to Dylan's suggestion.

"That's a terrible idea," Val said.

He shrugged. "Alyssa said she didn't care how stupid the idea was. That's mine."

"It's terrible because I already suggested it when I walked in," Brody said as he drizzled more syrup on his waffles.

"It was a terrible idea when Val said it first," Mom said on a sigh.

None of my three siblings appeared concerned that they'd all come to the table with the same plan. It wasn't one we were going to take. Not against a bunch of witches who'd armed themselves with the spirits of the dead. We already knew the elemental witch leading them was strong, and I had no doubt he'd surround himself with competent soldiers.

"We could wait until Chip gets back to us about the layout of the house," Dad suggested. "There might be another way in besides the front door. We could storm that instead."

"Henry," Mom snapped.

"What?" he asked. "I'm looking at our options here, Mary, and I'm not seeing many of them. They've got a strong coven working out of that house. They have all the advantages. The only thing we have is the element of surprise."

"And a coven of our own," Mom pointed out. "We have the numbers."

"Will we be enough?" I asked. "Even with how many we took down last night, we don't know how many they have. Would we be smart to call in another coven as reinforcements?"

"What about Simon?" Dylan asked. "You think he'd be up for the fight?"

I covered my worries on that point with a bite of waffle. During my very long attempt to fall asleep last night, I'd considered calling Simon. In fact, I'd gone back and forth on the matter until I'd seen four a.m. roll around. In the end, I'd decided to wait until a more reasonable hour, then touch base and see what sort of mood he was in.

"It would mean arranging ourselves to give him enough space to do his thing, but I'll message him," I said, and sent off a quick text. "He was ready to help save Gramps, so he'll probably be in. We'll get someone else to watch the pub."

"All right, so, there are fourteen of us. Add in Simon, that's fifteen," Brody said. "Do we not think that's enough to go after these people?"

I thought of how many witches we'd fought in the house on MacLaren. We'd taken down a few, but even so, I would have felt better with another dozen behind us.

"I'll put the rest of the cousins on standby," Gramps said. "If Chip comes back with information saying we need them—or if we scope out the place and don't feel comfortable—they'll be ready."

My throat tightened, and I set my fork down on the side of my plate. "Thank you, guys. It means so much that you're taking this risk for me. I know it's a lot to ask. There's a lot of danger involved, but not one of you has pushed back."

Dylan brought his plate into the kitchen and, after dropping it on the counter, punched my shoulder hard enough that I flinched. "What's a big brother for if not to save my little sister's boyfriend from a dark coven?"

Mom grimaced, but she reached across the table to take my hand. "Of course we're helping you, honey, and not only because he's your friend. This coven kidnapped your grandfather. They're trying to harvest souls for who knows what reason. We have a responsibility to this city to stop them."

Dad nodded. "The Mooney family has been a leader of Ottawa's witch community for over a hundred years. It's our place to step in where we can when we see something happening. SMOAC exists, and they have their place, but coven law should come first."

Avery snorted. "If that were true, we'd be handing this over to the council. Let's not pretend we don't all want a little revenge."

No one argued with her, but after a moment's silence, Gramps said, "Let's also not pretend we don't know why we're not turning this over to the authorities. It was my fuck-up. I know it. It's not revenge so much as atonement. I need to make up for not trying harder to get rid of the damned amulet."

Valery checked her nails. "As long as my helping you means we're square for that time I cut your hair when I was six and we *never need to talk about it again*, I'm ready to help where I can."

"I guess I can agree to that," I said, appreciating her attempt to raise the mood.

"Now that we know who's playing on our team, let's dig down on details," Grayson said as Kyle stacked up the nearby dishes.

Mom pulled a notebook out from somewhere—the woman always had one handy—and we got to work. Without knowing much about the location, the best we could do was prepare a wider strategy, but by the end of breakfast, we had something workable regardless of what information Chip provided. We were a strong family with hefty magic behind us. Working as a team, there was little that could get through our wards. Even if most of our magic leaned towards the defensive, I was certain we would find our way into the house. Once inside, our plan became murkier and the risk increased, but as long as we remained close enough to bolster each others' power, we stood a chance of keeping the strongest spirit magic away from us.

Anxiety fluttered in my stomach, and I did my best to ignore it. Yes, brain, we were walking into possible death. I got it. I didn't need the nausea or the sweaty palms or the racing heartbeat to point out how dangerous this was.

My rational thinking did nothing to make me feel better. What did help was Gramps. Throughout all the planning, he kept his cool, proposing suggestions and flagging possible flaws in our ideas.

This was not the man I knew. He'd always had a good head, but I'd only ever really known him behind the bar. After we'd discovered that Corrick was gunning for the amulet, Gramps had filled me in on a bit more of his history, but he'd focused on how he'd landed such a great deal on the pub—magic—and how the amulet had existed—a broken deal and four generations of Mooneys taking advantage of it. Only now was I starting to realize how much about him I didn't know. How much I was determined to learn.

We were due to set out around noon, figuring the odds were in our favour that at least some of the witches held jobs that would require them to be away from the house in the middle of the day. After everyone left to sort out their affairs—and possibly update their wills—I found myself alone in the kitchen with Gramps. We nursed our coffee cups to fill the waiting silence, and his green eyes followed me as though he knew what I was about to ask.

"You should have been terrified in that basement," I said. "You'd been there for days. They clearly weren't treating you well. But you acted as though it was nothing. Who are you, exactly?"

He released a breath and sipped his coffee. "My younger days weren't full of unicorns and fairy dust, Pip. You know about the amulet and how I almost lost your grandmother and your mother and aunts."

I nodded. I remembered him shattering the image I'd held of my family pretty clearly.

"Before I decided buying the pub was my best option, I had dreams of being a magical enforcer. A mercenary, of sorts. Even formed my own company. One of my brothers was a member, a bunch of the cousins, some guys I knew from around the neighbourhood. I even convinced a few of my buddies to join us, even though they thought it was a horrible idea. But I had the amulet, right? It didn't take much to persuade them."

A shudder ran through me at the thought. To wear down someone's free will like that was a power no one on this earth should possess. Yet how many of the spirit witches we were about to face had exactly that ability?

I pushed my coffee cup away. The thought of taking a sip of that bitterness turned my stomach. "I think I can guess what happened. You did some things you're not proud of, wound up falling too far under the amulet's influence, so you know what these people can do, and you believe because of all this you have a debt to pay by stopping them."

Gramps spun his coffee cup between his hands as he chuckled. "You've always been a quick one, Pip. That's exactly it. Fortunately, my moral compass, skewed as it was, and my love for your grandmother, a stronger force than anything else, prevented me from doing anything too horrible. In fact, I believe we made a difference for the better by taking down some nasty covens and convincing a few stray witches to get back in line before they followed the same path. A few of the people we stopped are now among my closest friends. And, as a result, I learned how to lead our family and coven properly. But I do regret how I did it and the short cuts I took to get there, and I do believe that my experience puts me in a good position to stand against them. But in the end, Pip, my helping you comes down to wanting to be a force for good in my waning years. I opened the first supernatural-friendly pub in Ottawa, and that's meant something to people for almost half a century—a legacy as you put it. One you're continuing. If this is something else I can offer, one last hoorah before I put my feet up and retire, so be it."

My heart twinged. Not only because over the past few days I'd abandoned our precious pub thanks to my plethora of personal issues, but because I didn't like the thought of Gramps's last anything.

"As long as you're careful," I said. "No heroics."

He smiled and scooched his chair closer to take my hand. "Don't you worry, Pip. I plan on being here for a good many years to come."

I prayed to the goddess that was the case. And that I wouldn't regret asking my family to come together on this.

My phone buzzed on the table, and I pulled it closer to check my messages. At Simon's name on the screen, I eagerly opened my phone to read his message.

My stomach plummeted.

Simon: I wish I could, Lys, but I'm out. You'll have to do this one without me.

Chapter 26
Trace

THE HEAT FROM that spirit spell had set my blood on fire. It raged through every vein, seeping into my bones and leaching through my marrow. My skin felt raw and tender as I thrashed against the chair. My hair was damp with sweat where it fell in my face, and splashes of blood from where I fought to loosen the bindings now splattered the pristine white floor.

Twice David had returned to check on me and adjust the mirrors so the spell hit new locations, creating fresh waves of hell, but despite the agony, I refused to give in. With my waning strength, I held on with everything I had against the spirits fighting back.

And oh, they were fighting back.

Despite the nullifying cuffs, they wriggled inside me, gaining more flexibility with my magic too suppressed to stabilize the bindings. They butted up against the offensive spell, searing my insides while the magic destroyed my outsides. What areas of my skin weren't throbbing with gashes and burns pulsed steadily with power, and I knew it was only a matter of time before my resident spirits burst free to claim their revenge.

I also knew the moment they did, David would be there to catch them, and once he had them, their freedom would be lost for good. So I exerted my dominance to contain them, willing them to remain still, remain calm.

When I'd stood in The Scorpio Lounge and broken my promise to myself never to dabble in spirit magic again, I'd convinced them to come to me by offering them a safe space. I'd promised them I would never make them act against their nature, and that when the opportunity arose, I would give them the end they'd been longing for since they'd given themselves to the gem that had harboured them. They'd come to me voluntarily, recognizing me as the better option over Corrick.

Now I begged them to keep that faith in me. They'd come out against Nathalie, and I sensed the regret of some mingling with the satisfaction of the others. They were at odds with each other, some having become increasingly corrupt after being cooped up and hidden away for so long, the rest clinging to the peace they'd found in existing outside time. I needed them to keep it together long enough for me to get out of here. Not only for their sakes but for mine. My sanity was hanging by a thread, and the closer the spirits got to the surface, the finer that thread became.

Once it snapped, I wasn't sure how I'd bring myself back.

The only thought that helped me ignore the pain and stick to my purpose was the look in Alyssa's eyes when I'd shoved her out the door.

I'd broken my promise to her as surely as I'd broken the one to myself. Goddess, I'd broken so many promises since meeting her.

Never use spirit magic. Never lose my heart. Never hurt her again. There was no doubt in my mind I'd fractured something between us. Something I hoped I could repair if I escaped this place, but until then it remained a divide—necessary but agonizing.

So between David's visits, I kept working on freeing my left leg. I'd made more progress over the past however long, having gained a few inches of movement. Not enough to slide my foot through, but a start. Left, right, left, right, pull. The dance had become a ritual. Every time I repeated it was another minute I remained myself. Another minute this spell hadn't broken me, and another minute I stayed in control. If I did one minute, I could do another, each one a single moment in time that, I prayed, would get me through until I stood free and could burn this house to the ground.

Chapter 27
Alyssa

GRAMPS AND I stuck around my place waiting for Chip to call me back as long as we could, but we finally agreed we'd be taking on more trouble by waiting any longer.

So of course, as soon as we reached the address in Rockland, Chip called, ready to heap truckloads of bad news onto our shoulders.

"You haven't gone in yet, have you?" he asked in greeting.

As all good conversations began.

"Not yet," I said. "We're parked about a kilometre away. Just waiting for the rest of the family to meet us here."

"What kind of numbers are you bringing?"

"Fourteen atmospheric witches. Some of the Mooney best. We should be able to keep ourselves well warded as we push our way in."

"You'd better hope so," he said. "I hate to break it to you, Cheers, but even with fourteen, you might be in for a bumpy ride."

Irritated that he was echoing every single one of my concerns, I looked at Valery in the driver's seat to gauge her reaction. Her jaw was set, and her hands tightened around the steering wheel. I'd opted to drive with her instead of in my own car in case—no, for when we got Trace out of here. I didn't want to have to worry about driving and offering any necessary healing at the same time. Yes, Mom would be on hand to do most of the medical stuff, but there was no way I would sit by and do nothing to help.

"Whatever you know, hit me with it," I said to Chip. "It's not like my view on this can get much worse."

"I wasn't able to bring up the blueprints, but I do have magically enhanced infrared visuals on the house."

I opened my mouth to ask how the hell he'd managed that, then realized it would be better if I didn't know. Chip had secrets he would never tell me, and he had secrets he'd probably kill me for learning. This one likely fell into the latter category. Right up there with his real name.

"If what I'm seeing is accurate, you're up against at least six people in that house. No, ten. No… twelve?—no, okay, that was some kind of glitch. There are six."

"Phew," I said blandly. "Because those extra few would have made me change my mind and turn around."

"Just be grateful it's a bungalow, because I can't really see anything beyond the first floor. But even if you outnumber them, remember these fuckers are powerful. My suggestion is get in and get out. Don't bother engaging if you can avoid it. There might be more of them in the basement, but I've only seen one person go up and down the stairs in the time I've been watching, so I think you're good."

My stomach wobbled. "Think they're keeping Trace in the basement, then?"

"They do seem to enjoy their underground pursuits."

"*Underground Pursuits*—name of my autobiography," I replied automatically. Ten minutes in my brothers' company, and I was spouting their nonsense. I gave myself a shake. "Okay, Chip, you're going to have to come in with me."

"Exsqueeze me? You may not have noticed, but I'm at home. Comfortable in my favourite chair, wearing sweatpants."

"And I'm sure Trace would be thrilled for you. Fortunately, you need neither remove your pants nor rise from your chair. Val, do you have your headset somewhere in here?"

I rummaged through her console and glove compartment until I looked over to find her holding out the earpiece.

"Did you move anything?" she asked, repeating our mother's usual refrain whenever we claimed something was lost.

I stuck my tongue out at her and went through the process of connecting the headset to my phone. "Now you can guide me through the house. If there are sixty-twelve people inside, I would rather avoid than confront."

"I like when you talk sense, Cheers. It gives me hope that you and Trace won't Thelma-and-Louise this shit. Let me know when you're in position, and I'll tag you so I know who's who."

I tucked my phone into my coat pocket and looked in the side mirror at the cars lined up along the road. I counted five vehicles, but there might have been more tucked behind the truck at the end. My heart thudded in my chest, and black spots danced in my vision.

"Are we ready?" Val asked. I sensed her nervousness creeping up with mine. Everyone was waiting for me to give the signal, and I was being selfish by freezing up.

Without thinking, I pulled my phone back out and opened my text messages to read Simon's latest.

Simon: I'm still sitting with your message feeling like garbage. I'm so sorry, Lys, but I do think it's better for me to stay away. I would probably make everything worse. If anyone can do this, it's you. You've got the power and the experience now. Don't underestimate yourself. Call me when you're done.

His words read like a hug, and despite my disappointment,

I understood. Having a chaos demon run in among the spirit witches would probably be a recipe for disaster. I just would have felt so much better with my best friend by my side.

I heaved a breath, put my phone away, and rested my hand on the door. "Yeah. I'm ready. Let's get this started."

Chapter 28
Alyssa

V ALERY STAYED CLOSE by my side while we waited for everyone to get out of their cars. We planned to go the rest of
the way on foot, with Aunt Hilary driving the pickup behind us
and staying out of sight in the vehicle. The idea was that once
we had Trace, everyone would pile into the bed of the truck to
return to the cars.

I acknowledged the flaw in this plan—if we had to bolt
to a getaway car, it meant members of this dark coven were
still alive and would be hot on our heels to stop us. But logic
trumped flaws. The odds of Trace being able to walk the kilometre back to Val's car were slim. The thought of dragging
him injured and unconscious across that whole distance sent
my pulse racing, and I nearly vomited my breakfast all over the

grass. Only the knowledge that Chip was in my ear and would give me grief over it kept me breathing through the nausea.

"You good, little sister?" Brody asked. He slung his arm around my shoulders and nudged me with his hip.

"No. I can't say I am. We've got this plan, and maybe it's good, but maybe it's garbage. Trace is in there, and they're doing goddess knows what to him. What if we find him and he's already—or what if they managed to break him? What if we're not in time?"

I thought of the rough shape Trace had been in when he'd found me in the parking lot behind Mooney's. By the time we'd stepped foot in the Labyrinth, he seemed to have regained some of his strength, but what if it wasn't enough to keep the corpsy witch out of his head? Once they got the souls out of him, they wouldn't let him walk away. The only hope he had was to cling to the magic that was slowly wearing him down.

I knew Chip heard every word of my freak-out, and his lack of commentary amped up my anxiety all the more. Was he quiet because he'd muted me for now, or was he quiet because I was speaking his fears? I wished he could pick Trace up on the infrared. If the magically enhanced tech was able to detect so much, why couldn't it go one step further?

Why were we stuck in the dark about the most crucial piece of information in this rescue mission?

"Breathe, Aly." Brody rested his hands on my shoulders

and dipped his head to catch my eye, then he drew in a slow breath and released it, continuing until I breathed along with him. "If he was dead, I think we'd know. They wouldn't be sticking around the house—they'd be out there using their new power for whatever they want it for. As for what state we'll find him in, we have some of the best healers in the coven with us. Between you and Mom, there's nothing you can't bring him back from."

That wasn't close to true, but I appreciated his attempt at a pep talk.

"What we need to stay focused on now is getting in there," he continued. "Once we start moving, you'll be so invested in holding your wards up you won't have time to panic."

That was truer. The anticipation was always what killed me.

He clapped me on the shoulder, then turned me towards the rest of the family and gave me a gentle shove. This was it. The rescue. If we turned back now, we were throwing away our best chance at saving Trace before this coven spread its evil through the city. I wouldn't let him, my family, or my city down like that.

Steeling myself, I strode towards Gramps, who'd taken position at the head of the group. I would be paired with him as we made our way onto the property.

During the brief moment I stood on my own, Chip spoke up. "Your brother's right, by the way. We'd know if something had happened to him. I've got ears in every corner of this city, and a win as big as taking Trace Wyatt out of the picture would spread fast in certain circles. If anyone stands a chance of dragging him out of whatever dark hole he's found himself in, it's you. Have a little more faith in yourself."

My throat grew tight. "That's the nicest thing you've ever said to me."

"Yeah, well, Trace is good people. He deserves someone willing to fight for him. But don't expect me to keep it up. You still don't get free access to my house."

I grinned and could have hugged him for raising my mood if only for a fraction of a millisecond. In the next, all smiles were gone as I took my place at Gramps's side.

"All right, Mooneys," I said. "We band together on this, and we don't let anyone through the wards. The goal here is to get Trace out. I've got magical intel on the locations of the witches inside, so with luck, we'll be able to move around without drawing too much attention. There are only six to our fourteen, so even if it does come to a fight, we have the witchpower to stand against them. Let's hope we can avoid it."

I thought of the witches we'd taken down in the house on MacLaren. Sure, Trace had been the one to strip them of their spirit magic, but if I could mimic his suppression spell, maybe I could achieve the same effect.

"We suspect Trace is in the basement. I want four people

outside guarding the exit. Once we get him, we'll need to move quickly. I want another four people inside the house protecting the front door to clear our way out. Whoever comes close, you take them down. Brody, Dad, Gramps, I want you with me heading downstairs."

Mom crossed her arms. "Where do you want me?"

Ideally back at home where she'd be safe.

"With us," I said. "We'll need Trace conscious and moving, and I don't know if I have that level of skill."

Mom gave me a look as though to say she knew I did, but she didn't argue with me.

I looked to Gramps. "Does all that sound good to you?"

He winked. "You're a natural, Pip."

I drew in a deep breath and turned towards the house. "Okay, then. Here goes nothing."

Chapter 29
Trace

I WANTED TO give in.

Goddess I wanted to give in.

Every muscle, joint, tendon—hell, every artery screamed as though it were on fire.

"Why are you making this so difficult for yourself?" David asked as he adjusted the mirrors again. The spell slid up my back and settled between my shoulder blades. "You could end all this pain, all this misery, by giving me what I want. Why do you insist on carrying this extra baggage? Look at the state of you. You look like you've been through the wars. They're putting too much strain on your system. Imagine how much lighter you'll feel once they're gone."

I tried to block him out. I didn't want to hear the temptation this devil whispered in my ear. I was too close to accepting his offer. Because nothing he said was a lie. These souls had been a burden ever since I'd absorbed them. I hadn't wanted them, and I didn't want the power they offered me. Not only was containing them draining my energy, but they scared the shit out of me. My control over them was slipping, and I didn't know how much longer I had before the bindings I'd woven around them cracked. Or my sanity did.

As though they heard what David was saying, they pressed against me, desperate to escape and destroy him. They would rather tear me apart to protect themselves than risk being harvested by him. I knew it as if they were screaming in audible voices.

I felt like I was being torn in two, and every second that passed pushed me closer to choosing one side or the other.

Probably the other.

Fuck this guy. Let the souls turn him to charcoal so he couldn't enslave them. Let my ravaged body give out, empty and spent, while the souls that had been stuck first inside an amulet and then inside me rampaged through this house and beyond. What would I care?

David made a noise of consideration and sat in his chair. "I will say, you've held out longer than I expected you to. I always thought your reputation had to be exaggerated, but no, you really are this stubborn. The way I see it is that I can continue to cause you physical pain in the hopes that it'll eventually push you over the edge… or I can switch to something a little more personal. A green-eyed, pub-owning witch? What do you think? Would Alyssa Mooney last as long in this chair as you have? Part of me would love to find out."

Rage seared through me, and the souls used that anger to fuel their escape attempts.

Every aching muscle in my body tensed, and I lifted my head to glare at this man in front of me who held the confidence of a king holding court. Except he'd seriously fucked up.

He could poke and prod at me as much as he wanted, but if he laid one hand on Alyssa, I would not only release the souls who wanted to flay the skin from his bones, I'd send all my magic with them.

David caught my expression and grinned, and it was the smile that made me snap. I was done playing games. I jerked my left leg free of the strap, shook my boot to the end of my foot and kicked it at one of the mirrors. The angle shifted, and the beam of magic struck David in the chest. The spell ignited a low fire that spread across the cheap polyester, melting the fabric and leaving the witch scrambling to pull off his shirt before the flames consumed anything else.

"That witch is as good as dead, Wyatt," he hissed as he fought with his burning sleeve. "And thanks to you, I'll make sure it's slow."

He rushed from the room cursing, and I set to work using my unbound foot to speed up the process on my right leg. I was getting out of here to shove David's threats down his throat, and he'd be lucky if that was all I did to him.

I'd just worked some flexibility into the second strap when shouts erupted upstairs. I couldn't hear what anyone was saying, but I recognized the tone. Shit was about to go down.

Chapter 30
Alyssa

CHIP'S CAMERAS GOT us closer to the house than I'd expected before anyone spotted us, but once they did, the situation sparked off like water in a grease fire and any chance of a sneaky rescue vanished.

"Two witches coming up on your left," Chip said in my ear. "Around the side of the house. They're showing a lot of heat, so I'm going to guess their magic is at the ready."

"On your left," I called to Kyle and Grayson. My cousins would be part of the team outside the house.

They broke off from the group, and in the corner of my eye, I spotted the seamless wave of purple magic as they raised their wards. Dad, Avery, and Mom summoned wards as well, wrapping them around the rest of us. Another moment later, the two witches came into view. Yellow magic burst from their hands as they released their spirit spells, but the magic bounced off our shield without causing damage. More spells—yellow mixed with elemental and necromantic power—followed up, and this time the wards wavered. Jennifer and Courtney stepped forward to bolster the magic, strengthening the barrier as Gramps reached the front door.

Instead of grabbing the handle as I'd expected him to, he summoned his magic and thrust the door in, sending it flying into the plaster of the bright and beautifully decorated foyer. A wise move on his part as a magical trap threw bolts of lightning across the doorway to catch the unsuspecting.

"Three moving through the house," Chip said. "Two from the left, one from the right."

That was five witches accounted for. I summoned power into my hands and moved in behind Gramps. As the witch came in from the right, I was ready to release my net. It caught the spell he threw at me, and both net and attack fizzled out in mid-air. He recovered first and launched a yellow-tinted magic bomb at me. I raised a ward at the last second, but the sourness of his spell hummed across my skin and left me gagging. I was grateful for the amethyst at my neck that repelled some of the magic, but I worried the enchantments had almost run their course.

Dad shoved me out of the way and wove a spell of his own. The witch rushed to put together another burst, but

Dad was quicker. He released his spell, and the spirit witch was thrown backwards against the wall, stuck there as though glued in place. I knew from experience he would stay there for a few hours until the spell wore off. At least he would have if Dylan hadn't followed up Dad's attack with one that crushed the witch's windpipe.

Val and Brody were already taking care of the other two. Purple spells flew between yellow and green. My brother dodged the incoming spells and hurled a few offensive ones, while my sister maintained a ward that covered them. The two witches they faced were older than any I'd seen so far in this coven. I placed them in their mid-forties, and unlike the angry power of the younger witches, these two were strong and fought with skill and experience the others lacked. But now that the third was down, Gramps, Dylan, and I joined my other siblings, overpowering the enemy.

Or so I thought.

The female witch, her bright red hair shorn into an uneven pixie cut, grinned at me as she drew more power between her palms. At first I didn't recognize the red magic mixed with the yellow, but when she unleashed it in my direction, I pinned what it was—demonic power. This woman wasn't only harbouring souls in her body but demon energy as well. I only had a second to dive and roll to avoid being hit head on.

Until now I'd accepted that Simon hadn't joined us, but

facing this bitch I would have given anything to have him here. Reverie, too, if she was in the mood to kick some ass. I would have risked his chaotic magic going haywire and tolerated Reverie's flawless beauty to let the demons go toe-to-toe with this thief-witch.

I jumped to my feet in time to watch the male witch launch an elemental-spirit combo at Gramps. My grandfather threw up a ward, but not quickly enough. The spell caught his arm, and he cried out as the magic burrowed through his flesh.

Dad grabbed him and shoved him towards Mom to get him out of the way, and I retaliated with a spell that pushed our attackers back. The man stumbled, looking shocked that I'd managed it, but the woman bared her teeth and followed up with a red-yellow spell.

"Ward!" I screamed to Avery, and she added hers to Val's, but it wasn't enough to keep out the demonic tempest that swirled around us. Pictures flew off the walls and smashed against the floor, spewing glass and cracked plastic. The paint on the walls bubbled and burst, spitting burning acrylic in every direction. We warded as best we could against it, but our wards worked best against magic, and this woman had launched a physical assault.

With a cackle as mad as any hatter's, she hurled spell after spell as though the expense of power didn't affect her at all. Dylan, Brody, and Tony fought hard to fend her off, but the male witch cancelled out almost every one of their strikes. Finally, one of Dylan's spells hit him in the chest, and the witch stumbled backwards into the dining table in a spray of blood. He wheezed on the floor, not dead but close to it.

I stared at my brother, wondering what the hell he'd been doing lately to have developed that kind of spell knowledge, but although he spared me a glance, he showed no sign of remorse as he turned his attention to the demonic witch.

Valery screamed as her ward gave out, and Mom rushed to step in and bolster Avery's. Dread filled me to see her on the front lines. My mother was a healer. She'd dedicated her entire life to easing people's pain with little experience or joy in defensive or offensive magic, yet here she was, putting herself at risk because of Gramps's bad decisions and my choice of friends.

And somewhere in this house, Trace had been at these people's mercy.

The horror I felt on my mother's behalf spread to encompass him. Had this demonic witch had a hand in whatever was being done to him?

Where was the ghoulish elemental witch?

The question had barely entered my mind when the door beside the living room burst open and a man with his shirt on fire sprinted into the room.

Chapter 31
Alyssa

THE DEMONIC WITCH stared at the new arrival in fury, and I took the opportunity to launch a binding spell at her. She noticed just in time to raise her hands, but not soon enough to prevent my magical net from wrapping around her and sending her to the floor.

I moved towards her to make sure she stayed down, but in my periphery I noticed that the ghoulish witch from MacLaren had shed the rest of his shirt and turned on Dad, who was covering Gramps. Valery's magic had given out, and Mom and Avery were holding their wards. Dylan, Brody, and Tony closed in on the demonic witch, and I stepped in front of Mr. Ghoul. The witch looked worse now than he had the last time I'd seen him. How was it possible his teeth looked even bigger?

His chest was covered in welts that had already begun to blister, and his eyes burned with rage, but when they landed on me, a deep satisfaction rose beneath the loathing. I did not like that look one bit.

"What luck," he said. "I thought I'd have to track you down."

He reached for me, but I evaded him, grabbed his wrist, and twisted. He landed on his back with a groan. One didn't work in a pub without learning a few self-defence tricks. The move might not have worked on a man in his prime, but Mr. Ghoul was well past, if he'd ever actually hit it.

Under my palm, his skin warmed, grew hot. My amulet buzzed, redirecting some of his spell back at him, but then the stone shattered, and the full brunt of his power soaked into me. I jerked my hand away and gave it a shake to relieve the pain. I'd missed the green glow of his elemental magic when I'd pinned him down, but the bastard had used it well. He pushed himself to his feet and came at me again, now with green fire licking from his fingertips.

"Should I start with your face?" he asked. "Or do you think Mr. Wyatt would prefer some other gift?"

His gaze dropped to my chest, and I curled my lip in revulsion.

A ball of purple energy flew from my left and struck him in the jaw, sending him careening into the wall. He slammed his head hard enough to crack the drywall and slumped to the ground, dazed.

"Keep your eyes off my daughter, asshole," Mom said, one hand raised against Mr. Ghoul while the other maintained the ward between her sons and Ms. Demon in case the witch got up.

Brody and Dylan rushed to the other elemental witch with the hole in his chest, who'd regained consciousness and was attempting to crawl to the door. Brody wheeled his arm back and punched the witch in his face, and Dylan followed it up with another spell that slammed the man's head against the floor and made him sag like dirty laundry.

Now that I was watching, I recognized the style. Dylan had been fighting in the Underground, the local—very illegal—fighting ring. Another conversation to set aside for later.

Silence fell over the house, and by the lack of noise outside, I guessed my aunts and cousins had taken care of those two witches as well. Which left me free to check on Gramps.

His arm was a wreck. The spell itself had punched through flesh and muscle, and everywhere around the wound had turned black. Necrotic.

"Let me see," Mom said, shoving everyone out of the way. Dad's face was tinged with green and my stomach was threatening to revolt, but her expression remained calm and unworried. "This doesn't look great, but no worries. We can patch you up."

Gramps wheezed a laugh. "If anyone could, it's you, Mary. I have no doubt about that." His eyes were glazed with pain, but they rolled towards me. "Go on, Pip. The coast is clear. Go get your boy and bring him home."

My throat tightened as I stared at him. I didn't want to admit that fear kept me rooted where I was. Mr. Ghoul had come upstairs with his shirt on fire. What did that mean for what I might find in the basement?

But the way Gramps had phrased it… *Go get your boy.* It left me no choice but to find my courage and move. Trace could have fought his way free in the MacLaren house, but instead he'd expended his energy to get Gramps and I out of the coven's range.

He'd kissed me.

In the rush of everything that had happened since then, I'd barely had time to sit with that particular life-changing event. Right now, though, it was exactly the push I needed to start towards the basement door.

"No other witches on the horizon, Chip?" I asked. He'd been so quiet, I'd almost forgotten he was hanging out in my ear. Only the faint sound of fingers tapping on a keyboard clued me in to the fact that he hadn't hung up.

"You're all clear, Cheers. Like Gramps said—bring our boy home. I'll leave you to it and meet up with you later. No one should be witness to this."

The disgust in his voice was so strong, I knew it could only be a cover for his true feelings. Like me, he was terrified about what I would find when I reached wherever Mr. Ghoul was keeping Trace. As soon as the line went dead in my ear, I wished Chip would call back. I didn't want to find out on my own.

With everyone starting to clean up behind me, however, I had no choice but to fortify. Trace deserved for me to hurry the fuck up.

With my shoulders back and my awareness on high alert for any magical traps in the doorway or along my route, I edged down the stairs. Although I spotted signs where those traps existed, none of them were active, and I guessed that Mr. Ghoul had run up so quickly and in such a state of chaos he'd forgotten to reset them. Luck was working on my side for a beautiful change.

At the bottom of the stairs, I took in the finished basement. Not finished as in vinyl flooring and a big screen TV. Not even finished as in shag carpeting, wood panelling, and a built-in bar.

No, those design choices would have been too basic for this lot. This place was beyond anything so plebeian. Nowhere close to trendy.

The concrete floors were painted white. The walls were white. The potlights were bright white. There were no paintings on the walls, though next to the door hung diagrams of… a spell? A potion? Metal shelving units stood along the edges of the room, with potion vials, tiny cauldrons, books, and various ingredients organized and labelled. I'd have to drag the rest of the family down here to take a look at what this coven was working with—or working on—but for now I ignored them.

All I cared about was the sickening tang of dark magic that hung in the air and the knowledge that Trace was down here somewhere.

I walked carefully through the room, making sure not to brush against anything that might shatter or spill or melt me into a puddle. Minutes felt like hours, but I finally reached the door on the other side. It had been left open a crack, and I peered through the doorway before stepping in.

I was glad I had, because it gave me a chance to brace myself. The whiteness of the space continued into this room, but there were no shelving units in here, no diagrams on the walls. Only a table covered in implements I didn't want to guess at, a narrow pedestal against the wall to the left with a spinning ball of yellow magic that shot beams to various points in the room, a dozen mirrors to catch and direct the beams, and two metal chairs. One sat empty, the other held Trace.

Whose still, hunched-over form made my heart jump into my throat.

All thought, all fear for my life, fled at the sight. I threw my magical net at the swirling spell as I ran across the room, extinguishing the beams and wiping out that suffocating tingle of magic. When I reached Trace, I dropped to my knees to get a look at him. His left leg was free of the leather strap that had bound him, and his right leg was halfway there, but he appeared to have passed out before he'd finished the job.

No fucking wonder. His shirt had been burned to rags across his chest, and through the destroyed fabric, I made out welts similar to what had covered Mr. Ghoul. The beams from that spell must have acted like radiation, slowly cooking him as the coven tried to what? Drag the souls out of him?

Part of me wanted to see if I could bundle up that spell so we could analyze it, but another part wanted to get as far away from it as possible. A third part of me wanted to crush it, destroying it and anyone who'd helped create it.

I rested my hand on Trace's knee and allowed a tendril of healing energy to flow into him. We didn't have time for me to patch up every injury—hell, I doubted I'd have the strength to do it by myself in one go—but I had to wake him up. More witches could arrive at any moment, and a good chunk of our forces had already burned themselves out against these six.

"Trace, can you hear me? It's Alyssa. It's all right, I'm here. We dealt with them."

He groaned, and his pale eyelashes fluttered. I moved closer to him, brushing his hair back where it had fallen over his face.

"Come on, Wyatt. Mr. Tough Bounty Hunter. You're not telling me a day of torture was enough to break you, are you?" I kept my tone light, channelling more magic into him. He twitched, and I caught sight of a blown-out pupil peeking out from under his eyelid.

While he worked on waking up, I turned my attention to the metal cuffs around his wrists. The same magic-nullifying cuffs they'd used on Gramps. Only this time no one was able to tell me where to find the key.

Cursing under my breath, I rose to my feet and looked around the room. There were no drawers, no handy keyring hanging on the wall. Although I wanted nothing more than to stay by Trace's side, I went into the other room with the creepy-ass diagrams to hunt for it. There were no desks, so I focused on the shelving units. Everything was so neatly labelled it gave me a lady hard-on, and I found myself searching for a convenient tag marked *Magic-Nullifying Cuffs Key*.

My luck didn't extend that far.

But I hadn't come all this way just to be put off by a lack of keys. I marched upstairs to where Brody and Dylan had dragged Mr. Ghoul to his feet. We'd only vaguely discussed what we'd do with any surviving witches, and I suspected this elemental witch was about to face the discomfort of lying in the truck bed while my brothers used him as a bench to cushion the ride. After that, well, if I never saw him again, I wouldn't ask what they'd done with him.

"Have you checked his pockets?" I asked, avoiding looking at the man's pale, bare paunch. "Whatever pockets he still has."

Brody and Dylan played rock, paper, scissors, and Dylan groaned as he reached into the guy's front pants pockets. Brody took care of the rear. They pulled out a wallet, an old candy wrapper, and finally, a keyring. I took it, left the rest with them, and hurried back downstairs.

By the time I got down there, Trace was awake, if barely. Sweat dripped down his forehead, and his wild eyes roved the room. They were more yellow than violet, with a few tendrils of spirit magic leaching out through the fine veins around his eyes into his cheeks. When his gaze landed on me, some of the yellow receded, replaced by a relief so fierce it stole my breath.

"I thought I'd imagined you," he said, his voice hoarse. "I swore I heard your voice, but when I opened my eyes, you weren't here."

I held up the keys in apology. "I had to go on a bit of a hunt. But it's me, Trace. I'm getting you out of here."

He squeezed his eyes shut and bowed his head into the crook of my neck as I worked to unlock one cuff, then the other. When both were open, I untied the leather strap around his right leg and had to catch him when he fell forward out of the chair. His arms wrapped around me, and he burrowed his face deeper into my throat.

I helped him put his boot back on, then held him just as tightly, breathing him in. For the moment, I overlooked the reek of sweat and blood and burned hair. All that mattered was that he was breathing and was himself enough to know who I was.

"What do you say we head outside and go home?" I asked. "Think you're able to walk?"

"With you here? I could fly."

My heart fluttered as I looped my arm around his waist, hooked his arm around my neck, and helped him to his feet. He wobbled, but I held him steady as we shuffled towards the door. With each step, I pumped a bit more healing energy into him.

"You're going to wear yourself out," he mumbled.

"Let me worry about that."

We made it to the door before his legs gave out, but Val had made it down the stairs and was able to help me get him the rest of the way up.

Mom and Dad already had Gramps in the back of the truck by the time we made it outside, and Grayson, Tony, and Avery were gone.

Brody, Dylan, and Kyle waited by the front door.

"Where are the others?" I asked.

"Jennifer and Courtney are taking another walk around to make sure we didn't miss anyone," Kyle said. "The others are taking the prisoners to the cars and bringing the rest of our rides here."

I expected them to look thrilled. We'd done it. We'd shut down the coven, rescued Trace, and—aside from a few wounds that I was confident Mom could heal—we'd made it out unscathed.

What I found instead was fear. Wariness. I looked from them to Mom and Dad, where they hovered around the back of the truck, eyes fixed on their surroundings.

"What's going on?" I asked, immediately on edge.

Dylan stiffened and shifted his back to me, but Brody rallied enough to meet my eye. "The leader and the one with the demonic magic—they slipped their bindings. They're gone."

Chapter 32
Trace

ISHOULD HAVE been sleeping, but I couldn't bring myself to close my eyes, no matter how hard it was to keep them open. In my efforts to stay awake, I stared around what had to be Alyssa's childhood bedroom. Even without her telling me, I sensed her essence everywhere. The purple bedspread, the posters on the walls. I tried to imagine her sitting in here doing her homework, talking on the phone with her friends. Enjoying a life that didn't include dragging my ass out of horrifying situations and putting herself in danger on my behalf.

Guilt ate at me, but it wasn't what kept me awake. Nor was it the fact that every time my eyelids sagged, I worried my rescue had been a dream and I was still tied to that stupid chair. That I was still in that room with its white walls and the promise of more torture to come.

It didn't help that my burns had begun to heal, making them excruciatingly itchy and painful. At least while the magical beams had done their thing, the pain had become one massive torment instead of these dozens of individual discomforts. But the pain also wasn't what chased all thought of sleep away.

No, what kept me from closing my eyes was the woman sitting on the bed beside me, holding my hand, stroking the back of it with her thumb as her magic flowed into me. How could I go to sleep now that I'd been lucky enough to be reunited with her? How could I waste a minute?

Alyssa had no idea how many ways she'd saved my life over the past twelve hours. Not a clue. I wanted to tell her, but while her grandfather dealt with the agony of having his wounds healed in the guest room, while her sister sat shivering in the living room, and while her brothers paced the hallways trying to figure out what they could do about the missing witches, now didn't feel like the time to bring it up.

"You should try to sleep," Alyssa said, smiling down at me. I noted the lines of tension in the corners of her eyes, the wobbliness of her lips, but her expression held nothing but gentle concern. "You're safe now. You're allowed to rest."

"I will." I winced at the scratchiness in my throat. "But not yet."

With a slight tug on her hand, I convinced her to shift so

she lay on her side facing me. Her green eyes scanned my face, ran down my body, and she frowned whenever they landed on a wound she felt should have been healing faster. I was getting to know her subtle expressions—the faint tuck of the corner of her mouth that meant she was frustrated; the way she bit down on the inside of her bottom lip when she was working something out. My condition combined with the dilemma of the witches had stressed her to her limits.

"I'm all right," I said, wanting to put her at ease on that subject at least.

Except my attempt seemed to make things worse. Her throat worked as she held back tears, and her nose and eyes turned red as she failed. "But you're not, are you? How much did that fight take out of you? What did that bastard put you through in that basement? Do you know how many times your guests nearly came out to play on the car ride here?"

I cringed. Yeah, that had been a dicey trip. We'd been in her sister's car, and my resident souls had taken offence to the amount of wild magic shooting through the vehicle as her sister and one of the cousins had come down from the rush of the fight. I'd accidentally blown up the radio and nearly set fire to the console. Great first impression for the family.

"They're under a lot of pressure," I admitted. "David made a good effort to get them out of me, and they're disappointed they didn't get a chance to play with him."

Her nose wrinkled, which I considered a fair reaction. Whatever the souls might have done, it wouldn't have been pretty.

"But I'm out of there now. They can calm down. They're safe." I brushed her hair behind her ear and cupped her cheek in my palm. "I'm safe."

"For now. Those witches…" A shiver ran through her, and I shifted so I could put my arms around her and pull her closer. She nestled against my chest. "I thought Mr. Ghoul was strong, but that woman has demonic magic, Trace. The spells she was slinging—the power—the *speed*. Between wards and attacks, it took eight of us to match her, and she still got away."

I hugged her even tighter. "This time. Next time will be different." I thought about everything David had told me when he'd believed I wouldn't get away. Hadn't he referenced someone giving him orders? "Do you think she's leading them?"

"It's possible. She didn't act like she was in charge, but with that kind of strength, if she's not, then I really don't want to meet the person who is." She groaned. "I just had to say that, didn't I?"

I laughed and kissed the top of her head. She smelled of smoke and sweat and blood, but I didn't want to let go of her long enough to let her shower, and by the way she sank against me, I wondered if she felt the same.

My eyelids tugged down again, and again I struggled to

keep them open. Sleep would help me heal faster but would also take me away from Alyssa, which was the only place in the world I wanted to be right now.

"Sleep, Trace." Her voice sounded so far away. "I'm not going anywhere."

With that promise winding through my head, I gave up the fight and allowed myself to drift off.

Chapter 33
Alyssa

To keep my promise to Trace or to not reek and feel like a disgusting bloody sweat monster? The struggle was real.

According to the clock, it was getting on five o'clock in the evening. I'd napped beside him for part of the last couple hours, but now I was awake and wanting to be clean and to join the conversation happening downstairs in my parents' living room. I was also warm, encased in a pair of muscular arms, and had never felt so comfortable or safe in my entire life. I wanted more of this, but the only way to ensure we got it was to help Trace not get taken by the spirit witches and figure out how to get the souls out of him.

So despite my reservations and with no small amount of guilt, I wriggled my way free of his hold and padded towards the ensuite bathroom. I did leave the door ajar in case he woke up. I didn't want him to wonder where I'd gone, and I wanted to hear him if he needed me.

The number of wounds I'd found across his chest and back had left me hollow. There had been over a hundred circular welts—I'd lost count halfway through. He'd filled me in on most of what David the Ghoul had done to him, but seeing it was a whole different kind of hell. It was no wonder Trace didn't want to be alone.

The thought of him waking up to find me gone squeezed my heart, so I shifted my plan. I would forgo joining the family summit for now and limit myself to the shower. At least then he could wake up to nice-smelling me instead of regurgitated-by-a-slime-monster me.

I stripped down, having borrowed a pair of Dylan's black sweats and one of Mom's T-shirts with a motivational *Keep Breathing* written on it. They were a cozy alternative to the blood-caked, tattered, glass-strewn clothes I'd tossed into the garbage earlier, and who didn't need a reminder to breathe every once in a while?

Once the bathroom filled with steam, I stepped into the tub and pulled the pink-and-purple-swirled shower curtain closed around me. The frosted-glass window beside me let in the lingering daylight, and I cracked it open just enough to vent the room. A cold breeze fought to take over the small space, but the hot water washed away the chill.

The external chill, anyway. My bones remained iced over at the idea of walking into Showdown 2.0 with that demonic witch. My thoughts lingered on her for a while, trying to figure out what exactly we were dealing with there. Part of me wanted to say she was half demon with her magic so strong, but the answer didn't hit quite right. Her spells had been all witch, and beneath the red-yellow magic, there had been a faint twist of something else. Green, maybe. The woman was a witch, but she'd somehow absorbed a demon's magic the way she'd absorbed the spirit magic.

That was some *dark* power at work. If she was aiming to level up again by taking on Trace's souls, I didn't want to imagine what the city would look like once she started using them.

Whether it terrified me or not, we couldn't ignore this threat. I doubted Gramps would stand for it, even if he had nearly lost his arm. My stomach threatened to revolt at the memory of my mother's healing magic winding its way through his torn-up muscles. His screams had echoed in my ears even though he'd been three cars away at the time. Mom and Dad had taken him to the guest room as soon as they'd gotten home, not wanting him to associate his basement apartment with his recovery, and the screaming had continued while I'd done my best to soothe the worst of Trace's injuries. I'd gotten the much better end of that deal. But the fact that no one had rushed Gramps to the hospital afterwards told me Mom had been successful at patching him up. The woman worked miracles.

A rush of cold air played around me, and the curtain billowed as the bathroom door swung open. I peeked around the curtain to find Trace in the doorway. His eyes were bleary with sleep and he wavered on his feet, but he was standing.

He caught me looking at him, and his cheeks flushed. "Sorry, not interrupting. Just… needed a glass of water."

His words sounded genuine enough, but the way his body swayed towards the door told me he'd woken up in a panic on finding himself alone.

"You're not interrupting. You can keep me company if you want." I closed my eyes on a sigh as I replayed what I'd said. "In the bathroom, I mean. Not in the shower."

A slow smile curled the corner of his mouth, and his violet eyes darkened.

My face flushed even hotter at the direction my dizzying thoughts took under that expression, and I prayed he blamed it on the water.

"Then again, I mean, we're adults, right?" I said. "You also need to shower and might need help, and I'm almost done, so—I mean—you could join me. If you wanted. In here."

Had I really just suggested he get naked with me? He'd been kidnapped and tortured, and I wasn't sure if his guest souls liked me or blamed me for their current prison. We had witches to catch and family members to check on. There was too much going on to explore whatever was growing between us.

But even as the objections rose, I dismissed them. All those reasons were exactly why we should indulge in the small pleasures. We would soon be getting ready to challenge some terrifying people. If that wasn't reason enough to seize the moment, what was?

I raised my gaze to his and might have laughed at the answering flush in his cheeks if I hadn't been distracted by the way he reached for the bottom of his borrowed T-shirt that was already stained with blood. His slow movements weren't a tease, more a limitation of his weakened, shaking fingers, but the result was the same. My attention followed the path of his hands, taking in the fine hair that trailed down his stomach, the definition of his abdominal muscles—though I suspected they were ghosts of his usual physique after weeks of nausea and waning strength. As he pulled the shirt off, I tore my gaze away from the lines of the V dipping into his jeans and focused instead on the semi-healed welts along his chest, the backs of his arms, the hints of more of them on his back. They had to hurt like a son of a bitch, but although he moved slowly, he never complained.

The sight stripped me of all—okay, most—of my desire, and I turned a practical mind to the temperature of the water, cooling it a touch to be more comfortable for him and adjusting the spray of the shower head to something gentler. Yes, he needed to get cleaned up, but I didn't need to take over as torturer to get the job done.

I heard the sound of his ruined jeans hitting the floor and pulled the curtain back, keeping my eyes fixed on his face, ready to help him into the tub if he needed it but otherwise giving him the space to do it himself. He'd never struck me as the kind of guy who enjoyed being fussed over. But I wasn't above showing a firm hand when it came to making sure his wounds didn't get infected. He wasn't about to enjoy what happened next.

He stepped into the shower, and I swallowed hard as I took in his closeness. His tallness. His nakedness. The first two details all the more noticeable thanks to the third.

"Hey," he said, staring down at me. So close, so tall, so, *so* naked.

"Hey," I replied, fighting to get the words out around the butterflies clogging my stomach, my lungs, my throat. The damned things were everywhere. A few had migrated further south, but for the most part that area had gone dormant. This was not a sexy-times shower. This was a this-guy-has-been-strapped-to-a-chair-and-burned-for-twelve-hours-let's-make-sure-he-heals-well shower. Totally different vibe.

Except, of course, for the close, tall, naked part. Those I

very much wanted to explore again at a less stressful opportunity.

By the way his kept forcing his gaze back up to mine, I wasn't the only one to feel that way, which was both frustrating and a relief. The water ran over his loose hair, and his lip-length locks fell over his face. I resisted the urge to brush them out of his eyes.

"I'll try to go easy on you," I said, "but we need to clean your burns." I twirled my finger, ordering him to turn around.

He stiffened as he obeyed, hissing through his teeth as the spray hit his back. I was glad he wasn't looking at me as I got a good look at the extent of the damage. In some places the spell had burrowed deeply enough to split the skin, and at each point of contact, red lines veined out, much as the yellow spirit magic did when it took him over. The welts began around his neck and spread down his spine, along his ribs—which were too visible for comfort. For all the muscle definition he still had, he'd lost so much mass over the past couple of weeks, I doubted he recognized himself when he looked in the mirror. The burns stretched around his sides, and I knew they continued across his chest.

Red swam in my vision. I wished Mr. Ghoul were here now. Dylan would be the one holding *me* back if I got my hands on him. I would pump the bastard so full of magic, his head would pop like a fucking cherry.

"Princess?" Trace said, and I looked up to find him staring at me over his shoulder. A touch of yellow had spilled through his violet eyes. "You might want to strap in that anger. My souls aren't reacting well to it."

Only now did I notice the way my magic had awakened with my rage and spread over my hands and up my arms.

I breathed deeply and did my best to let the negativity wash down the drain. There would be time enough for anger when we had Mr. Ghoul in our custody.

With a few more deep breaths, I reached a level of cool relaxation and rested my hands on Trace's back, mindful of the worst burns.

Gently, I channelled my healing energy into him, focusing more on numbing the pain so the water could do its work than trying to patch him up, but as I watched, a few of the smaller welts smoothed away, leaving only irritated red skin behind.

It took ten minutes for Trace's legs to start wobbling. I left off healing him and turned him to face the water so he could wash himself down. I pulled back the curtain to get out and leave him to it, but he curled his fingers around my wrist, and the expression in his eyes was so haunted, so lost, that I stayed right where I was.

He stepped closer and rested his forehead on my shoulder. I wrapped my arms around him and held him as the water spilled over us.

"Thank you," he murmured into my neck.

"For what?"

"For coming back for me."

My heart clenched. "Of course."

I started to say more, but the words stuck in my throat. One day I would speak them aloud. Right now the pain of almost losing him was too fresh. But honestly, after all we'd been through together, did he think I would ever leave him behind?

Chapter 34
Trace

THE WATER WAS cold by the time Alyssa and I finally rinsed off and she helped me out of the tub.

Our first shower together was nothing like how I might have imagined it. If I'd believed it was possible to experience one with her, I would have anticipated more high-intensity interactions than some gentle touches and even gentler mutual washing. My injuries and near death aside, I wondered if this had been better.

She was so incredibly beautiful. As I carefully patted myself dry with a clean towel, I watched her get dressed, taking in the sleek muscles of her legs, her taut stomach, her defined biceps and triceps. She was a woman who took care of herself—at least when she wasn't running around fighting witches. I noticed the tattoo on her hip: a series of three cat paw prints leading down her thigh. It was low enough that I doubted many people knew she had it, and I felt as though I'd been invited to some exclusive club of Alyssa Mooney secrets.

She pulled on a pair of black sweatpants and a purple graphic tee, and although the pants were too big and the T-shirt a smidge too small, she looked amazing. My body couldn't help but respond to the sight of her, even if the response was half-hearted. I was too exhausted, but even for that I was grateful. Being forced to keep my distance gave me a chance to appreciate the smooth column of her neck when she pulled her hair up into a messy bun and the curve of her cheek when she looked at me over her shoulder.

Once she was ready, she disappeared for a minute, leaving me to take care of the bathroom necessaries, and came back with a pair of sweats and a dark green, long-sleeved tee. "More of Brody's loaners," she said. "I'm afraid to raid my brother's closets too deeply. There are some secrets a sister shouldn't find."

"At least you know it."

I tried to step into the sweats, but my balance wasn't there. My shoulder slammed into the door jamb, knocking the breath out of me, and Alyssa came closer to steady me.

With her help, I got the pants on, and I raised my arms as she tugged the shirt over my head, carefully rolling it down so it didn't brush too much against my burns. She smoothed the fabric over my hips to remove the last creases, and her gaze lingered on my chest, the inside of her bottom lip once more tucked between her teeth.

I hooked my finger under her chin and lifted her gaze to mine. I wanted to know what dark thoughts were going through her head. Wanted to silence them.

Not knowing what I might say to reassure her I was fine, I dipped my head and brushed my lips over her cheek. Her breath caught as she closed her eyes and turned her head just enough that her lips met mine. The urge came over me to deepen the kiss, to clutch her against me and show her how badly I wanted her, but I forced myself to keep it as slow and gentle as she'd been with me. If all went well, there would be time enough for hard and fast, but right now I wanted to savour something sweet and good.

I ran my hands up her shoulders and cupped the back of her neck, stroking her cheeks with my thumbs. She curled her fingers around the collar of my shirt, drawing me as close as we could get with clothes still on.

She tasted like peppermint toothpaste with a hint of her aloe vera body wash, and I sank into it, teasing her lips with my tongue to memorize every facet of them. Her eyes were glazed over when I pulled away, and I pressed a final kiss against her forehead before letting her go and taking her hand. She looped her fingers through mine and raised my hand to kiss the back of it, which sent my heartbeat racing again. I could barely keep the dopey smile off my face as I followed her out of the bathroom, out of the bedroom, and down the stairs to the living room.

Her dad was puttering around in the kitchen when we arrived. Val was back in the armchair, though her shivering had stopped. She held a cup of something steamy between her hands, and my stomach grumbled at the idea of whatever she might be drinking.

"Already on it," her dad said, and Alyssa winked at me as she pulled me through the kitchen towards a stool at the island.

"You met each other over the video call, but Trace, Henry; Henry, Trace."

"Nice to meet you in person, Trace," Henry said over his shoulder. "I'd shake your hand, but I'm elbow deep in butter. How do you feel about hash browns, fried eggs, and bacon? Nothing says comfort like breakfast for dinner, am I right?"

"Those are three of my main food groups," I said.

"Good man. They'll be ready in a jiffy, so make yourself comfortable. Aly, there's coffee in the pot if you want to serve it up."

I could see where Alyssa had gotten her hospitality skills.

Movement stirred in the corner of my eye as Valery joined us in the kitchen. She grabbed the stool at the end of the island

and stared at me. The shape of her eyes was similar to Alyssa's, but their hue wasn't nearly as vibrant green. More a warm multi-coloured hazel.

"Trace Fucking Wyatt," she said after her sharp gaze finished its appraisal. "After all the years Aly's spent mooning after you, she finally caught you. Every girl's dream."

"Val," Alyssa warned. "You were always the one mooning, not me."

Her sister's eyebrows shot up. "Excuse me very much? Is someone having memory lapses? Or is it that you don't want me talking about it in front of Dad?"

Alyssa flushed. "Fine, but I wasn't the only one mooning."

I laughed, enjoying myself even more when Alyssa's blush spread across the rest of her face and she turned away from me. I tugged her closer and tucked her into my side.

Thumps on the stairs and the loud voices of two men stopped me from whispering anything inappropriate in her ear. Dylan and Brody rounded the corner into the kitchen.

"You're here," Henry said. "Everyone else has gone home?"

"They said they'll check in later," Brody said. He stopped short when he spotted me. "Oh hey, you're up. Nice to see you walking around."

"We would not have carried you anywhere else," Dylan said as he popped his head into the fridge and came out with a carton of orange juice. "You're a heavy mother—" He caught sight of his father and cleared his throat. "Guy."

"I appreciate you lugging me around as much as you did," I said, though I didn't know how much lifting they'd actually done. I'd blacked out in the car for a while, but I did remember making it from the car into the house. I was pretty sure anyway. It was all a bit hazy.

Valery rolled her eyes. "Don't be such a drama queen, Dyl. You didn't carry him at all. Alyssa and I are the ones who dragged him out of that house *and* up to her room. You were supposed to keep the balding guy pinned down, remember?"

Dylan dropped his gaze and his shoulders hunched. The flush that spread across his cheeks followed the same pattern Alyssa's had taken. I felt a pinch of pity for the guy, but Brody stepped in and punched his brother in the shoulder. "We know you let him get away on purpose so you could have the satisfaction of punching him in the face again, right?"

Dylan forced a laugh. "Totally. It was a cunning plan."

Alyssa grinned at her siblings, and I took in the warmth of her smile. The pride that glinted in her eyes. This was her family, her coven. I imagined the only place she felt as at home was at Mooney's, a place I was sure she missed. The sooner we got everything cleared up, the sooner she and I could go back there and have a drink. Another toast maybe. This one to a brighter, less violent future.

A warm glow took up residence in my chest, and I gave

Alyssa's waist a squeeze.

"Um, Trace?" Val asked, concern written all over her face. "Are you all right?"

I followed her gaze to the back of my hand and realized the warm glow I'd felt hadn't been metaphorical. Something about this scene had woken up my resident souls. They didn't seem about to attack, but they swirled across the surface of my magic, and I struggled to get them back into place. Alyssa watched me warily—though this time, thankfully, her worry didn't seem to be because of me, only for me.

"Yeah," I said as I tugged my sleeves down over my hands. "I'm fine."

None of them pushed the issue, thank the goddess, and almost immediately, Henry was ready with supper. He served while Alyssa left my side to pour the coffee. She moved around the kitchen like one familiar with the space and navigated around people as though she'd been born in a crowd. I watched her pull sugar from the cupboard, milk from the fridge, spoons from the drawer in a series of graceful steps that made it look as though she were dancing instead of carrying out mundane tasks.

When she returned to my side, I couldn't help but press a kiss behind her ear. Everything I learned about her made me appreciate all the more how special she was. How happy I felt whenever I was with her.

Whatever happened with these spirit witches, I didn't intend to let them separate us again.

"How's Gramps?" Alyssa asked once she'd finished pouring coffee.

Henry frowned. "He's healing. Your mother's done an amazing job. She's resting now, so I'm not expecting her to join us for a while. He'll keep the arm, but it'll take a few weeks before he's able to use it fully."

"Stop gossiping about me like I'm dead," Gramps said as he pushed his way into the room, Alyssa's mother trailing after him. His arm was in a sling, cradled against his chest. "You think a sore arm's going to put me out of commission? Come on, son, you know me better than that."

"Dad," Mary said, but he shrugged her away.

"You patched me up, and you're the best healer in town. You know I'm fine."

"That's not the point. You're still weak. You can't—"

"I'm not planning on riding out at dawn," he said. "I'll leave that to the youths. But I'm not going to sit in my room, either. Not when I can help plan for what's coming. Because you'll need all the help you can get."

Alyssa's hand tightened around mine. "Do you know something about those witches, Gramps?"

His green gaze paused on me before it landed on her. "I know they're strong, and I know they've been dabbling in power they shouldn't. That woman… The only time I've seen magic like that was in my darkest days. You think a demon gives up their power voluntarily? She pinned one down and tortured it until it was on the brink of death, and then she absorbed its magic while it was still breathing."

A shudder ran through me, and Alyssa leaned her weight into my side.

"We got her partner to SMOAC?" she asked.

"The one with the hole in his chest?" Dylan asked. "Yeah. Hilary and Tony took him in on their way home."

Gramps scowled. "We should have killed him and been done with it. Mark my words, the feds won't be able to keep him long. We'll be hearing about it."

Alyssa dropped onto the stool beside me, and I missed the warmth of her body. She buried her head in her hands, and I rubbed her back until Henry dropped a plate in front of me.

"I thought them abducting you was the worst this could get," Alyssa mumbled. "How do I keep winding up in these situations?"

I nudged her with my elbow. "You're welcome."

She turned her head enough to give me a wan smile, and I winked at her before satisfying my stomach's complaints and tucking into the food. On the first bite, my insides writhed, and I squeezed my eyes shut against the wave of nausea. Only it wasn't my stomach—and it wasn't nausea. As the tensions rose in the room, my spiritual guests fought their bindings. They swam under my skin and pressed against my pores. My hands trembled, and I braced them on the edge of the counter.

Alyssa's arms wrapped around me, and I sensed her magic rising, a cooling, soothing wave to counter the turbulent emotions everywhere else in the room.

Gradually, the other magics subsided and the souls settled down, and when I looked up, I discovered Alyssa and I were alone in the kitchen. When she turned my stool and stepped between my legs, I bowed my head against her chest and set my hands on her waist. Her arms were warm as she coiled them around my head and pressed a kiss against my hair.

I was falling apart. Alyssa was right—we were heading into war, and I had to pull myself together. Right in this moment, I didn't know if I had what it took. The woman in front of me was the only thing keeping me in one piece, but I couldn't heap that burden on her. I had to figure out how to patch myself up and keep these souls in their cage.

My breathing had just settled when Alyssa's phone rang. With a groan, she pulled it out of her pocket, and her brow furrowed. "Jet?"

Her face paled as her friend spoke, but the call didn't last long. When Alyssa hung up, she looked me in the eye and prepared to speak, but her phone buzzed again, interrupting her. She glanced at the text and pressed her lips together as she turned the screen towards me. I recognized Chip's brusqueness.

Chip: Right. Trace's phone is fried. We'll fix that later. Bigger problem. Hazel? She's out. Got transferred by SMOAC on some unknown business and was being kept here in Ottawa. Someone broke her out tonight, with a bunch of others. They headed back to Rockland, but I doubt they'll stay there long.

My head swam, and the souls struggled for freedom. I squeezed my eyes shut and breathed through the maelstrom of thoughts and emotions tugging at my frayed edges.

Someone cleared their throat, and Alyssa turned around. I forced my eyes open to find Val standing in the doorway.

"Turns out Gramps was right," she said, apology woven into every syllable. "The witches we dropped off? Someone broke them out of SMOAC's holding cells. They're still in the game."

Chapter 35
Alyssa

B Y THE TIME everyone returned to the kitchen, Trace had gotten control over himself, but I was still reeling. Jet's worried voice rang in my ears.

"That woman you asked me to look into? I don't really know how to tell you this… She's disappeared. I don't understand how, but I'm looking into it, because if the series of events happened as it looks like it did, it would mean—No, I'm not saying that yet. But she's not in Moongrave, she's on the loose. Watch your back, okay?"

Then she'd hung up before I could say anything. As though someone had walked into her office and she hadn't wanted them to know she'd told anyone.

I didn't understand it, either.

All the witches we'd captured had been released, and Hazel, the source of all Trace's worst memories, was free. There was a traitor in SMOAC working with these spirit witches. Someone supernaturals trusted for justice and oversight had been involved in Gramps's kidnapping.

We Mooneys had to stop them, and we wouldn't make the same mistake twice.

"They might not come for us directly, but they'll want to take another stab at getting Wyatt," Gramps said. "You're a soul buffet right now, my boy, and unfortunately, these guys are going for all they can eat."

I grimaced at the analogy. Was that really the best he could do—comparing my… Trace to a greasy, expensive, usually both too cold and too hot spread?

"We won't let them get close," Mom said, giving Trace a reassuring nod. "As we already told Aly, you're family, and we protect family." She shot Gramps a look. "There's also the little detail of the souls being our responsibility. You wouldn't be in this mess at all if it weren't for the decisions of Mooneys past and present."

"We'll get the rest of the Mooney coven back here," Dylan said. "These witches will be expecting us, but we didn't throw our all at them last time. They won't know what hit them."

Brody nodded. "I think it's the only way forward. And it should be tonight. If we give them too much time to gather their forces, who knows what we'll face."

I wriggled in my seat, my legs itching to throw myself at my brothers to keep them from leaving this room. "If we go tonight, we'll wind up facing more people than we might be capable of fighting. Even if we bring our biggest guns, we know they have the ammo to fight back. I think we should wait until midday tomorrow again. Go after them in smaller groups, whittle them down."

Gramps shook his head. "Your brothers are right, Pip. If we wait too long, we let them gain the upper hand. If we stay close on their heels, we stand a better chance of taking them by surprise."

My stomach lurched, and I stood up to put Trace's empty plate in the dishwasher, the smell of eggs and bacon testing my gag reflex. I'd come to terms with needing to track down the demonic witch, but I didn't want another big fight. We'd come so close to losing people the last time around, and there was no way we wouldn't be facing more of a challenge now. We couldn't afford to be cocky.

"I wish we'd had time to go back to that basement and see what they were working on," I said, my thoughts travelling to the diagrams on those white walls. "More information would probably help us here."

Dad carried over a few more plates. "Hopefully it won't matter. We'll stop them before they can do much to rally."

That was a pretty big fucking hope.

If only SMOAC had been able to do their jobs.

If only I didn't have to worry that asking them for help would get Gramps in trouble.

Unless…

As I set the plate in the rack, an idea bowled me over, and I stood up from my stoop so fast I cracked my head on the underside of the counter. I cursed and rubbed my skull.

"You all right?" Trace asked. He was half out of his seat, but I waved him back down.

"I'm fine. Do you remember why we couldn't bring Jet in to help us with Gramps?"

"Because you didn't want your grandfather getting arrested?" He shot a look at Gramps as though expecting him to be offended, but Gramps's expression didn't change.

"Exactly." I rested both palms on the island counter as I stared down my family. "What if we take this as an opportunity to throw that shadow off our family's back? We have information the department needs. If we work with them on this, it could put us in their good graces. We help them corral the witches they lost, and in return, they overlook the original crime."

Pride shone in Trace's eyes. "It's worth a shot."

Warmth filled my chest, and I looked to Gramps. "What do you think?"

He and Dad exchanged a glance, and Gramps shrugged. "I don't see the harm in asking, but you have to be prepared for your task force friend to take the whole thing over. If she's there in an official capacity, I don't think she'll leave room for us."

Jet's team had the training, the numbers, and the equipment my family lacked. If she offered to take over, there was no way I would complain about it.

"While you message her, I don't suppose anyone has a phone I can borrow?" Trace asked. "I should check in with Chip. The poor guy's probably losing his mind wondering how I'm doing."

"I wonder what that would look like," I said. "I didn't think he had that much of a mind left to lose."

"His fridge is empty, and he's on level seventy-eight of *Tetris*, I guarantee it."

"There's one in the living room, Trace," Mom said, then rolled her eyes at my sister's pointed stare. "Yes, we still have a landline, Val. Get over yourself."

Trace stepped out of the room, and I pulled my phone out of my pocket to text Jet.

Me: Call me when you can. We think we know where the missing witches are.

Only a few seconds later, my phone rang, and I walked into the hallway to answer it.

"Please tell me you have intel," Jet said when I answered.

I took a deep breath. Either I was about to ruin my friendship with an awesome, badass woman or I was about to solve most of my family's problems with a single proposal. "If you promise not to arrest Gramps for harbouring that amulet, I will tell you everything we know."

"Deal."

The lack of hesitation forced the breath out of me, and I dropped my forehead against the wall. "Really? You're not pissed that I'm holding my information for ransom?"

"I'm pissed at the people who brought Hazel and those other witches in and couldn't fucking hold on to them. Now it's on me to gather them up, which means I will make any deal it takes to get us there. The consequences can rest on the fuck-ups' heads."

I wandered down the hallway to the empty sitting room and stood at the window looking out at the snowy backyard. "We have a source that tells us they're heading back to Rockland."

"Goddammit. If they are, it's to pack up and leave."

"We plan to go back tonight to put an end to them. Any interest in joining us?"

Jet made a noise of frustration. "I should tell you to stay home and leave this to us, but you won't, will you?"

I opened my mouth to say that as long as they actually took them down, she was free to take the lead. But then I thought of my brothers and Gramps and the state of Trace when I'd found him, and my magic surged within me, throbbing at every joint. "Nope."

"I can give you an hour's head start," Jet said. "I'll limit my report to the fact that you called to give me the tip on where the house is located. Whatever happens before we get there is between you and this coven. I know how witch business goes."

All the fun with the promise of professional reinforcements, and Jet got her collar? Sounded like a win-win to me.

I gave her the address, she let me know her team would arrive around eight o'clock, and we hung up. Before going in search of Trace, I pulled up Simon's number but hesitated before sending him a message. He deserved to know what was going on. I'd been away from the pub for too many days with very few updates. I'd nearly died a few times already, and I might not survive tonight. The least I could do was give him the heads up that the management of the pub might be entirely his as of tomorrow.

Me: Hey

I thought I'd have to wait for a reply, but he must have been waiting to hear from me, because less than five seconds later, three little dots danced at the bottom of the screen.

Simon: You get him?

Me: Got him. Rough shape, but breathing.

Me: One of the witches had demonic magic. She got

Gramps. He's all right, Mom was there.

Simon: What are you involved in now???

I groaned, really wishing I knew the answer to that.

Me: Someone in SMOAC released everyone we brought in, along with Trace's old mentor. We're heading back out within the hour. Don't suppose you want to come? A little chaos might be just what we need to tip this in our favour. We could claim a plumbing issue at the pub. Davis would understand.

No little dots this time, and as the seconds stretched on, I sent him the address just in case but gave up waiting. Either he was free or he wasn't. He couldn't say I hadn't invited him to the party.

I headed into the living room to look for Trace and found him on the couch. He was still on the phone, head resting in his hand as he rubbed his brow. "Yeah, man, I told you, I'm fine. No, I'm good. Of course. As soon as we deal with things tonight, I'll swing by and see you, all right? We'll grab a beer, and I'll fill you in."

Trace raised his head and rolled his eyes when he spotted me, and I grinned for his benefit. It was good to know Chip had a heart tucked away in that graphic tee–clad chest somewhere. Even if he only brought it out on special occasions.

"So what do you say? Will you get us those infrared eyes on that house again? Perfect. Anything else you can send us?"

I sat beside Trace, so I was able to hear Chip's answer as though he were on speaker.

"Do you still have the spell-blocking amulets I sent you?"

I shook my head and mimed it exploding, and Trace pressed his lips together. "No. They took mine, and Alyssa used up her enchantment."

"Your tab is climbing fast."

"You love me enough to give me a discount." I sagged into the cushions, and Trace reclined next to me. "How many more of those can you send over?"

"I have another three lying around," Chip said.

"Three's a good start. Any way to make it ten?"

Chapter 36
Alyssa

I COULDN'T BELIEVE that only seven hours after our first visit, we were back at the house in Rockland.

I'd enjoyed all of a nap and a meal and had to rely on caffeine and no small amount of chocolate to gear me up for round two. So we were in a really good place.

Val had stayed home with Gramps. Her magic was only just returning, and everyone in the family agreed she'd be too high risk in a fight. Gramps had argued for a while before accepting he'd be at a disadvantage while he recovered, but he'd helped us come up with a plan of attack before we'd left.

Mom and Dad were with me, as were Brody and Dylan, because of course. Kyle's magic had taken a hit from one of the witches guarding the perimeter, so he had to sit out as well, but we had Avery, Grayson, Hilary and Tony. Three down against who knew how many witches, which wasn't the best start. Gramps had called as many of the other cousins as he could, but with our plans so last minute, none of them were able to join us in battle, and with SMOAC standing in reserve, I didn't see the point of more of our family risking themselves to play reinforcements.

At least this time we had Trace on our side, and while the souls made him a bit of a wild card, I felt much better about our odds. Worst case, he unleashed his guests and burned everyone around him to cinders. The thought that the souls might take control of him and refuse to release their hold didn't scare me even a little bit.

Which was why I didn't keep an iron grip on his hand as I drove us to Rockland. Chip was back on Val's headset, but this time Trace was our point of contact, using my phone to keep his friend in play, and already he was spouting bad news.

"There are more people at the house this time," he relayed. "We're looking at about twenty."

I swallowed around a cresting wave of anxiety. "Actually twenty, or is this another glitch?"

"Actually twenty. But he says he hasn't seen anyone go into the basement, so he's confident that's everyone."

"Thanks for the silver lining, Chip."

Twelve of us against twenty of them. I closed my eyes and

grounded myself in the present. We knew they had a few heavy hitters in their ranks, but we weren't powerless. Once we cleared out the lackeys, we could team up against the known power players. It would be dicey, and I couldn't guarantee we'd all walk out of here tonight, but we would dole out some damage.

I tightened my one-handed grip on the steering wheel and did my best not to crush Trace's finger bones on my other side. "This is ridiculous. We should call this off, shouldn't we? Why should I put my family at risk when Jet and her team are on their way?"

Trace stared out the window, his thumb gently stroking my palm. "It's true. We could absolutely leave this in their hands."

In the distance, we caught sight of lights shining from the house. Silhouettes appeared in the windows as someone closed the curtains. Far enough away that we wouldn't be noticed, I pulled to the side of the road, and the cars behind me followed suit.

For a moment, I sat staring at the house through the driver's side window, mentally jumping back and forth between our few options.

"We don't have to involve ourselves any more than we have," I said. "At most, we can sit on the house and make sure no one leaves before the task force gets here."

"It's true. Jet would be grateful for our help that far."

I frowned at him. "You're sitting there agreeing with everything I say, which means you have opinions of your own. What are they?"

Trace met my eye, then pressed a button on his headset to mute the call before shifting in his seat to face me. He took both my hands in his. "I want you to be safe. I admire you more than I can say for daring to come out here twice in twenty-four hours to take these guys down, but you're right. You don't have anything to prove. Do I want to go in there and rip off a head or two? Yes. Would it be wise? No. Is that enough to stop me?" He met my eye, but his expression was closed off. "Probably not. Hazel might be in there, and even if she's not, those people need to be brought in. It's what I do."

I squeezed his hands and fought against the anger that rose at his implication. "You think you're going in there without me? You must have been more damaged than I realized. I don't think so. I'm not giving them a chance to get their hands on you again. If you go in, we all go in."

"I have more power than all of you combined. I could make sure your family stays safe."

Fear curled its icy fingers around my heart. "To tap into that power, you'd need to give your guests full control."

Sympathy cut through his previously blank stare, and I scoffed in disgust as I jerked my hands away and threw myself out of the car to get some air. I couldn't believe what he was suggesting.

Behind us, Dad started to open his door, having taken my exit as the cue that we were moving, but Mom rested her hand on his shoulder to stop him, and he quickly retreated.

Trace slid out of the car and came around to my side. "Come on, princess, I'm not saying it'll come to last-resorts, but we can't ignore the possibility that we'll need to strike hard. You've got more power than most of these witches. I know we stand a chance without my souls." The lines around his eyes hardened, and silver-yellow magic danced through his irises as his voice filled with desperation. "But I'm terrified for you. If Hazel touches you—If anything happens—"

"But if something happens to you, I'll be fine?" I snapped, fear and anger and a sense of inevitability clawing at me, making it so damn difficult to breathe. "Did the whole summoning-my-family-and-raiding-the-house-to-rescue-you not register at all, Trace? You keep making these sacrifices for me, throwing yourself into boiling oil to save me, and I have to wonder if it's because you care or if you just have some hero complex."

As though my words were a slap, he jerked his head back. For a breath, the yellow in his eyes brightened, then yellow and silver disappeared as he wrapped himself around me and pulled me tight to his chest. "A fair point. To be honest, I'm not used to doing this job with someone at my back." He bowed his forehead against mine. "All right. What do you want to do? Spread out around the perimeter and tell Jet she's free to move in? We can help pick off the dregs as they scatter."

My chest relaxed, and I nodded. "I think so. We'll spread word back through the cars. Monitor and report, no engage—"

The surge of power that burst from the house stole the rest of my words, and Trace tightened his grip on me as the ground rocked beneath our feet.

I looked around. "What the hell was that?"

No longer waiting for a signal, the rest of my family piled out of their cars and hurried towards us.

Trace tapped his headset to bring Chip into the call. "We just had an energy surge here. Any idea what's going on?"

I couldn't make out Chip's reply, but I heard his urgency even from a foot away, and Trace paled. "Stay on top of it, let us know if anything changes."

He waited until the others moved closer, then levelled a stare at me. "He says if we plan on moving, we better do it fast. He can't get a read on what the magic is, but it's creating one hell of a heat source. If I had to guess, they took that spell they used against me and are using their souls to amplify it. They must know we're here—or at least that someone's coming."

I looked at the eleven people with me, trying not to think too hard about the twenty waiting inside. Jet wouldn't be here for another half hour. Who knew what kind of power the dark coven could draw in that amount of time? We might not be able to stop them, but with a solid enough strike, we could keep them busy until SMOAC arrived.

"Anyone who wants to back out now can, no judgement. Chip was able to courier us five spell-blocking amulets, which will deflect any stray magic and do some of our warding work for us, but we'll still be on the hook for defence, and seven of us will be unprotected."

"Mary, you should get one," Dad said, pushing Mom towards me. "Our healer needs all the safeguards she can get."

Mom flexed her jaw. "If that's the case, Avery and Aly should each get one too."

I looked at my cousin in surprise. I hadn't realized she'd been training. Avery flushed but stepped forward, and Trace handed one to her.

I hesitated to take one for myself. Much as I wanted to make sure my dad and brothers were safe, I couldn't leave Trace vulnerable.

"We'll flip for the rest," I said.

"Like hell we will," Trace growled. "You're taking one. You know they'll target you because of me."

"He's right," Dad said. "You both need to take one. My wards are strong, and so are Brody's. We'll be all right."

"And I'll stick close to Dylan to protect his ass," Brody said.

Anxiety squeezed my stomach. So many members of my family would be standing in the line of fire, and I would be limited in how I could help them. We needed more reinforcements.

Before we could agree on who took the fifth amulet, shadows stirred behind the cars. As one, we summoned our magic. Trace's eyes took on their yellow glow, and I cursed that the spirits already had such a hold on him. Avery threw a ward over the whole group, and Dad channelled some of his magic into it to bolster its strength.

The shadows approached, two people with their hands up, and when they stepped into the glow of the headlights, the air rushed out of my body.

"Simon?" I tamped down my magic, then flew across the grass to wrap my arms around his waist.

He hugged me back with an especially tight squeeze. "You didn't think I'd let you go in twice without me, did you? I learned my lesson after this afternoon. The guilt isn't worth staying away."

I stepped back and noticed Reverie beside him. She looked as out of place here as I would in her swanky club—black minidress, black heels, plump red lips, deeply shadowed and lined eyes that made her full lashes and star-filled irises blend in with the darkness.

"I can't believe you're here," I said.

She grinned, showing off a faint point to her teeth. "Simon mentioned there's a witch involved in stealing demonic power. How could I resist?"

I shot a wary look at the house. "I'm grateful you came, but I don't know if it's safe for you to be here. Or for us. Whatever they're doing in that house, it's huge. If it sets your chaos magic off, you could turn the entire property into a mess of necrotizing vines or something."

Simon frowned and rolled his neck. "I know what you mean. I've never felt magic like this before. It's tugging on me from here."

"We shouldn't risk it," Reverie said, and I looked at her to find her staring at Simon with genuine concern in her starry eyes. "Not with your family here."

Did I imagine the way she put a slight emphasis on *family*? As though she needed to remind him why we might be important? While I appreciated her acknowledging the role we played in his life, I wanted to know why she thought it was necessary. What did she know about my friend that I didn't?

Simon scowled and his eyes flashed red. "You're right. Rev and I will stay out here and deal with anyone who tries to run." He grabbed my hand and squeezed until I met his eye. "You do whatever it takes to stay safe in there."

His worry was like a soul hug, and I bundled him up in another real one. Just in case it was our last. "I promise."

The spell inside surged again, and Simon's bronze magic trickled over his arms—a good sign that it was time to give him space.

Trace and I exchanged a glance, and I exhaled a sharp breath. If we were going to do this, we'd best do it.

I turned to face the house. "All right, everyone. Wards up. Be prepared for anything."

Chapter 37
Trace

IT FELT STRANGE coming up on the house from the front. The first time I'd come here, I'd been unconscious. I'd woken up in the basement bound to that chair. Now that I was back, I appreciated how normal the place looked with its perfectly manicured lawn and freshly painted shutters. A person driving by might imagine a well-to-do family lived here.

Until anyone with even a smidge of magic made it halfway up the driveway. Then they'd want to turn and run as badly as I did.

Whatever purpose this coven's spell had, it was overwhelming in its dark, acrid tang. It slid over my skin and into my pores, coating my insides with a thick sludge that clogged my joints and made me want to retch. The souls within me writhed in discomfort, and they pressed so close against the limits of their bindings that their power seeped through my skin, so strong I felt it like fissures that spread from my nail beds and crept up my arms.

Alyssa kept a close eye on me as we approached the house, and I was certain she saw my struggle. She'd double-checked that I was wearing my amulet three times since we began our trek, and her worry gnawed at me.

"If you're focused on me, you're not paying attention to your own safety," I said in a low voice. "Don't worry about me. I've got this."

She nodded and scanned the porch instead, but I caught the way her attention flicked my way as we approached.

Simon and Reverie disappeared into the shadows of the property, and the rest of Alyssa's family trailed behind us. Their wards were up, and I sensed the hum of their magic as they gathered it between them. With the perimeter guarded by our demon allies, it meant we were free to bring everyone inside. Courtney—the stronger offence and wearing the fifth spell blocker—Grayson, and Jennifer would stick near the front door, ensuring our way out remained clear. Mary would stay with them, throwing wards and providing healing energy to anyone who needed to retreat, while Avery would come with the rest of us to patch people up on the go.

Hilary and Henry were the stronger warders, while Tony,

Dylan, and Brody would be on take-down duty, clearing out the low-level witches so we could focus on the three we knew were a problem—and any other surprises that might be waiting for us.

The thought that Hazel might be inside curdled my blood, but I refused to let it distract me. She either was or she wasn't, the end goal was the same. None of them would walk out of here freely tonight.

We were as prepared as we could be. Even if all we did was keep the witches busy until SMOAC arrived, so be it. They wouldn't make it past us.

I drew in a breath, summoned my magic into my hands, then threw it at the front door so it burst off its hinges and struck the wall on the opposite side of the foyer.

Two witches immediately stepped into the doorway, spells ready. Dylan and Tony gave them no time to attack first, unleashing their atmospheric magic in pulses that made my eardrums rattle. The spirit witches were thrown off their feet. One landed on his back, his head cracking against the ceramic tile, and the other one smashed into an end table against the wall, reducing it to splinters.

Four more witches approached, two coming through the open archway of the dining room to the left, two from the living room on the right, but Mary and Henry threw their double ward over the family, and the spells bounced off it, sending the two witches on the left hurtling out of the way, while the two on the right threw up wards of their own.

Avery launched an atmospheric pulse at the first witch who'd come from the dining room. She dodged it, but it landed in the chest of the other, who flew backwards and struck her head against the china cabinet. I took advantage of the smashed pottery by grabbing hold of a larger shard with my telekinetic power and aiming it at the first witch's throat. Blood spurted from the slashed carotid, and the witch clapped her hands to her neck in a futile effort to staunch the flow as she sagged to the floor.

Alyssa gagged and turned away, pushing further into the house.

I moved so I stood between her and the gore, wanting to save her from seeing more than she had to.

Shouts and screams erupted outside, and Chip spoke up in my ear. "Not sure how I missed them. Five closing in on the house. But looks like your demon pets have it in hand."

I didn't have time to update Alyssa before another four witches came into the dining room from the kitchen beyond. They'd combined their magic, and the swell of it made my ears pop. I drew my mixed power into my hands and felt the moment Alyssa added hers to it, taking it from me and expanding it. Another bump of power filled me, and I glanced over my shoulder to find Henry with his hands raised behind us.

Their spell slammed into ours. The impact was a punch to my solar plexus, and it took all my strength to hold our counter spell steady. Alyssa's brow furrowed with concentration, and sweat beaded along her hairline, but she stepped forward and released a cry as she shoved a second spell behind the first and threw it at the quartet in front of us.

One woman fell to her knee, and the man beside her keeled over, clutching his chest as the light faded from his eyes. The other two drew on their natural powers, and fire sprouted from the man's hand as the woman summoned a knife from somewhere behind her and threw it towards us.

I caught the blade with my magic and redirected it at the witch on one knee, driving it deep into her chest. Without giving myself time to breathe, I threw my power at another piece of broken pottery and hurled it into the fire-wielder's eye.

The knife-throwing witch backed up against the wall, drawing more power around her. Alyssa cried out and shoved me to the side as the spell flew, and the mirror behind me shattered. Alyssa stomped her foot, sending the tiles shuddering beneath her, and pushed out with her hands. The woman against the wall let out a sharp scream before her chest caved in and she sank to the floor.

Alyssa wavered on her feet, tears in her eyes, and Henry made it to her before I could. He wrapped his arms around her and held her close.

"You did good, baby girl. We can't afford to hold back. No guilt."

He brushed the tears off her face, kissed her forehead, then gave her a gentle push towards me. I led the way, and we found ourselves in a large kitchen filled with stainless-steel appliances, black granite countertops, and dark green backsplashes. It was striking and might have been cozy with the right family cooking in it, but all I could see were the jars filled with body parts lined up on the table.

Alyssa groaned and walked through the room without stopping. The Trace Wyatt without souls contained in his centre would have done the same. Unfortunately, the Trace Wyatt with souls struggled to withstand the rise of fury at the idea that all these people and creatures had been pinned down, tortured, mutilated, and now stored for whatever magic the various elements contained.

The rage began as a creeping heat from my centre to my face and spread to my fingers with rising force. My vision blurred, and I raised my shaking hands in front me. Unable to stop myself, unable to control whatever the souls were trying to do, I swung my arms and watched the jars fly off the counter and smash into the wall in a spray of glass and preservation potion. Someone shrieked behind me, and magic buzzed over my skin as a ward was summoned.

Alyssa stood in the doorway of the next room looking back

at me, sympathy and no small amount of worry in her eyes.

I heaved a few breaths through my tight lungs until my anger subsided enough that my legs unlocked, and then I strode forward, not slowing when I hit the doorway even though everything that lay beyond it was unknown. I had the spell-blocking amulet and the power of hundreds of spirits within me—what did I need to be afraid of?

Alyssa stayed close behind me, her hands raised, power pulsing from her fingers. The rest of our team wisely held back, not only allowing us to go first but keeping space between me and them. I didn't want them to get caught up in whatever happened next, but my hold was so fragile.

As we turned into a larger sitting room, the power we'd sensed from outside the house grew more intense. It rushed in my ears and skittered over my skin, making my hair dance. Alyssa's neck was spattered with goosebumps, and I didn't miss the way her hands shook as she wove a spell, readying herself for whatever might come.

"I think we need to get a move on," Brody grumbled somewhere behind me.

No one argued with him. We'd walked into a timebomb. The only way to get out of here alive was to diffuse it.

So far we'd taken down ten of the twenty witches, which meant somewhere in this house, another ten were pooling their power, including the three—or more—magical Godzillas.

Whatever spell they were brewing would be enough to level this place.

"You're closing in on them," Chip said in my ear. "From what I can make out, you should be right on them. You don't see anything?"

"If we did, you think we'd be standing here?" I snapped, but I knew he was worried about what we might face. For all his snark, he was a momma hen whenever I stepped in over my head. Which was often enough.

Alyssa looked at me, and I filled her in on Chip's warning. She frowned and glanced around the empty sitting room, which was a giant dead end.

"Basement?" she asked, keeping her voice low. She sounded skeptical, and I agreed. We'd both been down there. While I'd noticed a lot of nasty stuff on those shelves during our exit and nothing in the room they'd held me in, there wasn't space for ten witches and a spell that big. Plus Chip wouldn't have been able to see them on the infrared if they were downstairs.

"Any magic to follow?" I asked.

Alyssa shook her head, the furrow between her eyebrows deep.

They had to be here somewhere. Even if they had a cloaking spell strong enough to hide the entire group in this room, there was no way they'd contain the source of that spell.

I stepped farther into the living room and walked a path

around the perimeter. Alyssa got the hint and began on the other side near the windows. I thought it unlikely that there would be any hidden room along the exterior wall, but I appreciated her thoroughness.

With my hand pressed to the drywall, I opened myself to the flow of magic in the air, following it as one would a draft. The faint tingle of power made the hairs on my arms stand on end and pulled me towards a wide bookcase in the back corner.

Alyssa finished her side of the tour and met me there. We exchanged a look, and she scanned the bookshelf at eye level. I ran my fingers over the spines, testing each book as I passed it. Alyssa sucked in a breath when her gaze landed on an old, worn copy of *Great Expectations*. I dropped my hand so it covered hers, and together we pulled out the book.

The door opened, the magic hit us with the force of a light-rail train, and the souls inside me broke through their barrier and took over.

Chapter 38

Alyssa

I STUMBLED BACKWARDS into my dad, who caught me before I could hit the ground. He steadied me, and my attention jumped to Trace, who'd barely staggered at the force of that magical punch.

When I moved up beside him and caught a look at his face, I understood why.

Trace was nowhere to be found.

His violet eyes were gone, turned full yellow with veins flowing down his cheeks. It was exactly the way he'd looked when he'd turned Nathalie into a crispy witch but even more intense. Fissures of yellow magic seeped out from under his shirt and glowed through the fabric, his hair seemed to float in the air around his head, and when I got too close, my magic crackled as though he'd turned it to static.

My mouth went dry, my heart raced, and I didn't know if I should burst into tears or step out of the way and let him charge through the hidden room.

I did neither. Forcing myself to accept the turn of events, I embraced my new partner's strengths and pushed my way through the doorway first. We'd known this might happen. The moment we'd noticed the brewing spell, I had accepted the likelihood that he'd lose control. I couldn't back out now that it had happened, so we'd have to see it through, whether it was Trace at my side or the hundreds of souls he carried with him. As long as he remembered who his allies were, we could get through this.

After we'd won, I'd worry about getting him back.

Anxiety crawled its tendrils through my brain, threatening to choke every conscious thought with worst-case scenarios, but this was neither the time nor the place. I stretched my neck to relieve the suffocating tension and stepped down the two steps towards the full working coven.

The ten witches we'd yet to face sat in a circle, seemingly unconcerned at our intrusion. Mr. Ghoul was there, and beside him was the demonic bitch. Next to her was the other elemental witch who'd fought beside her earlier—the one whose chest had almost exploded under Dylan's attack. The rest of them, as yet unknown, channelled so much power my legs grew weak.

I scanned each face, wondering if one of them might be Hazel, but no one paid me the least bit of attention. Their eyes were closed, and their lips moved in a low, murmured incantation. As though they believed there was nothing we could do to stop them.

As though they believed they'd already won.

I took a moment to assess the room and come up with a speedy plan. The space was long and narrow, an obvious extension on the house. In here there were no bookcases or comfy furniture. It was as bare as the room they'd kept Trace in except for the cushions the witches sat on. Two windows faced the massive backyard that sloped towards the Ottawa River, but there was no other door out of here. If they wanted to escape, they'd have to come through me and Trace—and I suspected we wouldn't be much of a deterrent. Especially not once their spell was complete.

Now that we were here, I could make out exactly what it was. A body lay in the middle of the circle, back arched and limbs twitching, mouth open in a silent scream, as yellow magic wrapped around it and burrowed into it. So many souls spun through the air, attempting to escape the barriers of the ritual but stuck within it. For now. As soon as the incantation was complete, these witches would absorb the power between them and level themselves up times a bajillion or so.

Standing so close to the power source, my spell-blocking

amulet warmed, repelling stray wisps of magic that split from the spell to seek me out. Even with the protection, my magic churned within me, rising to meet it, and I firmed my concentration to remain in control.

"Well, well, well," a woman said as she rose to her feet. Long black hair fell over her shoulder, and her brown eyes were lit with yellow. "Andrew Wyatt. I knew you were nosing around, but I hoped rather than expected to cross paths while I was in town."

I stiffened. This was her. The woman who'd seduced an eighteen-year-old into a life of dark spirit magic, then thrown him under the bus to save her own skin. Rage flooded me, and I balled my fists to keep my magic close. I looked from her to Trace, but no recognition sparked in his eyes. Nothing showed in them at all beyond his deep, widespread loathing for everyone in the room.

Hazel canted her head. "Or is Andrew Wyatt in there at all anymore? Looks to me like someone indulged in a bit too much of the forbidden." She smiled. "Don't worry, darling. We'll take care of you."

Trace's eyes brightened with the same pulsing glow as the spell, and when he raised his hands, the barrier around the corpse glowed in response.

"Stop it, Trace, you're fuelling it," I warned, but he was too far gone to hear me. He unleashed his mixed silver-yellow power towards Hazel. She warded herself and redirected his spell towards the bubble around the corpse. His magic skittered across it like tiny electrical charges before sinking into the spell and strengthening the ward.

"Add these souls to our arsenal, would you, David?" Hazel said. "I have somewhere else to be."

She blew us a kiss, gifted me an extra wink and a yellow-tinged spell, then climbed out the window and was gone.

I threw myself into the wall to dodge her spell, cursing our missed opportunity to grab her. Trace made to follow her, but Mr. Ghoul grinned and raised a yellow-wrapped hand. Trace gasped and lurched forward, and the glow on his skin grew brighter. I stepped towards him, not understanding what was happening but seeing enough to know he was in danger. Somehow this elemental witch was casting two powerful spells at once. How many souls did he carry to give him that much strength?

My amulet grew warmer, uncomfortably hot, as more magic bounced around the room.

A gasp sounded behind me, and I half turned to find Dad and Brody in the doorway, both of them pale as milk and shaking on their feet. They couldn't be here. The only reason I was still standing was because of the amulet. This spell was targeting souls. Anyone unprotected would risk losing theirs.

I summoned a small amount of magic into my hand and

sent a gentle pulse towards my family, pushing them out of the room.

The distraction cost me. When I turned back, a witch with ashy hair was on her feet. She didn't even stumble on the words of the incantation as she lobbed a yellow-hued spell my way.

I dropped into a crouch, and the magic burrowed into the wall. The drywall crumbled as though it had aged a century in a second, and mould spread like tendrils along the exposed studs.

My heart in my throat, my palms sweaty, I launched a counter spell. The witch crossed her arms in front of her and shielded herself with ease. The unfinished spell had to be fuelling them already. We needed to end it. To lure the witches out of the room and cut down their advantages.

My brain scrambled to come up with a plan. Trace had proved he was the idea guy, but right now, his ideas were blocked by the rage of the souls inside him. Our survival rested on me to get us out of this, which meant I needed to be rational.

Or maybe I needed to take a page from Simon's book.

Thinking only of unleashing as much chaos as possible, I launched myself at the two witches closest to me, knocking them out of the circle. We collapsed in a heap of limbs. Stray magic burned my exposed arms, and I threw up a ward to keep the worst of it off me. Breathing through the pain, I curled my fist and drove it into a woman's face. Her head thwacked against the floor and her dazed, yellow-tinted eyes rolled towards the ceiling.

The other witch grabbed my leg, and the tingle of spirit energy buzzed along his palm. By luck, he wasn't as strong magically as the others and couldn't uphold an attack and his connection to the barrier at the same time. In prioritizing the barrier, he left me open to swing my other leg out and kick him in the nose. Bone crunched and blood spurted across his face. He cried out and released me to protect his nose from further attack.

With my blood rushing in my ears, I rolled to my feet, moving away from the recovering witches, and launched a pulse at another two.

"Someone stop her," the demonic witch ordered. Mr. Ghoul's concentration was still focused on both Trace and their bigger incantation, but I caught the twitch of rage in the corner of his flattened mouth.

Another witch gathered up a spell and aimed at me, but before she could throw it, Trace stepped in front of me, his eyes shooting magical sparks, and released enough magic that half the witches around the circle skidded away from it, Mr. Ghoul included. The incantation fell silent, the spell interrupted. The power emanating from the barrier waned, and I used the opportunity to catch my breath and put my back to Trace's.

As the last of the central spell fizzled out, the demonic

witch laughed and rose from her seat around the circle. Red power wrapped around her fists, and I gulped as I braced for the force of it. The first blow hit me in the stomach, the second in the chest—right on the amulet. The stone shattered, and the defensive enchantments it contained spilled into the room. The witch grinned, and I rushed to strengthen my ward. I sensed Dad's energy bolstering it, but there was only so long he'd be able to help before his strength gave out. There were still eight witches in this room ready to fight, and I was now vulnerable.

Sweat dripped down the back of my neck, and my lungs burned with my heaving breaths, but I rushed to raise another ward to guard myself against the demonic witch's next attack. The ward held, but I flew backwards away from Trace into the wall. I doubled over, gasping, struggling to maintain even a thin shield to protect me.

There was no way we could win this, not the two of us against so many.

Even as I thought it, my family poured into the room, no longer affected by the tugging, soul-stealing spell, and the chaos I'd started turned widespread.

A heavy ward fell around me, powered by at least three witches. Brody came up by my side and tackled one of the rising witches to the ground while Dylan charged another one, his fists wrapped with magic to give his punches extra weight. He moved like someone sure on his feet, and I wouldn't have worried about him against the older guy he fought if it weren't for the demonic witch who'd drawn so much power from the incantation she was levitating.

Mr. I Survived a Hole in the Chest tried to sneak up behind me, but I caught a tendril of green magic in the corner of my eye and released my spell first, a one-two pulse that sent him careening into the window. The glass smashed, and blood oozed down the windowsill from where he'd landed on his throat.

Trace let out a cry and stumbled forward. I whirled around and grabbed his arm to steady him, then jerked my hand away when he turned his furious gaze on me. His power surged, yellow tendrils homing straight for me, and I warded myself against him as I darted out of his way.

Trace stepped towards me, ready to destroy another threat, and Mr. Ghoul grinned, his massive teeth sparkling in the reflection of the magic bouncing through the room. His attention was focused entirely on Trace, and strings of yellow bound the two together as David attempted to tear the souls from Trace's body.

Trace wavered on his feet, his face red, his jaw taut, as he fought to hold back. He was weakening, keeping his feet by sheer willpower. The air around him shimmered, and even as I threw a spell at two witches trying to close in on me, wrapping their heads in a vacuum that left them purple-faced and clawing at their throats for air, I caught the moment that the expression in Trace's eyes shifted into one of horrifying determination. There was no fear, no uncertainty. He was scrabbling at a mountain cliff, struggling to find purchase, and in another few seconds he would throw himself into the abyss to destroy this coven.

I wouldn't let that happen.

Allowing my power to rise to its highest levels, fully aware of how much it would drain me, I lifted my hands. The air crackled with the strength of my magic. It prickled my skin like a million tiny bee stings and resisted my draw, trying to reserve itself, but I pressed beyond all safe limits.

"Alyssa!" Dad called from behind me.

I ignored him. He'd said it himself—whatever it took to get out of here. No guilt.

Trace was falling. If someone didn't catch him, I would lose him. That mattered more to me than my limits. Right now, I had no limits.

As though he heard me or sensed my intentions, Trace craned his head to look at me. His eyes were still yellow, no sign of *him* to be found, but the tendons in his neck were strained and his muscles were so tightly wound his shoulders had bunched. Whatever was happening to the souls within him, he was putting every effort into breaking their hold.

He would never succeed. The only way for him to get free was for Mr. Ghoul to die, and the only way to achieve that was for the demonic witch to go first.

The red light around the woman spread, and the air wavered with rising heat. The bitch was brewing hellfire, and if she let it loose, the entire room would be ash.

Brody grabbed Dylan by the back of his shirt and tugged him behind his ward. The witches they'd gone after were down, either unconscious or dead. The others had pulled back to the corners of the room to avoid the demonic witch's attack.

Her eyes flew open, red-yellow swirls of power. My time was up.

With a last look at Trace, who put everything he had into freeing himself so he could reach me, I unleashed my magic.

It flowed through me in purple waves, streaming in thick, heavy ribbons as it wound around every witch, awake or otherwise. I was the kraken and they were the ships that had trespassed too far. They'd threatened my family, threatened my safety. They'd spread their cancer through my city. Clyde Corrick had shown me how far some witches were willing to go for power, but in doing so, he'd taught me how far I'd have to go to stop them.

The weaker witches on the floor thrashed against the squeezing tentacles of my magic. Their faces turned red, then a darker shade of purple before they stopped flailing.

Two mid-level witches attempted to raise their defences, but in focusing on me, they forgot about the witches behind me. While Tony, Dad, and Avery held the ward, Dylan added his power to mine, wrapping the witches from head to toe in a thick net and squeezing until their magic was fully bound beneath it.

Their terror at finding themselves powerless lasted only as long as it took for them to draw the ritual daggers at their waists. They ran at us, but Dylan and Brody were ready for them with a well-honed offence. One pulse cracked the first witch's ribs and almost hollowed out his middle. The second witch made it within a few feet of me before she was thrown backwards into Mr. Ghoul's spirit magic. Her screams rippled through my ears as she decomposed before us, leaving nothing but aged bones on the ground.

Only the demonic witch and Mr. Ghoul remained. By the woman's smile, she was just gearing up, and I feared what it meant that I'd already spent almost everything I had. My magic wrapped around her, but she moved as though she didn't notice it. She raised her arms in front of her, revealing ruby-tinted flames that danced between her fingers. Hellfire burned significantly hotter than regular fire and was nearly impossible to extinguish. One ember could consume the entire room.

I tightened the leash I'd thrown around her, and she reached down and sliced through it with her flaming hand. The tentacle snapped, and I cried out as I dropped to one knee. I couldn't stay down—not if I wanted to save Trace, who'd fallen onto all fours, sucking in breaths, the air around him thick with the souls that were being dragged from his pores.

I shouted and threw another pulse at the pair at the same time the demonic witch released her fire. She was thrown backwards as my magic mixed with hers, and both spells scattered across the length of the room. A spark landed on a cushion in the corner, another by the window. Two of the still witches on the floor were immediately devoured in a flashfire that turned my whole world white for a heartbeat.

One spark landed on Mr. Ghoul's sleeve, and that spark was the straw that broke him. He jumped to his feet and smacked at his arm to extinguish the ember before it could catch, but he should have known it would be useless. In another moment, the entire sleeve was aflame, and once more he was tearing at his clothes to save himself from a worse fate.

Trace collapsed, and Brody and Dylan dashed to his sides to drag him backwards, far from the demonic witch, who was shaking off my spell. She was moving, but I could barely make her out through the fire that was rapidly sweeping across the room.

Heat pressed in on me, drying my sweat as soon as the beads formed. The ward around me wavered, weakened now that my brothers had dropped their ends of it.

We had to get out. Had to take the loss. The demonic witch raised her hands again, but with the last of my strength, I threw out a final pulse. This one caught her at the perfect angle to knock her into the support beam. She cracked her head against the wood and wavered on her feet.

Fire licked towards my shoes, smoke filled my lungs, and I toppled into the wall to brace myself. The world went dark as the shouts of more people arriving in the house echoed behind me.

Chapter 39
Trace

THE DRIVE HOME was quiet, each of us lost in our thoughts. Or lack of them, in my case. I was too exhausted to have thoughts. Too drained to be able to do anything but sit and stroke Alyssa's hair as she lay sleeping with her head on my shoulder. My guest souls were silent, likely as wrung out as I was.

Mary sat in the backseat with us, while Avery drove us home.

Henry drove the other car with Brody and Dylan, and I assumed Hilary, Tony, and Grayson travelled with Courtney and Jennifer in the third. Grayson had been hit hard, and although Mary had been able to patch him up, they were on their way to the Peaview Supernatural Hospital to make sure he'd survive the night.

Simon and Reverie hadn't said anything, but I had no doubt they'd be at the Mooney house when we arrived. Simon had nearly burned down the rest of the house when he'd climbed through the window to get Alyssa out of the fire, but he'd been the only one able to withstand the heat.

I might have felt jealous that he'd played hero to save her, but I'd come too close to being magically flayed. As it was, every inch of my body, inside and out, was tender from having the souls nearly stripped from me. They'd hung on tightly, anchoring themselves in my veins, digging themselves by spiritual claw and tooth into the essence of my being, and still David had almost won.

A few more seconds, and I'd have been a shell of a man, my borrowed magic and my natural abilities nonexistent, my mind snapped, invisible wounds bleeding. As soon as the connection had broken, my own magic had instinctively pulled them back. The barrier was in place, if less stable than it had been.

Alyssa had saved me. But at what cost?

She hadn't woken since her final blast of magic at the woman with the demonic power.

Even when Jet had ordered us to stay put while she and her team cleared the house, Alyssa didn't stir. Dylan and Henry had settled me in the backseat as we waited, and Alyssa had slept. She'd stayed unconscious when Jet's lieutenant had emerged a few minutes later with the final tally. Including the witches our team had taken down outside, we were looking at twenty-two dead, one unconscious.

David had survived the fire, but had not evaded capture this time. The demonic witch, however, was gone again. As was Hazel.

For tonight, I didn't have the energy to lose myself to the spinning thoughts of having seen her again, but they lurked like shadows in the back of my mind.

Hazel was free. She was back. And she was coming for me.

My heart gave a lukewarm thrash, and I gritted my teeth. At least we knew who was behind this coven. We could plan for her. We had time.

After a few more questions, Jet had let us go, giving us the heads up that someone would be around in a day or two to get a full report. Stumbling with fatigue, we headed back to Ashton.

The lights were on at the Mooney house when we arrived. Val opened the door and ushered us into the living room, where Gramps was sitting on the edge of the couch, a bottle of whiskey close at hand to offer anyone who wanted a glass. Everyone partook except Mary, who stayed with Alyssa after Brody brought her to her bedroom.

I wobbled on my feet, torn between joining Alyssa and sitting on the couch, but in the end I'd dropped down next to Gramps, too exhausted to make my way upstairs.

Gramps handed me a drink, and I sipped it with a trembling hand.

"You made it," he said, looking at me and then at each of the other battle-worn witches around the room. "Whatever else you did doesn't matter. You're breathing, and that means you won."

Dylan scowled. "That bitch got away again. I could have stopped her the first time. I fucked up."

"All right," Gramps said with a nod, "so you fucked up. You think we all don't fuck up a billion times a day? You learn, you grow, you adapt. Next time, you take her down."

The thought of a next time made me sink into the cushions and close my eyes as I took another sip of my drink. I couldn't wrap my head around the idea that we weren't finished. Tomorrow I would. Tomorrow, I'd be ready to go, ready to stake my claim and show Hazel and her lackeys I wouldn't be pushed around again. Tonight, I wanted to curl into a ball and lick my wounds.

And at some point, I had to let Chip know I was alive. David's spells had fried the headset, which meant, aside from the moving figures on his infrared camera, he had no idea who'd walked out of that house.

It was a miracle the answer was all of us.

Other than Grayson, the closest we'd come to losing anyone was Alyssa, but I had to believe she'd pull through.

Though when Mary staggered into the living room, pale and haggard, I snapped to my feet, striding towards her as though I'd been sitting home on my ass all evening.

"Is she all right?" I asked.

She forced a smile. "She'll be fine. She drained herself. Almost to the breaking point, but there's a spark of magic still in there."

Henry put his arm around his wife and escorted her to the couch. She squeezed my hand as she passed, and I took it as her suggestion for me to go to her daughter. I didn't need to be told twice.

I set down my drink and trudged up the stairs. By the time I reached the top, I was out of breath and clinging to the banister, but I found my footing to walk the rest of the way to the closed bedroom door.

It was dark inside, the blinds having been pulled down to protect against the rising sun when it came in the morning. I appreciated how optimistic Mary was that she'd considered it. More than once tonight, I'd wondered if I'd see another sunrise.

Unfortunately, the darkness meant I couldn't make out anything about Alyssa except the rough shape of her body under the covers. I couldn't see her face or even the reassuring rise and fall of her breath as she slept.

I headed to the bathroom first, careful to leave the light off until the door was closed so I didn't disturb her. A quick look in the mirror guaranteed that a quick look was all I'd take as I changed out of my soiled clothes—another set for the trash—and hopped in a speedy shower to wash off the blood and magic. The tub seemed empty without Alyssa to share it with me, so I didn't dawdle. Once dry, I pulled on a clean pair of grey sweats and a *Legend of Zelda* graphic tee, more loaners from Dylan and Brody, and finally made my way to bed.

For the third night in a row, I tucked myself against Alyssa. Her skin was chilled, so I held her close, nuzzling her neck to take in the soft scent of aloe vera. A quiet, happy murmur escaped the back of her throat as she wriggled against me, and I relaxed. She was alive, and Mary was right—as long as she had a single spark, she would recharge and come back fighting. My princess wasn't a quitter.

I swore to myself I'd stay awake for a while to ensure she slept well, but before long, the drain of the day swept over me, and I joined Alyssa in sweet oblivion.

Chapter 40
Alyssa

One week later…

I FINISHED WIPING down the last table of the night. Mooney's had been closed for a while, and I knew I should go home and get some rest, but there was something relaxing about puttering around in my natural habitat. Especially after so many days away.

Despite all the horrible, terrifying events in my life that had taken their first steps in this pub, it was one of the few places I felt safe. And I needed safe right now. There were two witches on the loose who were hunting for power, and I doubted their defeat in Rockland would be enough to get in their way. If they were quiet, they were planning, and I feared what their next attempt would look like.

But they weren't the only ones making plans, a detail I took to heart. They wouldn't catch us unawares again.

"You're good if I go?" Simon asked as he came in from the back office.

I smiled at him. "I told you to get lost an hour ago. You don't need to stick around. I'm fine."

He crossed his arms. "You've had to sit down three times tonight. Don't think I didn't notice. Are you sure you'll be okay to get home? I can stick around another half hour and drive you."

"Thank you. Thank you for being amazing." I wrapped my arms around his waist, and he held me tightly before pressing a kiss into my hair. "I'll be all right. I'll text you when I get home."

"Promise?"

"Promise."

I pushed him away, and he gave me one last pointed look before he headed out. Since the events with the spirit witches, Simon and I had rediscovered our balance, but something about him still struck me as *off*. I'd tried to bring his attitude up a few times, but he'd brushed his issues aside as fatigue. He was helping Reverie with her new club as much as he was working his shifts at Mooney's, and the split attention was wearing on him. Or so he claimed. I wasn't sure I believed him, but until he decided to open up to me, that was the best I'd get.

I locked the door behind him and continued with my clean-up.

Only when the knock sounded a few minutes later did I accept the real reason I'd stayed as long as I had.

With a flutter in my chest, I unlocked the door and opened it enough to peer through the gap. Trace winked at me from the other side, and I opened the door wider to let him in. He closed it behind him, locked it, and followed me to the bar.

"You're looking good," he said, and my face nearly combusted.

I poured us both a pint and set them between us. "Thanks. Amazing what a few days of sleep can do for a person. I think I've de-aged." I played with the ends of my highlighted brown hair to show it off, and he gave the strands a gentle tug.

"Your beauty is timeless, princess. No amount of sleep can improve perfection."

I shoved the glass towards him. "Drink more and continue. I like where this is going."

He chuckled and made himself comfortable on the stool across from me.

"How about you?" I asked. "You've been okay?"

Unlike last time, Trace hadn't disappeared after the night in Rockland. He'd been an almost constant presence. I'd stuffed him full of food and ordered him to sleep until his eyes couldn't stay closed any longer. Only in the last couple days had he gone off. To pack up his rental on Metcalfe, he told me, and it had taken all my self-control not to give him shit for having been only a few blocks away and never reaching out to me.

I only held back from letting him have it because of what he had to be going through right now. Hazel was free. He'd seen her for the first time in a decade, and she'd ordered her people to kill him. She hadn't even had the decency to take him on herself. He had to be reeling, but I didn't want to press.

"I've been good," he said. "The spirits have settled in again. A bit more comfortably this time." He grimaced. "For better or worse."

I frowned and leaned on my elbows. "What do you mean?"

He shrugged. "Before, I had them on a tight leash. They were inside me but not part of me. After what David did, after all the exercise they got trying to stay put and not go over to him, they've sunk in a bit deeper."

"So getting rid of them…"

"Will be more of a challenge," he admitted, and rested his hand over mine. "But we'll find a way. They still want to be free, and I want to free them. I won't sit on this."

I sipped my drink and considered what he was saying. The spirits that had called him a temporary home were starting to renovate. What would happen if they claimed squatter's rights? Would they leave space for the man they'd invaded, or would they try to force out the previous tenant?

I tried to tell myself it wasn't a tonight problem, but the anxiety remained. Or maybe it was that all the anxieties of the past weeks had piled up and this was the final one to tip me over the edge into a full, uncomfortable attack.

"Hey." Trace tugged on my hand, guiding me around the side of the bar until I stood between his legs. "Don't stress about me. Whatever happens, we'll see it through, okay?"

I raised an eyebrow and cupped the back of his neck. "You're not going to run off on me again?"

He hit me with the full force of his violet gaze. "How could I? I can't see my way clear of this mess without you guiding me. I'm staying right here."

I slid my arms around him, and he quirked an eyebrow. My heart fluttered, my core warmed, and I leaned in to brush my lips over his. He curled his hands into the back of my shirt to pin me against him as a low moan escaped his throat.

My tongue darted out over his lips, and I tasted the chocolate, nutty notes of his beer, nudging me to deepen our kiss. I sank into him, needing the closeness, and he responded as though he were starving.

My thoughts raced with where we went from here. He'd packed up his rental because I'd invited him to stay with me until we sorted out the spirit witches. I felt better having him close and he was determined to keep me safe, but where were we headed? So far we hadn't progressed beyond kisses. The desire was there, but, at least for me, the fear was stronger. Was there any point making plans when there were so many threats hanging over our heads?

"Stop," he said against my mouth.

I pulled back with a frown. "Stop what?"

The corner of his mouth kicked up in a knowing smile, and his eyes sparkled with amusement. "You're overthinking things again. I can hear it."

I rolled my eyes. "Don't look at me as if you're not."

"With you this close? Believe me, princess, the only thoughts I have are what I'd like to do with you. When you're ready."

He pulled me back into another kiss, and this time I tried to follow his lead, to let my worries drift away and be present in the warmth of him.

Until a low vibration buzzed against my thigh.

I jumped away from Trace, moving so quickly his teeth caught my lip and I tasted blood.

He reached for his new phone, and dread coiled in my stomach when he read the screen and his face went pale.

I didn't ask. Part of me didn't want to know, and the rest of me was too terrified to utter a syllable.

But Trace didn't need me to ask. He set the phone on the bar and nudged it towards me, the text message showing in all its ominous glory.

Unknown Number: Hello, darling. Sorry our reunion was cut short, but you know how things go. So much to do. But we should meet again. Soon.

When I looked at him, his jaw was set and yellow veins stretched from his eyes towards his temples. I swallowed hard, and he closed his eyes and bowed his head against my chest. All I could do was put my arms around him and hold on tight.

After the events with Corrick, Trace and I had toasted to whatever came next.

How I envied Past Me her optimism.

All I could hope for now was that one day we'd look back at this and have a true *next* to toast to.

Thank You for Reading

Thank you so much for taking a chance on an independent author. We're living in a wonderful age where it's easy to upload a book to the internet, but that doesn't reflect the blood, sweat, and tears that go into making a book the best version it can be. It takes time, patience, perseverance, and to have the final result end up in a new reader's hands is the best reward. You are the reason we keep writing, so thank you.

If you enjoyed the read, please help support the author by leaving a review at the retailer where you purchased the book. Reviews make a world of difference for an author, helping us reach new audiences and bringing more people into the worlds you've spent time in.

For exclusive character content, announcements, promotions, and special offers, sign up for Krista's mailing list at https://www.kristawalshauthor.com/pages/about-the-author

Acknowledgements

Two books in, and I'm already in love with these characters more than I was before. Especially Chip. I don't know how a guy who is so totally unlikeable could be so lovable, but I'm sure he's furious about it.

But of course I need to acknowledge the people who continue to help me bring them on the page:

Kate Sparkes, because you are my buddy, my pal, and the best hand-holder a girl could ask for.

Emily Stewart, my editor. Thank you for helping me navigate this treacherous English language with all its questionable commas, not to mention cleaning up my prose so these characters can shine.

My beta readers, Noelle and Traci, for helping me catch those last minute inconsistencies that made it through a dozen previous drafts.

My author groups! Every step of the way, you're there to help me choose the best path for my books, and I'm grateful.

My Patrons, Wyverns, and Ravens—you are the best cheerleaders. My pep squad. My motivators. Thank you for keeping me accountable with all the deadlines I juggle.

My husband and daughter. You make me feel all the emotions, which helps me figure out how to put them into words. Frustration, amusement… and always love.

And always my readers. Thank you for being here! I'll see you at book three ^.^

About the Author

Known for witty, vivid characters, Krista Walsh never has more fun than getting them into trouble and taking her time getting them out.

When not writing, she can be found reading, gaming, or watching a film – anything to get lost in a good story.

She currently lives in Ottawa, Ontario with her husband, toddler, and epileptic blue heeler.

You can find her at www.kristawalshauthor.com or at the local Second Cup coffee shop... but only if you come bearing a Vanilla Bean Latte, half-sweet.

Other Works by Krista Walsh

Epic Fantasy

The Meratis Trilogy

The Cadis Trilogy

The Nayis Trilogy

Urban Fantasy

The Dark Descendants Series

The Ghostmaker Trilogy

The Immortal Sorceress Series

The Hour of Witches Series

www.ingramcontent.com/pod-product-compliance
Lightning Source LLC
Chambersburg PA
CBHW030746310726
48969CB00005B/1332